THE
LAST THING

A Baker Girls Romance

BETHANY
MONACO SMITH

For more information about this book, visit the author's website.
www.bethanymonacosmith.com

Editing by Lacey Braziel of On the Page Publishing
Cover Design by Chelsea Kemp
Formatting by Bethany Monaco Smith

ABOUT THE LAST THING

The Last Thing is the fourth book in the Baker Girls
interconnected standalone series. All books in the series can be
read as standalone novels.
The Last Thing is a low angst, surprise pregnancy rom-com
featuring the spunky, sarcastic nanny Hallie Baker, and the
slightly grumpy single dad Wilson Decker. *The Last Thing* is full
of ridiculous nicknames, lots of banter and tension, an age gap, a
precocious eight-year-old, and plenty of swoony and steamy
moments.
Ready to fall in love with Hallie & Wilson?

MEET THE CHARACTERS

The "it's just a one-night-stand" lovebirds:
   Hallie Baker
   Wilson Decker

The Baker Girls crew:
   Frannie Baker
   Kennedy Baker
   Justin Ayers
   Brian Ackley
   Ryan "Hardy" Hardison
   Devon McGregor
   Jade Jackson
   Mark Abbott

Wilson's family & co-workers:
   Sophia Decker- Eight-year-old daughter
   Linnie Decker- Mom
   Leo Barone- Boss (and single dad role model)
   Nick Ardito- Co-worker

TRIGGER WARNINGS

If you're looking for possible triggers in this book, this page is for you. If you're not, you can skip this page and dive into the story.

trigger warnings may contain plot spoilers

As a lighthearted read, I tried my best to keep this one as trigger-free as possible. **In case you missed it, this book features a pregnancy as the main theme.** If pregnancy is problematic or a trigger for you, drop this book like it's hot and run. There is mention/depiction of a possible miscarriage in this book. It's scary for a second, but everything is absolutely fine and ends with a healthy delivery for the baby and mother. Again, if miscarriage is a trigger for you, you may want to set this one aside. Other briefly mentioned possible triggers: mention of general pregnancy complications with a non main character's past pregnancy, discussion of past loss and grief.

Any updates or changes to this information can be found at bethanymonacosmith.com/triggers

To anyone who has gotten frisky on a carnival ride. Keep living the dream for the rest of us.

CHAPTER ONE

Hallie

"I GOT WHAT I DESERVE! What I should've had! What I would have had if you hadn't slept with that whore of a nanny and destroyed our relationship."

Rule number one of being a nanny: never get involved with the client.

Unfortunately for her, the quivering girl a few feet from me with tears in her eyes did not get the memo.

To a degree, I feel sorry for her. She obviously knew she was getting in the middle of a marriage, but I don't think she's a whore or a gold digger. She's got a soft heart and fell for the smooth words of a man who was desperate to relive his twenties with the night nanny taking care of his five and three-year-old daughters.

Not a concern for me. Before I started babysitting in high school, my mom had a long talk with me about what behavior was appropriate and inappropriate with the parents, and told me to come to her right away if they ever made me feel uncomfortable. She also plainly told me, no matter what words they say, never get *involved* with the parents of the children I babysit—or nanny—for. When I was young, she said it to protect me from predatory men. Now, as an adult, I use that as my hard and fast rule.

Not that I need to worry about it, anyway. My heart is far too locked up to fall for some sweet words and longing looks. But my rule extends beyond matters of the heart, to matters of the body, which I'm happy to partake in.

But never with a client.

As the jilted ex-wife continues screaming at her ex-husband and the nanny-turned-lover, I make my exit, stage right.

These people have taken enough of my time and sanity. When their affair came to light and everything blew up, my job as their daytime nanny was blown to pieces too. I had to say goodbye to two little girls I adored. I cried. They cried. The Brazilian manny the ex-wife revenge hired cried. But the fun didn't stop there.

Since they're high-profile people in New York, the press has followed it all, which means no one has wanted to touch me with a ten-foot pole. So, now I have the joyous task of finding another job when my name has been dragged through the trenches with those idiots.

My sister Frannie's boyfriend, Mark, is the quarterback for the New York Bandits, and though he put my name out to everyone in the Bandits organization, most people already had nannies. Though I'm a backup or babysitter for a few, it's not full-time income.

I have to come up with some kind of plan, but right now, I'm too exhausted to think of anything.

Theoretically, I could finish my teaching certification and do that, but I got two weeks into my student teaching and realized I hated it. Running a whole classroom brought out my chaotic side in the worst way. Turns out I'm not great with a room full of kids. I like having only a couple of kids at a time. I can bond with them in a different way, and really get to know them. So, I went back to nannying, which I'd done throughout high school and college.

Now I'm here.

Whatever. At least I'm free of all that family drama I didn't ask to be a part of.

I take a deep breath as I walk down the courthouse steps and pull out my phone.

I laugh at the text I see.

GRAN

How did it end? Spill the tea.

I take a right and aim for the nearest subway entrance while typing a text back to my grandmother.

She's eighty-three going on twenty-eight. She lives her life wild and free and loves a good dramatic story—fiction or reality—and always has a sarcastic quip in response.

Gran is one of my favorite people. She's off traveling the world, so I don't get to see her as often as I did when I was young, but it's the way she's chosen to spend the rest of her life.

She had a beautiful love story with my grandpa. He died unexpectedly when I was fourteen, and she struggled for years before she found some great widowed friends and started traveling the world with them—living their best lives.

Long story short... it was a lot of drama. The wife got more than the husband wanted her to, and they were in the middle of a screaming match when I left.

GRAN

Good for her. She should make him pay. Glad you're finally free, even though I'll miss the regular updates.

I'll try to find some new drama to update you on. Preferably further removed from me. What about you? How's Greece? What trouble are you getting into?

Rather than a text, my phone buzzes with a call from her. I answer, weaving through the people on the street, and let Gran distract me from my career uncertainty and general cranky attitude.

It's time to let it all go.

I'm going home and getting changed, because most of my favorite people are in the city for the day. We're going to spend the afternoon at the New York Metros game, and if I'm lucky, we'll spend the night at our favorite bar, where hopefully I can find a hookup to fuck all the bad energy right out of me.

"LOVE IS NOT COMING FOR ME," I say pointedly, looking around the booth at our favorite little bar, McGills Tavern. It's a safe space, it's never overcrowded, the drinks are good, and the burgers are amazing.

Unfortunately, I'm surrounded by hopeless romantics.

The game this afternoon was fun. Frannie, who now lives upstate in a tiny little town called Ida, came down for the weekend—though she and Mark went back to their apartment here to bone as soon as dinner was over. I can't blame them. If I had someone to give me regular phenomenal orgasms, that's where I'd want to be too.

Though I'm happy for her, I miss her. It sucked when she moved upstate, but at least when she visited, it was our time together. Her, me, and our cousin, Kennedy—who is more like our sister since our moms are sisters and our dads are brothers—the Baker girls.

We grew up together until Kennedy's family moved to California when she was eleven and I was six. She moved back here after college, but a couple of months ago, she went back to California for her high school reunion and decided to stay since she and her best friend Devon *finally* admitted they were in love after denying it for years.

I miss them, but I'm happy for them. They deserve to live their best lives—and love stories.

Just because I don't want one doesn't mean I'm not happy for them.

With me tonight are two of Mark's teammates—wide receiver Ryan Hardison a.k.a. Hardy, and Brian Ackley, a giant lineman with the softest of hearts—and my brother from another mother, Justin Ayers. He met Kennedy and Devon ten years ago at college in Chicago and moved back here with them when college was over.

From the first time I met him, we had big sibling energy, and he's always acted like my brother, giving me shit and protecting me. He's moved around a bit, and now lives upstate in a neighboring town to where Frannie lives. With his wife, Jade, who is also here. Because the man got married six weeks ago to someone he'd only known for two weeks because she needed health insurance.

Yet, with the way he looks at her, it's obvious that has nothing to do with why he married her.

He's stupidly in love. Just like Frannie and Mark. And Kennedy and Devon. The love bug is chomping its way through our friend group.

But. Not. Me.

I don't do love.

I love seeing the people I love happy in their relationships. I believe love can last. But I also know it can catastrophically destroy you. And that's not a risk I've ever been willing to take.

But Hardy just pats my hand. "Baby girl, I don't think you get to choose that."

"He's right," Brian says. His voice is soft, filled with longing, and there's a deep ache in his eyes.

A look that only increases when Hardy gives him a gentle look and squeezes his arm. "You will find it when the time is right. When the person is right."

And if the love bug is looking for its next victims, it needs to open its eyes because they're sitting right there.

I've known Brian is bisexual for a while. He told me soon after we met, though I'm not sure he's told anyone else. We both have an emo-kid side and we bonded over that. He's never admitted his feelings for Hardy to me, but I see them. I have no idea how Hardy identifies or if he has any feelings for Brian, but with the tenderness in his eyes when he speaks, it's impossible to believe he doesn't feel *something*.

So, crossing my fingers those two figure it out, because I hate seeing that hurt and desperation in Brian's eyes.

But as quickly as all that angst filtered into his eyes, it disappears again.

"Yeah. You're right. And I don't need to mope, so let's go grab another drink."

I slide out of the booth to let them go to the bar, and as I'm slipping back in, the bell over the door goes off.

And *hello*.

Walking in is a deliciously hot man with dark hair and a face full of dark stubble. His jaw is set tightly, and he's loosening his tie like it's the most restrictive thing in the world. He's a little older than me for sure—not hard since I'm only twenty-three—but he looks like exactly my type.

Smiling, I sit down in the booth, watching him as he walks to the bar and orders a drink.

Target acquired.

CHAPTER TWO

GET me out of this fucking monkey suit.

I hate fitted button-downs. I hate suit coats. I hate uncomfortable shoes. I *loathe* ties.

A choker of oppression. And not in any kind of fun way.

If it's not a tee or a flannel shirt and jeans or sweats, I don't want it.

But an old buddy of mine got married today, so here I am, in a city—not my place, not somewhere I ever enjoy being—in a fucking suit and tie so I could stand up with him while he got married.

I don't regret it, but I'm praying no one else asks me to be in another wedding any time soon. My few high school buddies I kept in touch with are married or uninterested in the idea, so hopefully I'm out of the woods.

Not until I'm home tomorrow, though.

Enjoy yourself. Have some fun.

I'd like to believe my mother's words when I left her house were not encouraging me to hook up, but they might've been. She's been on me to find a partner for years now.

Not necessarily a woman. She doesn't care how I identify or who I choose, but she thinks I should have someone. And Soph should too.

Though my eight-year-old daughter Sophia loves that it's just the two of us, she occasionally asks about having siblings. Even though that's the last fucking thing I can think about right now.

We're moving into a new apartment next weekend. It's a beautiful space right in a small town about twenty minutes from my hometown of Lacy Creek, and it's closer to the offices of the construction job I've been working for the past few years.

Though we've been living with my mom in Lacy Creek for most of Sophia's life, it's time to break out on our own.

It's time for me to have some space.

Pulling the tie over my head, I set it down on the counter and order a drink.

It's time for me to enjoy myself.

I crack my neck a couple of times, and when a cold beer is placed in front of me, I take a few long gulps, then look around the bar.

I picked this one because it was the closest place to where my buddy had his reception that didn't seem seedy or too upscale.

I'm a blue-collar country boy and feel out of my element enough here. All I wanted tonight was a chill place to grab a drink and food—so far, it's hitting right.

In the corner are a few people playing darts, and as I skim the rest of the bar area, I notice two guys who look strangely familiar. It takes me a second to place them, but when I do, I school my features.

Two of the New York Bandits are a few feet from me.

Part of me wants to go ask them for autographs for Sophia. She's been obsessed with the Bandits ever since she got to meet one of their players earlier this summer when the company I work for renovated an apartment for him back home. Apparently, he's a small-town boy at heart. But I'm not going to be the weirdo who walks up and claims to know their teammate, and they deserve the ability to get some drinks without someone stalking them.

Still, my eyes follow them as they walk back to their booth, and when they get there, I can't look away, but for an entirely different reason. A gorgeous woman with an athletic body and long dark blonde hair gets up so they can sit back down.

Fuck.

If I don't want to bother the football players, I really should not be staring at their friend like that.

I spin on my stool, but can't stop myself from peeking over my shoulder again. When I do, I find stunning amber eyes staring back at me. She winks, then goes back to her conversation.

My cock thickens in my pants and I curse myself because all I want is for my night to end with her body trapped beneath mine while she screams my name.

I'M NOT STARING like a total creep. It's forced me to keep my eyes on the Boston Revs game playing on the TV, but staring like a knuckle-dragging moron isn't how to get the girl.

But when I hear movement behind me, I look over my shoulder.

The football players are headed toward the end of the bar where the cash register is.

"Hey, Ronnie. Can I get another beer?"

The dulcet voice comes from my other side, and as I spin toward it, my arm brushes hers, setting off a volcano inside me. The woman I'm determined to spend my night with. All honey-brown hair and a beautiful smile. For a moment, I almost second-guess myself. She looks young. But as long as she's over twenty-one, that's all I care about.

"Sure thing," the bartender says.

The woman's eyes land on me. "Hey."

My full attention turns to her. "Hi."

She tilts her head slightly, watching me with a smile. "Let me guess. You're not from around here."

I chuckle at that. "What gave me away?"

"This is my favorite little hole in the wall. And most everyone who comes here is either a regular or meeting up with someone. Plus, you look like you'd rather set that suit on fire than wear it."

"Very perceptive."

She shrugs. "I'm good at reading people..."

I offer her my hand. "Deck."

She stares at me for a moment, then shakes my hand, a wicked smirk on her face. "Like a porch?"

I instantly groan, but she just laughs. Trouble dances in her wild eyes, and it only makes me want her more.

"It's a real name."

She nods dramatically. "Of course it is. I know lots of people named Terrace. I even have a close friend called Veranda."

Behind the bar, the bartender—Ronnie, I guess—stifles a laugh.

"Fine, what's your name, then?"

"Hm... you can call me H.B."

"H.B.? That's not a name."

"So judgmental, *Deck*."

The bartender gives up and walks away from us, laughing loudly.

"Plenty of people use only their initials. Or would it be better if I added a name after it? H.B. Wells?"

I give her a flat look, but can't stop the corners of my mouth from tipping up.

"Fine, you've got me. It stands for Heavy Bananas."

"Well, I believe the bananas part."

She gasps in mock offense, running her hand down my arm and making flames erupt beneath the surface of my skin.

"Okay, really it's Honey Badger."

"I'm glad you're having fun with this."

She shrugs. "Life's too short not to have some fun, right?"

Her voice takes on a sensual tone, and my gut heats.

"Fun was exactly what I was looking for tonight. Then I saw you..."

"I promise, I'm plenty of fun, Patio."

I let out a huff of a sigh, and her smile grows.

Goddamn.

"How old are you? And I need the real answer for this one."

"Twenty-three," she says easily.

Above my minimum age limit. Still a smidge younger than I usually go for, but I can't deny the hold she has on me.

"Any proof of that?"

"I could show you my ID, but since you started the whole stupid name thing, I feel like it'd be giving you an unfair advantage. Hey, Ronnie!"

He appears again, eyes set on me.

"How old am I?" she asks.

His brow furrows and he glares at me. "You put something in her drink?"

She laughs and waves a hand. "No. He's being upstanding and making sure I'm not a lying high schooler. But you don't serve underage kids."

His gaze hardens. "No. I don't."

"And did you ever buy my fake ID?"

He grins at her. "Not for a second." Then he looks at me. "She's twenty-three and has been driving us all insane for years now."

"Aw, thanks, Ronnie."

He shakes his head as he walks away, then she leans in closer to me.

"He knows my parents, and I used to babysit for his kids.

He'd never serve anyone alcohol who's underage. Especially not me. Good enough?"

I nod.

"And how old are you?" she asks.

"Not old enough to be your dad."

"The perfect age, then, Back Deck."

"You're going to drive me crazy with that, aren't you?"

"I don't know, *Deck*. Am I?"

I swallow the throaty growl that tries to come out.

"It depends if that's how you're planning to say my name all night."

She swirls her finger in a circle over my hand, and the sensation goes straight to my cock.

"Well, *that* depends on how good you are at giving me what I want."

A dark laugh slips out. "You're going to get me into trouble, aren't you, Hells Bells?"

"Hells Bells, huh?"

"It fits." Leaning in, I whisper, "You seem like a little hellion."

She leans in even closer, her lips almost brushing mine. "You have no idea." Then she lightly pinches my arm and smiles at me. "You want to find out?"

I throw fifty bucks down on the bar—enough for my meal, drinks, and a tip, then turn to her.

"As long as you're good with this being one night. You're right, I'm not from around here, and frankly, I'd like this to be a night of fun that can be a fond memory of the city."

"Thank God. I was worried you were going to ask for my number—or my full name. I'm here for fun, and that's all."

I slide off the stool and offer her my hand. "Let's go."

"One thing we have to do first."

She leads me over to the table where she was sitting earlier. The football players are gone, but there's still a blond guy who looks a lot like her minus a different eye color and a woman with dark hair and curves for days.

The guy stands up, expression hard, and crosses his arms over his chest.

"This is who I have to get approval from?" I ask, trying to seem trustworthy but also not look meek.

"I'm Justin, the older brother. The guys who just left are the two professional football players that'll help me hide your body if you hurt her." He looks at the little hellion next to me. "Location on?"

"Yep. Shared with you."

"Good. Now, for posterity..." He digs his phone out and takes a picture of me. Then he spins his finger. "Turn to the side." I stare at him for a moment. I don't like being told what to do, but I can appreciate him taking care of his sister. So I turn to the side and let him take another picture.

"Thank you..."

"Deck."

He gives me a derisive look that quickly turns menacing again.

I hold up my hands because as fun as a little shit-giving might be, I want him to know she's safe. It's different, but if it were Sophia, I'd be a hard-ass too.

"We're not doing full names, but I don't have a secret identity, I promise. With my picture, you can find me. I won't hurt her."

He stares at me for a beat longer, then gives a subtle nod.

"Ready to go, Hells Bells?"

Hells Bells? the other woman mouths.

But the hellion just puts a finger to her lips.

"I'll text you that I'm alive later."

"You better," her brother says, keeping his voice low and grumbly.

I almost want to tell him I'm not interested in fucking around —but in a very literal sense, that's exactly what I'll be doing. Not in a fuck around and find out way.

Tonight is not about me getting my dick wet, it's about having fun with this wild woman at my side and making sure she enjoys every second of it too.

"Let's go," she whispers.

Hand tightly wrapped around hers, we leave the bar.

"YOU KNOW, when you said you wanted to have fun, this isn't quite what I thought you meant."

She laughs, eyes bright, as she stares at the carnival across the street.

"You look like you need to relax a little. Have some fun. Let loose. I'm fully invested in all forms of fun tonight, but you'll enjoy yourself more if you loosen up first."

"Okay. I'm in."

At least I'm wearing sneakers and jeans now. We passed a department store, and she sent me in to put on clothes that didn't make me "look so cranky."

Now I'm in my standard attire. White tee, jeans, and sneakers, plus the backward Metros ball cap I grabbed while I was waiting to check out.

Again she takes my hand, and it's impossible to ignore the crack of electricity I feel. It burns up my arm, going straight for my chest, every time she touches me.

"Let's go."

I can't remember the last time I went to a carnival.

My mom usually takes Sophia to the local fairs in the summer while I'm working, but me?

Fuck, when was the last time I let myself have fun or did something just for me?

The tenth of never.

So I let all my inhibitions go and follow the hellion as she drags me through the carnival.

We laugh our way through the funhouse with all the mirrors, then she dashes over to get some cotton candy.

Her smile is bright and intoxicating.

She's just... free.

And it lets me channel that feeling, if only for a night.

She sways back to me and holds out a piece of cotton candy. I take the whole thing in my mouth, my tongue brushing her fingers.

Her eyes lock with mine, going a little hazy for a second... until she spies something over my shoulder.

"Games!" Grabbing my hand, she drags me over to a row of carnival games, going straight for the one where you toss darts at balloons.

We both get four darts, and as she picks her first one up, she looks at me. "Want to make it interesting?"

"How so?"

"Winner decides what we do next."

"Okay. What do you want to do if you win?"

"Hm. Carousel. What about you?"

My eyes go up and to the right. "Ferris wheel."

She smiles brightly. "You're on."

We throw at the same time, lightly shoving and trying to distract each other, but when all is said and done, I get three and she gets one.

"Looks like we're going on the Ferris wheel," I say smugly.

She shoves my shoulder. "You're lucky I don't cry on them like my sister does."

"Don't forget your prizes," the attendant says.

"Which one am I picking from?" I ask.

The attendant points to the prizes for scoring three points, and my hellion whispers, "You should get the rabbit."

It's a floppy, light gray rabbit, and when I look down at her face and the expression shimmering in her eyes, that's exactly what I get.

"Where are my prize options?" Hells Bells asks.

"Right over here."

She runs around the side of the booth to where there are a

variety of necklaces, then she laughs loudly and grabs one. "Perfect."

She's tearing the plastic open as she walks over to me.

"One for you and one for me."

She holds something out, and it takes me a minute to realize it's one of those necklaces that's half a heart, and she has the other half. The one she gave me says "true." Hers says "love."

She smiles brightly. "Now you'll always remember the night you met your true love."

The sassy, spunky look on her face sends me over the edge, and I grab her by the side of the neck and pull her lips to mine.

And fuck.

Fuck me.

She pulls me closer, twisting her tongue around mine as she kisses me back.

God damn it. It's been too long since I've gotten laid.

I must be desperate, because I swear a kiss has never felt this damn good before.

Her fingers curl into my hair, and I wish we weren't at this carnival. I wish I was buried deep inside her.

When a groan slips out of me, she breaks our kiss and stares up at me, wide-eyed, but then her face morphs into a devilish smile as mischief dances in her eyes.

"Race you to the Ferris wheel."

She takes off running, and for a second, I stare at her.

I was fully prepared to be a sulky, grumpy asshole with only my hand to get me off in a lonely hotel room tonight, but this woman changed everything.

Her sassy brightness makes me want more. So much more. Since this is the only shot I get, I'm going to make tonight count.

CHAPTER THREE

"YOU LIKE FERRIS WHEELS?" Deck—if that's his real name —asks as it quickly moves us up to the top, then down and around again.

"Yeah. I've always liked heights, exploring, adventure. I don't know… one time, my cousin and I took my sister cliff jumping, and we literally had to drag her over the edge with us. She's terrified of heights. She was scared to fly for the first time. But me? I don't know. Not much scares me."

Except love. Or what happens when love ends.

That's why I have my rules. No love, only hookups. Nothing more than one night.

Though this is more than I usually do with a hookup. I wasn't initially planning to bring him to a carnival, but it's like I could sense this other part of him deep down that desperately needed to be set free. And carnivals are always magical.

The Ferris wheel slows and comes to a stop at the top as people get off and others climb on.

"Good. Because it looks like we're going to be up here for a few minutes."

I lean back against the seat and look out over the carnival and the small piece of the city I can see from here.

Deck's warm hand comes to rest on my thigh, and it's impossible to ignore the way that warmth spreads all over my body.

Then his hand moves up, slipping under my flowy tank and skimming the waistband of my shorts.

"You want a little adventure?"

My exhale is shaky with excitement, though I try to hide it.

"What did you have in mind?"

He kisses the side of my neck and undoes the button of my shorts, gliding his hand inside them.

"Let's see if you can come before the ride's over."

A little whimper slips out of me as he brushes his fingers over my clit.

"But you have to be quiet. Can you be quiet for me?"

"Yes," I whisper, but it's not in response to his question but to him slipping two fingers inside me as he works my clit with his thumb.

Wrapping my arm around his bicep, I bury my face in his shoulder.

"You have no idea all the things I'm going to do to you tonight. All the ways I'm going to make you come."

His voice is gruff and rumbly in my ear, and it takes everything in me to keep from crying out.

My labored breathing tells him how much I'm enjoying it though.

"Right there," I gasp when his fingers hit the right spot inside me.

The Ferris wheel moves forward slightly.

"Time's running out. Are you going to come for me? I want to feel your sweet little pussy clench my fingers."

"Fuck," I whimper.

My head lolls back as I cry out, my orgasm bursting through me in hard waves.

And then, perfectly timed, fireworks go off from somewhere behind us and the Ferris wheel starts moving again.

Deck pulls his hand out of my shorts, then *licks his fingers.*

He groans and looks at me, his voice low and rough. "I can't wait to taste even more of you."

And that's it.

I'm done for.

Completely screwed.

Because this devil of a man wants to let my wild side out, and I am *so* ready to play.

"JUST LIKE THAT. Hollow those cheeks. I want to see you swallow my cock."

His words send another burst of heat straight to my core.

He's holding my hair with both hands as he controls the movement of my head.

Rough, dirty, raw, wild, *consensual* sex is my favorite thing.

I learned at a young age that I have a high sex drive and lots of fun fantasies. I started watching porn before Frannie did, and my mother didn't know what to do with me.

I lost my virginity at sixteen and was so underwhelmed, I asked my mom if I could have a vibrator.

She *really* didn't know what to do with me.

But she never shamed me. She got me one. She got me romance books that showed safe, consensual sex, and encouraged me not to watch porn because too many people on porn sites are forced into it or taken advantage of.

Now I know how to source it from people who actively choose to make it themselves.

I unapologetically love sex and all sexual things.

Which is why I'm on my knees, mascara tears running down my cheeks as I choke on Deck's cock and beg for more.

I've been imagining this since we got off the Ferris wheel and I dragged him the three blocks back to my apartment.

It's been too long since I've had a good hookup. Not one quickie and it's done. But a night of passionate sex.

I'm actually a little worried this is going to ruin me. If him touching me on the Ferris wheel was that good, I might be a little devastated in the morning when I have to face the reality that I can't have it again.

But for tonight, I'm going to enjoy every second.

"You like choking on my cock, baby?"

I try to nod, but he grabs my hair tighter, thrusting faster.

"Fuck, you have no idea what you do to me."

His body shakes, and I know he's close. Letting my eyes slip closed, I steady my breathing.

"You gonna swallow my cum like a good girl?"

I whine, again trying to nod in response.

He grunts and pulls most of the way out, then with one last hard thrust, he spills inside me.

He keeps hold of my hair as he pulls out, staring down at me. The pad of his thumb swipes under my eyes, wiping the smudged mascara away. Then he hauls me to my feet.

"Show me the bedroom."

Right. Because we ditched our clothes and I blew him in the middle of the living room.

I tilt my head and give him my sweetest smile. "You think you'll be able to get it up again this quickly?"

He leans in and slaps my ass. "If you give me what I need, I'll be ready again in no time."

A shiver runs through me, and I take off at a sprint. The growl that slips out of him as he chases after me sends my insides fluttering.

I come to a stop just inside my bedroom, and Deck whistles as he looks around. "This is big."

"Perks of living alone." But my voice gives away how I really feel about that. For a second, his gaze shifts and the intensity in his eyes falters. That's the last thing I want. Tonight isn't about feelings. Not emotional ones. It's all about the physical. One night is all I get, and I'm going to make the most of it.

"So, what is this magic thing I can do that's going to get you hard again?"

Heat sparks in his eyes again, and he leans in and brushes his lips over mine. "Ride my face."

My eyes fly wide, and he laughs.

"Have you done that before?" he asks.

I nod, though it was only a couple of times with a guy in high school. It wasn't great, but he was determined to learn, which is a lot more than most guys that age will do.

Deck sweeps a strand of hair over my shoulder. "Have you ever done it standing up?"

I squint at him. The math isn't mathing.

"How?"

"I'll show you."

He leads me over to the bed and lies down so his head is partially over the edge.

"Now you step over me and settle in. From that angle, you can control everything."

I stare at him for a beat, desire coursing through me.

"Come on, baby. Drown me with that pussy."

I've never moved so fast.

He palms my ass as I settle over him, running my fingers through his thick, dark brown hair. I notice a few strands of gray right at his temples, which only makes him hotter.

I lower all the way down and the second his tongue sweeps over me, I let out a moan.

With a few swipes of his tongue, it becomes clear I've spent too much time playing with boys. Deck is a man. A man intent on making sure his partner gets as much—if not more—than he does.

My legs tremble, and I use my hands in his hair to reposition him slightly.

Fuck, I'm a slut for having my clit played with. Everything else is fun too, but that gets me there faster than anything else. And Deck might have a magic tongue because I swear I'm seeing stars.

"Yes," I whine, rolling my hips.

I'm close. So close.

He sucks my clit into his mouth and my vision goes spotty. I yank on his hair, pulling him tight to me as he sputters. My orgasm rips through me, and my legs shake so badly Deck grabs my hips to steady me.

When I'm finally finished and step out of his grasp, I spin around and find him stroking his hard length.

He smirks like the devil as he sits up. "Told ya."

"It's about time."

I reach for my bedside table and pull out a condom. We talked about protection before I ever got on my knees for him.

He reaches for the condom, but I step closer.

"Let me." I climb on the bed beside him and push him backward, rolling the condom down his thick cock.

"Get on your back, let me—"

I smile to myself as I ignore his words and climb on top of him, sinking down his length.

The second he's buried inside me, I cry out.

His fingers bite into my hips, and then we both move, thrusting together.

Sparks dance along my skin as awareness prickles through me.

It's never felt like this before. This good. This *everything*.

When I meet his gaze, he smiles wickedly, then flips us and pins me beneath him.

With his hand holding my wrists above my head, he drives into me while kissing my neck. And as he nips at my earlobe, it's clear he knows... he's ruining me for every other man.

CHAPTER FOUR

"PULL OUT."

I glare down at my little hellion, who arches a brow in response.

"Pull. Out."

My abs go tight, and it takes a deep breath to get enough oxygen to my brain to do as she says.

I instantly reach for my throbbing cock, but she slaps my hand.

"Touch your cock and you won't be coming again tonight."

I grit my teeth and drop my hand.

"Are you having fun?"

Her devious smile answers my question.

"Torturing you might be my new favorite thing."

I grumble in response, but as grumpy as I try to play it, I'm having the best night I've had in a long time. At least as myself. Not as a dad or anything else, but just as me.

This is our third round of sex after that rough blow job and frantic face riding.

Between each round, we explore each other's bodies, kiss everywhere, and tease each other to see who can be ready again first. It's always her, but that's nature's fault, not mine. Though it's been a long time since I've spent all night having sex, I still have plenty of stamina.

This little hellion brings it out in me.

Grabbing the clit sucker—since she'll whine and beg to have her clit sucked—I put it on the middle setting and find that perfect spot.

In seconds, she's bucking beneath it, desperate to come. Painfully desperate. Just like me.

So I turn it off again and set it aside.

"No," she cries.

"If I don't get to come, you don't get to come."

She stares me down. "Maybe you should make me."

"Make you come?"

That wicked grin spreads across her face again. "No. Make me let you come."

I grab her by the thighs and pull her to me. "No more teasing?"

She shakes her head.

"Fucking finally."

I plunge inside her again, and she throws her head back.

"Look at me, baby. I want to see your pretty face when you come on my cock. Work your clit. I won't last long."

She slips her fingers between us, furiously stroking her clit as I pump in and out of her in punishing strokes, hand wrapped around the side of her neck.

I'm barely holding it together. We've been teasing each other for almost an hour, and I'm about to bust the damn condom when I come.

"God, yes," she cries.

"God's not here. I am. Say *my* name."

Her pussy shudders once.

"Deck."

The soft, breathy whisper goes right to my balls, and I move faster.

"Fuck, fuck. I'm almost..." A moan rips out of her.

"Me too. Come on. Show me how you come for me."

"Deck!" Her screams bounce around the room as her pussy clenches my cock in long, hard pulses.

"Fuck!" I cry, grabbing her hips and holding her tight to me as I fill the condom.

My vision is hazy and my heart's beating so hard it feels like it might explode.

She lets her hand fall to her side, eyes slipping closed as she lays her head on the pillow. I flop down beside her, my body melting into the mattress as my hazy eyes drift closed. Without looking, I pull the condom off and toss it toward the side of the bed where the garbage is. Then I pull her close, kissing the side of her head before we both give in to sleep.

I DON'T HAVE VERY many natural talents, but waking up five minutes before my alarm each day is my shittiest one.

Though it came in helpful today so I didn't have to wake the hellion.

It makes me feel like a bit of a shithead, but I can't wake her up.

Last night was one of the most incredible nights of my life, and if I'm thinking only about sex, it was the best of my life, no contest.

If I wake her up, it'll go from the one night we agreed on to something more. Because I won't be able to look at her and not think *mine*.

I've been thinking it since she stuffed that cotton candy in my mouth and then I touched her on the Ferris wheel.

But she's not mine.

I don't get to keep her.

So it's time to go.

Pausing in the open living room and kitchen, I grab the stuffed bunny I won last night and set it on the counter. Then I find a piece of paper and scrawl a quick note.

My little hellion,

Last night was one of the best I've had in a long time. Might sound cheesy, but this will be a fond memory for me—maybe my only one of the city. Take care of yourself and keep the bunny. I got it for you.

Deck

With that, I pull the half heart necklace from my pocket and set it on the counter.

But as I turn to go, I look back at it and stupidly pick it up again.

One souvenir from an amazing night won't hurt, right?

My eyes sweep the apartment again, and I smile, remembering every moment, then force myself to leave and let it all become a memory.

CHAPTER FIVE

WHEN I WAS A KID, my mom used to tell me that the consequences of my actions were important. I could learn from them so I wouldn't repeat them.

I've learned a very important lesson.

Condoms are useless.

Tears crest in my eyes as I dive forward and puke again.

No one to hold my hair.

No one to tell.

No one to buy me ice cream and let me cry until they can make me laugh.

Sure, the football boys are in the city, and I love them, but it's not the same.

My sisters—Frannie and Kend, who I'll always consider my oldest sister—aren't here anymore. Justin, my surrogate brother, left before they did.

If Frannie hadn't met Mark when she did, I would be completely alone here.

My parents are close by, but I'm not ready to let them in on this dumpster fire yet.

I miss my people.

Frannie left because she never felt at home in the city. She's a quiet, small-town girl at heart. Kennedy left because she found her home building a life with Devon. Justin left initially because he was looking for a place that felt like home. He's closer now that he's finally found it. Not far from Frannie upstate. And I'm here alone. This apartment doesn't feel like home anymore. Nothing does. For me, it's never been a place that makes a home, but who I'm with, and most of the people I love left me behind.

And now I'm about to start sobbing in the middle of my bathroom.

Why am I so easy to leave?

I put my hand on my stomach. "Don't leave me, kid, okay? I've got you and you've got me. Deal?"

I sniff and wipe my eyes, then get up and make my way out to the living room. Collapsing on the couch, I grab my stupid, gray bunny and hold it close. The one thing *Deck* left me with.

Well, not the only thing anymore.

I don't know what the fuck to do with that. Start looking on social media for random guys named Deck? If that's even any kind of real name?

I don't mind being a Lorelai Gilmore—with better parental boundaries—and raising a kid alone. It's what I was planning to do one day. Settle into some type of career, find my stability, save up money, visit a sperm bank, and use the turkey baster method.

I've always loved kids and I have always wanted to be a mom.

While Frannie was playing bride and Kennedy was playing reporter, I was pretending to be a mom. That's what I wanted.

That doesn't mean I want Deck to miss out on having a relationship with his child.

I look at the bunny's face, then give it a shake, as if it's a Magic 8 Ball that will randomly give me his contact info.

Fuck.

I need to get my shit together.

A loud bang on my door makes me jump.

"Hallie, baby girl, you in there?" Hardy calls.

Unsurprising. I haven't returned anyone's calls or texts in days. Since I went to the doctor and had the suspicion I didn't want to admit to confirmed. Then I spent the next two days lying on my couch—or praying to the porcelain god—staring at the ultrasound picture to make sure I didn't dream it all up.

Even from a distance, Frannie and Kend love to meddle.

I wish they were here.

"We need to know you're alive," Brian calls.

"Coming," I grumble at the door, then shove myself off the couch, dropping the bunny on the coffee table.

I catch my reflection in the small mirror near the door. I look like straight up hell, but at least that'll sell why I haven't been answering. Sort of.

After unlocking the door, I pull it open to find two football players standing there. I'm five-six, but they still seem giant to me. Hardy mostly because he's just over six feet and muscular as fuck. Brian because he's a literal giant.

I gesture for them to come in, and they follow me, neither saying a word.

Surprising. Hardy usually has something to say.

The second my butt hits the couch again Hardy's intense stare is on me.

"What's going on?"

I give a little shrug. "Just having a rough few days. Emotionally speaking."

His brow furrows, and he drops onto the coffee table in front of me. "What's wrong?"

"I don't want to talk about it. Not yet. I'm okay. Just wallowing... I guess."

I glance up at Brian, who is staring at me intently, concerned, and clearly not convinced by a word coming out of my mouth.

"Frannie and Kennedy are both worried. You haven't answered any calls from them, and when they called and asked if you'd responded to us, we were out the door before they could tell us to come check on you. If you're not ready to talk yet... well, I'm still determined to get it out of you, but we need to know you're okay," Hardy says.

I stare at him for a beat. "I'd say I'm the definition of that word." I rub a hand over my face right as my stomach growls.

"When was the last time you ate?" Brian asks.

"Breakfast."

Brian folds his arms over his chest. "Hal, it's almost three in the afternoon."

"Tell us what you want, and we'll go get it," Hardy says.

I close my eyes and think about what doesn't make me want to barf.

"Can you get me a vanilla milkshake and some fries from that diner a couple of blocks over?"

"Coming up." Hardy stands and smacks Brian on the shoulder. "Coming?"

"Actually... would one of you stay?"

I glance at Brian, and he instantly knows I mean him.

He sits down on the couch next to me. "I will."

"Thanks," I murmur.

"Be back soon." Hardy looks at Brian. "I'll grab some stuff for us too."

Brian nods, then Hardy leaves. Once I'm sure he's far enough away from the door, I turn to Brian.

"Can I ask you something?"

"Of course."

"Do you have feelings for Hardy?"

Brian's eyes slowly widen, then his face falls. And then he looks horrified. "Is it obvious?"

I chuckle lightly. "I don't know about obvious, but I've picked up on something. Justin has too, but he's a romance nerd."

"I try not to be obvious about it." He runs a hand through his short, dark blond hair. "I'm officially the guy who falls for his straight best friend. Fucking pathetic. And the last thing I want to do is make him uncomfortable. Is there something I'm doing?"

I blink at him a few times. "No. I picked up on it a bit because I don't know... I can read you, I guess. And it's more of how you look or talk about him when he's not looking or not around. But Justin questioned it because of Hardy's reaction to you. The way he talks at you, touches you, speaks to you... there's a tenderness there."

Brian's face morphs into utter confusion. Like he can't even process the possibility.

Finally, he shakes his head. "No. That's just Hardy."

"That's Hardy with *you*," I counter. "He loves and supports us all. He's kind and easily loyal. But with you, it's different. I'm not saying you should jump him. But don't write it off either."

He sighs and rests his head against the couch, silence settling between us again.

"Hey, Bri?"

He flashes his eyes open and looks at me. "Yeah?"

"I'm pregnant."

He shifts on the couch and grabs my hand. "I was wondering why you wanted me to stay. Nice mislead with the question about Hardy."

I laugh, though tears well in my eyes. "A truth for a truth."

"When did you find out?"

"Couple of days ago. I've been... processing."

"And what do you want to do? If you want an abortion, I'll go with you. Pretend to be the father. My agent might kill me, but—"

I throw both arms over my stomach.

"I want this baby. I've always wanted to be a mom."

Brian reaches over and swipes a tear off my cheek. "Hal... you know we've all got you, right? Why didn't you call us?"

"I love you guys, but—"

"You needed your family."

I nod.

"Who's the father?"

"That guy from the bar. When Justin and Jade came down for the Metros game."

"Have you told him?"

I shake my head. "We didn't exchange contact info. Or even full names, just silly nicknames."

"Shit."

I shrug. "It sucks because I don't want to be the mom depriving a kid of having their dad in their life, but I'm not ready to dig through some social media black hole in an attempt to find him. I need to breathe first." I drop my head into my hands, groaning. "Find a job so I can afford to pay for a baby."

"About that. Frannie mentioned she might have a job for you. Either way, you should call her, but if she does... maybe you should think about it."

I look around the apartment. I have no idea what living in a small town would be like or if I'd enjoy it, but it's never been about the place.

Frannie would be right there.

Justin would be close.

I rest my hand on my stomach.

Maybe this is a sign to start a whole new chapter. A fresh page for whatever comes next.

I DIDN'T THROW up the fries and milkshake, so they're all I

want to eat now. Thankfully, grocery delivery exists, and I got some milk, vanilla ice cream, and frozen fries to cook up.

Hardy, surprisingly, let me off the hook and didn't push me to talk, but I think that may have been because of the stern look Brian gave him. Brian, unsurprisingly, kept my secret.

I'm still not ready to tell Frannie. Not about the baby. But… if she thinks there's a job for me in Ida, I want to hear about it. At the very least, I'm going to visit her for a bit.

I don't have to worry about paying rent since my parents own the building I live in, so I can float by for a little longer without stressing about a job.

When I push the call button next to Frannie's name, it only rings once before she answers.

"You're alive!"

"For the moment."

"Hallie."

"What? I'm fine. You worry too much."

"Says the person who threatened to call Jack Bauer when I didn't answer fast enough on vacation with Mark."

"We didn't know he wasn't a serial killer yet."

"Well, you could've been mugged or drugged or chopped into bits."

I laugh at that. "Have you been reading murder mysteries again?"

"Sorry I care."

"I'm okay. Just been in my feelings for the last few days."

"Anything job or no-job related?" she asks, sounding hopeful.

So I lean into it. "A bit. It sucks that I can't find anything."

"Well, I might have the perfect solution… if you're willing to move to Ida."

"Ida, huh?"

"Our new downstairs tenant needs sort of a babysitter/housekeeper combo. Not in a pristine white-glove housekeeping kind of way, but someone to make sure the apartment stays generally clean, can cook meals, and look after his eight-year-old before she goes to school in the morning and after school before he gets home from work. And since you could move into the apartment directly across the hall from them, it would be very convenient."

"You've got it all figured out, don't you?"

"What do you think?"

I blink back tears yet again. I could say it's hormones, but really, I'm processing everything.

"I really miss you."

"Hallie..."

"I'm okay. The city just sucks without you and Kend. I don't know how I'll like small-town life, but I'm willing to give it a shot."

"Really?" she squeals.

I laugh at that. "You've been trying to get me up there for a while now."

"I know, but you never said yes."

"Kend was still here."

Frannie's quiet for a moment.

"Now we're both gone."

I clear my throat. "Yep."

"I'm sorry, Hallie."

"It's fine. I'm fine. You got your wish, and I'm coming to Ida. And please, don't tell Kennedy I said anything about her leaving. I don't want her to feel guilty. I'm glad she and Dev are finally together and living their best life."

"I know you are. So... when will you be here?"

"What day is it? Friday?"

"You're scaring me if you don't know that, but yes."

Ignoring that, I continue on. "Okay, then I'll pack tomorrow and head up on Sunday."

Again, she squeals. "I'm so excited. I can show you all the best restaurants. The coffee place and café down the street are the best. Oh, and we can go bug Justin and Jade in Woods Junction. I promise you, this is going to be amazing."

Her excitement lifts my spirits a little. "I hope so. Anyway, I should get started organizing things. I love you."

"Love you too. See you Sunday!"

Her cheery voice rings in my ears as she hangs up.

Looking around the room, I inhale deeply. This is it. New adventure. New start. Next chapter.

I pick up the stuffed bunny and stare at it for a moment. "What do you think, Veranda? Ready to find a new home?"

Maybe my baby's first home.

Then I rub my hand over my flat stomach. I can't believe there's a baby growing in there. And now I'm packing up my life and moving to a small town that I've briefly visited twice.

What's that saying? When it rains, it pours.

I guess I'll find out if it's the kind of rain that ends a drought or the kind that destroys everything in a flood.

CHAPTER SIX

"HEY, DECK."

I spin around with my hands out in front of me. I never know when one of my idiot crewmembers might decide to chuck a tool my direction without so much as a "heads!"

But it's just my carpenter strolling toward me, thumb over his shoulder.

"Bossman and little bossman are here."

I suppress a chuckle and shake my head, adjusting my hard hat.

"Don't let Ardito hear you call him little bossman. He'll give you the shittiest job he can find."

I smack his arm and jog up the small hill to where the driveway of the house we're working on is situated.

Leo Barone and Nick Ardito are looking things over while slowly walking in my direction.

I'm a project manager for AB Construction, which Leo

started with his best friend Noah—Nick's dad—in their early twenties. They've grown to be one of the biggest in the area, and they're certainly the most well-respected.

I've worked a lot of construction jobs, and a lot of them are toxic as fuck. It's unfortunate, but the trades can be that way. They're either great or filled with assholes, and the people you work with and for make it that way. Leo and Noah expect the best from their employees, and over the last few years, I rose from associate carpenter to project manager.

This is a whole house reno, and the biggest project I've been in charge of so far.

"Leo. Nick."

I give them an up nod, and Leo walks over to shake my hand.

Nick is still in school, learning the business side of things, but he'll be working as the general manager eventually, so he spends a good chunk of his time shadowing Leo. Even though he grew up on sites and already knows his shit. His brother, Vince, just finished his bachelor's degree in architectural design, and he's been working on a lot of our building plans over the last couple of years.

"Deck, how's it going?" Leo asks. "It's looking good on the outside."

"It's coming along. I'll take you inside in a minute. We've caught up pretty well after we found that natural spring in the yard and had to adjust the drainage. The new windows are all in and, as you can see, we're working on siding now."

He nods, looking at what a couple of the workers are doing with siding.

"Any concerns from the homeowners?" Nick asks.

"They ask about the timeline for completion regularly, but that's typical. We're on track to be within a few days of our original projection. If that spring hadn't set us back, we might've finished early."

"Good, let's see inside."

I lead them up the back deck, which was finished a week-and-a-half ago, and inside the house.

"Electric was run on Monday, Tuesday, and Wednesday. The electrical inspector will be here bright and early Monday to sign off on it."

"Any major issues?" Leo asks, coming to a stop in the middle of the gutted and reframed living room.

"Might need you to step in with the door company. They sent us two warped ones and one of the replacements was also warped."

He blows out a breath. "Yeah. We might need to switch suppliers. That's not isolated to you."

"I'll look over all the info we've got," Nick says.

"Anything else?" Leo asks.

I look around to make sure no one is close by. "That new kid we hired isn't a good fit. He's missed two days in his first two weeks, and from what I'm hearing around the site, they weren't legitimate call-offs. He went to a casino out of town with his buddies one of the days. It's on his social media." Nick snorts at that. "He also didn't have a reliable work ethic when he was here."

Leo grinds his teeth. I know how much he hates when they mishire someone.

"Thanks for letting me know. I'll deal with it on Monday."

It sucks that anyone would come in and take advantage of working here. Leo and Noah are flexible about people calling off. They were both single dads and understand life happens. They get hard shit and value empathy and compassion when dealing with their employees. That said, Leo Barone is just about the last person you want to play fuck around and find out with.

"All right, well, keep us updated if anything changes. Otherwise, it's looking good," Leo says, patting my shoulder as he walks by me toward the door. "Oh, hey. Any luck finding a sitter?"

I sigh and rub my chin. "Working on it, but not yet."

He nods in understanding. "Well, Lara is happy to keep helping out until you find one."

"Thanks, Leo. Take care, guys."

He and Nick wave as they leave, and I sigh and check the clock.

Just under an hour until we wrap up for the day.

Moving was a great plan minus the fact that I don't have anyone to look after Sophia now that school is in session. In the summer, she spent the days with my mom. I'd drop her off in the morning before work since my mom is always an early riser and pick her up after. It was out of my way, but it worked well enough for the last month while we got settled in our apartment.

Now that Sophia is in school, though, it's been harder to manage. Having my mom drive out and back twice a day to watch for a couple of hours—less in the morning—is ridiculous.

Leo's wife runs a daycare, and though it's meant for younger kids, she's had Sophia act as her helper in the mornings and afternoons for the last few days since school started. I've got to find something soon, though, because that's not an ideal situation for Sophia. Plus, I need some help with food prep. I hate eating out, but I'm exhausted by the time I get home.

Marion's Café just down the road from our apartment is a staple, but it's not a substitute for me cooking my daughter the meals she deserves.

Single parenting is hard as fuck.

But other than my mom, I've been in this alone since the beginning, so I'll do what I always do—put my big boy pants on and get on with it.

WHEN I CLIMB out of my truck at Lara's daycare, Sophia is in the backyard, showing Leo's five-year-old granddaughter Harper how to do a perfect spin while Lara—who used to be a dance teacher—laughs in the background.

"Hey," I call.

"Hi, Decker, how are you?"

"I'm good. Busy as usual, but that's life."

"Isn't it, though? Sophia, your dad's here!"

Sophia gives Harper a hug and a kiss on the cheek, then runs over and jumps into my arms, knocking me back a step with the force of her hug.

"Hi, Daddy."

"Hey, sweetheart." I look into her sparkling green eyes and see nothing but happiness. She is joy personified and I couldn't be luckier that I got her for a kid. "How was your day?"

I set her down and rub my sore back.

"It was good. I think a girl I met could maybe be a friend."

"Nice." I give her a high-five. "How come it's just a maybe?"

"Well, we're still getting to know each other. You always say I shouldn't trust people until I know them."

Damn. She's always paying attention. And sometimes takes my words a little too literally.

"That's true, but if you don't give them a little trust to start, they might never feel safe enough to get to know you."

Her little brow furrows. "Oh. Okay. I'll spend more time with her tomorrow."

I catch Lara's gaze, and we both laugh. *That easy.*

To be a kid again.

"Oh, Daddy! Guess what?"

"What?"

"Miss Lara is going to teach dance classes again! Can I sign up?"

I glance at Lara, who nods.

"No pressure. Nick's wife has gotten back into dance recently, so we're going to do some small classes together. It won't cost much and it'll only be a couple of afternoons per week."

"We'll talk about it. Thanks."

Sophia gives me her grumpy look, but waves goodbye to Lara and lets me help her into her booster seat in the car.

Once I'm in the driver's seat, she hits me with the question I was expecting. "Why do we have to talk about it? I really want to learn to dance!"

"I get it, kid. I want that for you too. But when do I ever make a decision without thinking through everything?"

She huffs. "Never."

And even though my brain shouldn't go there, it takes me right back to the carnival. The night with my little hellion. Making her come on that Ferris wheel. It was the first time in a long time I didn't think every little detail through. I felt more alive than I had in years.

But it was a moment in time. A fleeting memory. Pulling into the small parking area across the street from our building, I push all those thoughts away. That was a night outside of my reality, and I have to get back to living in the real world.

I grab my backpack and Sophia's from the trunk, then help Sophia out of my CRV. Not the most glamorous car, but it's better than a minivan.

After looking both ways, we cross the street and head inside the building to our apartment.

We've just gotten to the landing when the door at the top floor swings open.

"Hi, Wilson. Hi, Sophia," Frannie Baker calls. She's our land-lady, though that word is far too frumpy for her. She's in her mid-twenties with a warm smile and upbeat energy. Her boyfriend, Mark Abbott—the starting QB for the NY Bandits—bought the building back in late April and AB Construction did a bunch of renovations for them. When I found out the apartment was up for grabs, I jumped on it. Mark's away right now since the season's on, but Frannie works as a social worker here in Ida.

"Hi," Sophia chirps, waving happily.

"I just got home and was hoping I'd catch you quickly. Are you still looking for someone to nanny for you?"

I wouldn't use that word exactly, but... "Yes. Know of anyone?"

She comes down the stairs to me, smiling the whole way like she's solved all my problems. "Yes. I finally convinced my sister to move up here, and she's worked as a nanny for years. She's looking for a fresh start because the last people she nannied for had a messy divorce that she was dragged through. She's amazing, though. I've never met a kid she nannied for who didn't adore her." She pauses thoughtfully. "And she has a big heart. She'll be here Sunday, if you'd like to meet her."

I glance up at the ceiling. I'm not much of a believer in God, but fate... are you really dropping the solution to all my problems at my door?

"Sunday might be busy, but we'll try to stop by. If not... she could come down early Monday morning?"

Frannie nods. "I'll let her know. She'll be in the apartment right across from you, so it'll make things easy."

I let out a sigh. That would make things so much simpler.

"Thank you, Frannie. Really."

She waves a hand. "It's nothing. I'm just helping two people who need problems solved to find each other."

I chuckle at that. "Well, again, I appreciate it. Have a good night."

"Thanks, you too."

"Go Bandits!" Sophia yells.

"Go Bandits," Frannie calls back as she makes her way up the stairs.

Once we're inside, Sophia scampers off to her room to unpack her backpack, but I lean against the closed door, hoping that for once fate is here to help me out.

CHAPTER SEVEN

Hallie

I WAS BORN in the wrong time. At least by like a decade. I wish I could've been a teenager at the height of the early 2000s emo-pop-punk days. That's where my soul resides.

And as I cruise off the highway exit in my 2008 custom baby blue Jeep Wrangler with the top off, belting out the lyrics along with Taking Back Sunday, I feel a shred of peace.

I'm a strange mix of sarcastic, playful, and upbeat with a dash of doom and gloom. Very Peyton Sawyer *people always leave* vibes. Yeah, I really would've thrived as a teen in the early 2000s.

Frannie's apartment is right on the downtown strip in Ida, overlooking the river, and when I pull to a stop in one of the spots in front of her building, I pause to look around.

Is this my home?

Is this where I'm supposed to be?

I don't know, but at least Frannie's here, and that's a start.

I'll have to come back out and put the top on my Wrangler later, but for now, I'm going inside to see my sister.

Frannie throws the door at the top of the stairs open before I've made it halfway up.

"You're here!"

"Is there an elevator?" I tease.

"Mark wants to put one in, but he hasn't figured out how. He's tired of lugging his stuff up and down two flights of stairs. But we'd have to cut into your apartment to do it."

I stop when she says that. *My* apartment. And I knew that, but something about it really hits. I'm moving here.

We're moving here. I may not technically count as two people yet, but it won't be long until I do.

I hurry up the rest of the stairs, then throw my arms around my sister.

She hugs me back tightly, closes the door behind me and locks it, then leads me over to the actual entrance to their apartment.

The last time I was here they were still unpacking, but this time everything is laid out and absolutely beautiful.

"Wow. This is amazing."

"Thank you. I love how it turned out."

The whole living area is charming and open, with a huge row of windows on the back wall where the kitchen is.

"I'm so glad you're here," she squeals. "I know you've seen your new apartment since it used to be mine, but I'm so excited to show it to you again." She pulls me in for another hug, then lets me go, putting her hands on my shoulders. "But first, how are you? Are you okay?"

Well, no point in lying about it.

"I'm pregnant."

Frannie goes as still as a statue.

"You. What? Who? How? Hallie!"

"Great sentences."

She smacks my arm. "You just dropped a bomb on me. Words are hard."

I deflate a little. "Yeah. I know the feeling."

Grabbing me by the arm, she drags me over to the couch and plops me down onto it before sitting down beside me.

"When did this happen? And who's the father?"

"The day we all went to the Metros game. And the father is a guy."

"That is usually how babies are made."

"I met this guy at McGill's, and we had this whirlwind night. It was all sexy and fun. We went to a carnival, he made me come on the Ferris wheel, then we went back to my place and fucked like rabbits. Now here I am."

"Well, have you contacted him? If he tries to skip out on you, Mark and the boys will hunt him down. Then Kend and I will cut off his di—"

I hold up my hand. "Oh my god. As much as I appreciate the sentiment, we didn't exchange contact info or even last names. The name he gave me might've been fake. And I told him my name was Honey Badger or Hannah Banana. He decided to call me Hells Bells."

Frannie laughs. "That actually tracks."

"Anyway, other than a baby, the only souvenir I have from that night is a stuffed rabbit named Veranda."

"Why?"

"It was a whole thing." I wave my hand. "But unless I want to reverse image search the photo Justin took of him and hope I find a social media post of him looking pensive with the caption 'thinking of my hot hookup' I don't think I'll be finding this guy again."

"Wow, if this wasn't so insane, this might actually be romantic. Or be a romance in the making."

"Mm." All my playfulness wanes as my stomach sours.

Frannie runs her hand down my arm. "Hal?"

"Nauseous." I groan. So far, this has been the worst part. I've always hated throwing up.

There's a knock on her door right as I clutch my stomach.

"Go to the bathroom, I'll be there in a second."

I run down the hall as she answers the door. I don't overhear any of the conversation because I'm too busy violently puking.

The front door closes again right as I'm rinsing my mouth out, so rather than wait for her, I make my way back to the living room, exhausted. Apparently, puking sucks the energy right out of you. That and growing a human.

"Who was that?" I ask as I sit down in the corner of her couch and grab a blanket.

She sits down next to me. "Oh, that was Wilson. The guy who lives downstairs and needs a nanny. He was going to say hello to you, but he and his daughter were heading to his mom's for the day."

"Probably for the better. I can meet him in the morning after I've had some sleep. And hopefully haven't thrown up yet."

"Are you going to tell him you're pregnant?"

"That's my plan. I know it's early, but I figure... I'm good at being a nanny and there's no reason I can't keep doing it after I have a baby. Yeah, I'll need a bit of a break, but even then, I could still keep an eye on his daughter, even if I'm not cooking and cleaning and stuff. It's sort of the best of both worlds because I'll still get to have my baby with me. Being right across the hall will make it easy. So yeah. I'd rather be up front with him because obviously I'm keeping the baby and if he's not comfortable with that potential distraction slash complication in my life, then it's better to handle it right away."

"Look at you being mature. I'm so proud."

"Yes, getting knocked up by a stranger I spent one night with and only exchanged nicknames with is my proudest moment."

She sighs and pulls me into her arms. "I really missed you."

I squeeze her back as tight as I can. "I missed you too."

"So you're really planning on staying in Ida? For good?"

I try to sigh, but I can't. "Yeah. I think you're stuck with me. I want to be with my family. I know you won't always be here, but a good chunk of the time I'll have you. More than in the city. And Justin's close too. Think we can get Kennedy to move here?"

"I don't think she has any intention of letting Devon or Brighton go."

"Lame. But whatever. She did her soul searching. Now it's time for me to grow up. Nothing like seeing an ultrasound of your baby to do that."

"You have an ultrasound?" she squeals.

"Yeah. Hold on." I pull it from my purse, then turn back to her. "What?"

"Have you told Kennedy?"

"No. Why—oh."

"She's going to be so mad if you wait longer than thirty minutes after telling me. You need to call her now."

"Mm. Better idea." I grab my phone, select video call, then hold the ultrasound in front of the camera as Frannie squeaks with excitement next to me.

When the call connects and Kennedy's face appears—her short brown hair longer than when I saw her last—her eyes instantly go wide.

"Hallie—who's calling me—not Frannie. Hallie? You're—are you? Hallie!"

I laugh and switch the camera around so she can see Frannie and me.

"Hi."

"You're pregnant? Who and how?"

"I had sex with a guy."

Her nostrils flare. "I know how babies are made!"

"Then why does everyone keep asking me *how*?"

"I'm not wondering how pregnancy happened. I'm wondering how you, in particular, ended up pregnant."

"Had a hot as fuck one-night stand and he left me with a goodbye present."

Kennedy's face softens, and I spill the whole story before she can give me pity eyes.

"Wow. Well, you always wanted to be a mom," Kennedy says.

Frannie bumps her arm against mine. "You did. I remember you stuffing pillows under your shirt and pretending to give birth."

I swipe a hand over my face as I laugh.

"You're going to be amazing," Kennedy says.

And there are those stupid tears again. I'm not the crier in my family or this friend group.

"I wish you were here."

"So do I. I don't care that it's only been a couple of months. We need another Baker girls reunion."

"Yes, we do," Frannie says.

"At least you two are together, so I only have to make it to one stop to see you both. And Justin too. Let's get everyone to Ida, then Dev and I can visit a few times a year and see you all."

I let out a sigh, surprised over the words about to leave my mouth. "That sounds amazing."

THE APARTMENT I'm living in is beautiful. Like Frannie's, it overlooks the river, and there's a little bench seat next to one of the windows. It's where I've been living for the last two hours, intermittently reading books and snacking.

I've found a few more foods that settle well. Mostly potatoes. Microwaved tater tots with sour cream have been my go-to for the last hour, though I've managed to keep down some baked apples as well—which I ordered from the café down the street along with the chicken soup which is supposedly magical.

When I hear the downstairs door open and footsteps

rumbling up the stairs, I consider going to say hello, but I'm exhausted and feel gross and I'd rather make a good first impression.

I look out at the sky darkening over the river.

This is home now. And tomorrow is the first day of my new life.

CHAPTER EIGHT

Hallie

WHAT DO I take to meet a client for the first time?

Usually, I have a portfolio and references and all kinds of things, but usually it's an interview. It seems like this Wilson guy really wants to hire me. And I'm cool with that, as long as he passes my vibe check. Though with Frannie's endorsement, I don't know how he could not.

He said to come over around 7:45, so I'm waiting one more minute before walking across the hall.

I'm dressed in my typical summer nannying attire. Relaxed fit thick canvas shorts with a simple V-neck tee. My hair is tucked back in a braid, and I'm ready for whatever the day might bring.

And I'm praying a lot of nausea won't be a part of that.

But that might be wishful thinking.

I grab one of the ginger hard candies that have become my saving grace and head across the hall.

There are faint footsteps and then heavier ones, and finally the door swings open.

"Hey, thanks for coming over this morning, I'm—"

"Deck," I breathe, my heart stuttering as I take in the devil of a man who I was only supposed to have one night with.

One night. And now... oh fuck. Oh *fuck*.

"Hellion?" he rasps, eyes locked on mine.

"Also known as Hallie," I chirp.

We stare at each other, eyes wide.

What in the fucking fuck? Of all the places and all the neighbors and all the jobs... Deck?

Here?

My hand almost goes to my stomach.

My baby daddy.

At least I found him?

I open my mouth to speak, but before I can say a word, a little girl flies over, coming to a stop in front of her dad.

She's beautiful with big green eyes and light brown hair.

"Are you my new nanny?"

I look at Deck, because—*what the fuck*—am I?

"Ooh, do you know how to braid hair?" she asks, bouncing on her toes.

"I do."

"Good." She gives me a big smile. "You're hired."

Then she grabs my hand and drags me inside and right past Deck.

Or Wilson?

I don't know.

I don't know much of anything right now. I'm so overwhelmed I couldn't think straight if I wanted to.

"Can you do two braids? One on each side?"

My focus goes to the girl standing beside the couch and staring up at me.

Right. This is why I'm here.

"What's your name?"

She smiles brightly. "Sophia."

"That's a very pretty name. I'm Hallie. And yes, I can do two braids. But I need your help. Can you go get me your hairbrush?"

She nods firmly, then I get up and go to the kitchen, opening a few cabinets until I find the bowls, then I fill one with water. I can feel Deck's eyes on me as I get back to the living room and take a seat on the couch, but I tune it all out.

If this is an interview, I'm going to prove my worth. Everything else can be dealt with later.

Sophia returns and hands me her hairbrush.

"Here, sit down on the couch in front of me." I turn sideways on the couch and she sits down in front of me.

After dipping the brush in the water to wet her hair, I part her hair and separate a few strands, then get to work on two Dutch braids. It takes about ten minutes, but she holds still the entire time.

"Okay, ready for the reveal? Do you have a small mirror we can use so you can see the back?"

"Yeah, come on."

She drags me down the hall to the bathroom, and I try to ignore the roiling in my stomach at the fast movement.

She pulls the mirror out and hands it to me while she gets a stool. Once she's standing backward on it, I hand her the mirror and her little mouth drops.

"Oh my gosh! Thank you, thank you, thank you! Daddy says his fingers are too big and meaty to do braids. And Nana can't because of her arthritis. I've always wanted someone who could braid my hair like this."

I gently rub her shoulder. "Well, I'm happy to help."

She throws her arms around me in a hug, and I hug her back.

This is why I love nannying. The amazing connection I form with the kids I nanny for is like nothing else.

Although I have a feeling the connection with my own child will surpass even that.

"Anything else you need to do to get ready for school?"

"Nope. I ate my breakfast, packed my backpack, and brushed my teeth. I just need shoes."

"Soph!" Deck calls.

"We better hurry."

I grab her hand and she jumps off the stool.

She runs over to her dad, and my stomach flips.

Her dad. Who is also my baby's dad. Which means she'll be my baby's sister.

My brain is scrambling all over again.

Deck throws a backpack over his shoulder, and it takes me a second to remember what Frannie said he does. Construction.

Slowly, I make my way to the door instead of standing there awkwardly and staring.

Deck looks at me hesitantly. "We'll talk this evening?"

I give a quick nod as I follow them out the door. "Yeah. No problem, Mr. Decker."

He freezes for a second, then makes a strangled noise, and I'm not sure if I want to laugh out of playfulness or at how absurd this all is.

"Bye, Miss Hallie." Sophia waves as they walk down the hall.

I wave back, smiling as they go. But the second they're out of sight, the facade falls. And when the door at the bottom of the stairs slams shut, I run upstairs to Frannie's apartment, praying she hasn't left for work yet.

I hit the bell at her outer door, and she buzzes me in.

She's walking across the living room when I throw open her door.

"Hey, how was your meeting with Wilson?" Her brow furrows. "You look frantic. Are you okay?"

"It was an interesting meeting. Of sorts. And okay? I'm not sure what okay is right now."

"You're freaking me out. What's going on?"

"He's the guy."

"The guy—what guy?"

I gesture to my stomach. "*The* guy."

Her eyes fly wide. "Oh my god," she whisper-screeches. "*The guy*? But wait, how did you not know? I've said his name a billion times!"

"You said *Wilson* a billion times. And I told you we didn't do full names. That night he went by—"

"Decker."

"Deck, actually, but yes."

She paces in front of me, then spins to face me again. "Did you tell him?"

"No, I didn't tell him!"

"Why not?"

"Because it's one thing to give professional courtesy and tell this stranger that I'm pregnant but it won't affect my ability to do my job. It's another to have a personal rule about never sleeping with the parent of the child I'm nannying, then showing up at their house to find out I already did and I'm pregnant with his baby."

"Okay, yeah. That's not the best."

"Thank you. Plus, I couldn't do that in front of his daughter. She seems sweet and wonderful. I'd love to be her nanny. But how? How would any of this work?"

"Maybe instead of her nanny you could be her step mommy."

My mouth drops open and I give my sister a little shove. "What is wrong with you?"

She laughs. "I'm just saying..."

"Well, don't. We're so *not* going there." Even if he's hot as sin and I'd love to take another spin on that ride. But no. Nope. Not an option. Especially if I work for him.

"Okay, well, do you want to be Sophia's nanny?"

"Yes. It's literally across the hall. Sophia seems awesome. I think it could be a great fit for me. Minus one particular complication."

"When do you think you'll tell him?"

"He said we'll talk tonight. If he wants to do this... maybe I'll work through a contract first. Then I can tell him so he doesn't get weird about how he'd pay me or anything else."

Frannie stares at me for a moment. "Will you be able to work with him? With your history and now your present?"

I rest my hand on my stomach. "If he's anything like the father he seems to be, I'm going to need to work with him one way or another. And this baby is Sophia's sibling. Even if it makes things weird at first, this could be a great fit for both of us."

Frannie pulls me in for a hug. "Then I hope it works out for you."

"Me too."

FRANNIE KEPT ME FOR TEA, then she had to get back to work. She's been working from home more lately since a lot of what she does working for CPS she doesn't have to be in the office for.

When I get to my room, I flop onto my bed, then pull Veranda into my arms. Who knew a floppy gray bunny could hold so much meaning to me?

My eyes flit to the half heart necklace hanging on a small nail on my mirror.

What are the chances of Deck being the guy I'm supposed to nanny for? What were the chances of us randomly meeting that night at McGills?

What if none of it was random?

I immediately chastise myself for that thought, but it's impossible to deny. How coincidental is life?

Were we meant to find each other again?

I don't like the feeling in my heart when I think that.

A silly little flutter that wants to cling to the romantic idea of soul mates and fate.

It's a feeling I instantly want to squash.

But that feeling is tied to my baby too. So I can't squash it.

Instead, I tuck it away in a box and try to ignore it.

Then I grab my phone and make a group message with Justin, Jade, Brian, and Hardy.

> So, remember that guy from McGills after the Metros game? Funny story…

CHAPTER NINE

Wilson

I'M NOT FIRING on all cylinders this morning.

Actually, I take that back. I *am*, but all those cylinders are devoted to Hallie.

My little hellion.

My hellion who is supposed to be Sophia's nanny.

I drop my pencil onto the table in front of me when I come too close to snapping it in half.

Monday morning is my late morning. We have our project managers meeting at the AB Construction offices at 8:30. It worked out perfect for me to stay home a little longer and meet Hallie before heading here.

Except that meeting Hallie wasn't the relief I hoped it would be.

She was supposed to be a memory. One I looked back on reverently, but a memory nonetheless. Because to have her here, right across the hall from me... whether she works for me or not, it's going to be pure torture. It's impossible to deny there was more than sex between us that night. There was an underlying passion—connection—that drove everything.

I don't let random hookups drag me to carnivals, and I don't finger them on Ferris wheel rides.

This is why I don't do fun things. This is why I overthink and over plan. It drives Sophia nuts, but it keeps these exact situations from happening.

And of course, Sophia had to instantly fall in love with Hallie.

I mean, who wouldn't?

I've yet to see anything about her that isn't incredible.

I'm in so much fucking trouble.

Especially because I *need* a nanny. And her living across the hall would make life so much easier. It would uproot her life less, and it would make it easy for her to be there in a pinch.

My cock is very angry about this because it means he doesn't get to play anymore.

If Hallie is going to be Soph's nanny, anything else has to be done.

If her being Soph's nanny is even a smart idea at this point. Maybe it's too tangled.

Fuck.

I have zero frame of reference for this.

As the meeting ends, I grab a cup of coffee, and try to think about who I can talk to. My mom is usually my go-to person for this, but this is one area of my life I don't need her to know about or have an opinion on. Thankfully, I think of a better option, and I make my way up to Leo's office, hoping this isn't crossing any boundaries. He's always supportive of his workers and tells us to come to him with anything, work-related or not, so here I am.

I knock on his door frame since his door is open, and he looks up from his computer.

"Hey, Deck."

"Hey, boss. Got a minute?"

He waves a hand. "Sure thing, come on in. What's going on?"

"Nothing construction-related. This is a personal thing. Question. If you're okay with that. I don't know many single dads, especially ones who have already been around the block. I could use some advice."

Though he's only forty-eight, Leo had kids in his mid-twenties and his youngest daughter was a teen mom, so he's been through the ringer already.

"Yeah, of course. What's going on?"

"Well, I may have found a nanny for Sophia."

"That's great."

"It's Frannie's sister."

"Ah, she moving up from New York?"

"Apparently. The thing is... back in August, I was down there for a friend's wedding and I had a one-night stand..." I clear my throat and his brows go up. "With Frannie's sister. But we didn't exchange full names, so I had no idea and she had no idea and this morning we found out."

"Wow."

"Yes. And she's worked as a nanny for years. Lives across the hall from us. Seems to have a good heart. Soph already loves her. But would it be crazy to have her be Sophia's nanny after what happened between us?"

"Look, I'm just going to ask... do you want it to happen again?"

"In a perfect fucking world, of course. But in reality, I can keep my dick in my pants."

"Then you've answered your own question. If you can both be professional, then I don't see a problem. Assuming you feel she's comfortable with it."

"I think so."

"Then talk to her. Worst case she's not, and she becomes the fun neighbor Sophia talks to now and then. But if she is, and you can both be professional, it should be fine." Then he laughs and shakes his head. "But I get it. It's complicated. I told myself over and over I wasn't going to sleep with my daughter's dance teacher and I've been married to her for over fifteen years now, so what the fuck do I know? I guess what I'm saying is, play it by ear, but don't write it off because of your history. Maybe fate's bringing you back together for a reason."

I let that settle in. It makes the most sense. No matter how incredible that night was, I can put it aside and be professional, and if Hallie can do the same, there's no reason we shouldn't do this.

"Thanks, Leo."

"No problem. Have a good day, Deck."

"Yeah, you too."

"IS Hallie going to be my nanny?" Sophia asks through a yawn as I'm tucking her into bed.

I'm surprised it took her this long to ask, but she was busy telling me every detail of her day, then I distracted her by telling her she could take dance classes with Lara. Because as long as Hallie is on board, I'm determined to make this nannying thing work.

"I hope so. I'm going to talk to her about it tonight. But you have to go to sleep first."

She gives me her grumpiest face, and I lean in and kiss her nose, then gently run my fingers through her light brown hair.

Even when the entire world is a dumpster fire, Soph is perfect. She's the best part of my life, no question. Even when one or both of us is struggling, we make it through together. Usually with a little help from my mom.

Mom's always been my biggest supporter. My dad died ten years ago, so when Sophia was born eight years ago, she devoted her time to being our rock. I didn't know what the fuck I was doing when Sophia's mom told me she was pregnant.

We'd been dating about six months and it was all just okay. We were young. Still figuring ourselves out.

She didn't decide right away about keeping Sophia, and I gave her my full support with either option. I love Sophia with all my heart and I have no regrets, but at barely twenty-three and in an iffy relationship, I wasn't longing for a kid then, either.

Soph changed it all, though.

Her mom struggled through the pregnancy. It was high risk. She was uncomfortable and unhappy. She had to quit a job she loved because she couldn't work and was hospitalized all the time. I worked two shitty jobs to make sure every bill was covered, and even then, my mom helped out a lot. Between my dad's pension and his life insurance, she's set for the rest of her life and uses the extra to help everyone around her, especially me and Soph.

Sophia was born by an emergency C-section, and though I'd like to say I was more worried about Soph's mom, I wasn't. Our relationship was dying and neither of us really wanted to keep it alive. She had a long recovery and held a lot of resentment toward Sophia because of it.

But I respect her because she knew it. She knew she wasn't in the mental space to be the kind of mom Sophia needed. After a lot of talks, she decided to take some time away, pursue the master's program she wanted, and see how she felt.

She ultimately signed her rights away. Not because she felt like she had to choose between Sophia and a future, but because she realized she didn't want her future to include motherhood.

I've raised Sophia telling her that her mom loved her enough to let her go because she knew she couldn't be the mom Sophia needed. That will probably hurt more as she gets to her teen years, but for now, she's okay with it.

And I'm okay having Soph all to myself. Though I've always left the door open to her mother. She can change her mind, and as long as she's sure, she's welcome in Sophia's life. I refuse to let there be any bad blood there. It destroys kids.

Sophia is my whole world, and I'll do everything I can to protect her from that kind of needless ache.

"Night, Daddy," she whispers sleepily as I leave the room.

"Night, kiddo."

I switch the light off, then head out to the kitchen. I don't know what the fuck I'm doing or what I want, though, so I prowl around the apartment, trying to be quiet as I wait for Soph to drift off.

Unlike when she was young, she's a great sleeper now, so I don't have to worry too much. Still, I'll take the video monitor over to Hallie's place when I go.

I just want to talk to her. Get it all out. Move on.

Because if I don't do that, my mind will keep wandering to what-ifs, and that's a dangerous place to be.

Carefully, I creep down the hall to Sophia's room and stick my head inside. She's snoring softly and cuddled up with her favorite purple bear.

Grabbing the video monitor, I quietly walk back down the hall and to the door, grabbing my keys and then locking it behind me. Even though there's a door at the end of the hall that automatically locks along with the one downstairs, I'll never risk Sophia's safety.

In the hallway, I let out a long breath, then take the three diagonal steps over to Hallie's door and knock.

There are soft footsteps on the other side, then the door swings open.

The slightest smirk appears on her lips. "Deck."

Her playfulness relaxes me a little, and a smile slips out. "I told you it was a real name."

"A *nick*name. For Decker. Wilson Decker."

"Hallie Baker. Though I still prefer Hells Bells."

She laughs lightly. "Where's Sophia?"

I shake the monitor in my hand. "Asleep."

"Ah. Well, come on in. We should talk."

"Yeah. So... this morning was a surprise."

"You're telling me."

She takes a seat at the far end of the couch, and I sit down at the opposite end. That's good. Keeping space between us.

Whatever it is about her that attracted me to her after only a look across the bar hasn't gone away. As much as I'd like to pin her to this couch and hear her scream my name again, that's not an option.

"Do you think Frannie knew?" I ask.

Hallie immediately shakes her head. "No. I mean, I wouldn't put it out of the realm of possibility for her to meddle like that, but I never mentioned to her that I hooked up with anyone. It's pure coincidence."

Or fate. But I'm not stupid enough to say that.

"So, what do you want me to do?" Hallie asks.

My gaze darts to hers, and she laughs.

"As your nanny, Deck."

I clear my throat. "Right."

"Assuming you still want me to take on that role."

"I do. It's the perfect situation. You're close by and Sophia already loves you. I saw a flash of your abilities this morning, and I trust Frannie when she vouches for you. And Sophia needs someone like you."

"Someone like me?"

"Upbeat. Fun. Not a curmudgeon like me."

She bites her lip, and *fuck me.*

Don't growl. Don't move. Don't think of her naked.

"I don't think curmudgeons make people come on Ferris wheels."

I groan before I can stop myself, then shake my head. "The guy you saw that night is a guy I haven't been for a long time."

"Because you have to focus on being a dad. And a grump."

I stare at her for a beat. "You really think I'm grumpy?"

She shrugs. "You have a gruff side. Like you're closing a part of yourself off. It might be subconsciously, but I think it comes off slightly grumpy."

Running my hand through my hair, I lean back against her couch. "I keep things locked down tight so I don't have to worry about major things being out of my control."

Her features cloud for a moment. "That's not how life works."

"You're right. It's not." I wave my hand and move on because I don't want to get into my baggage right now. "Anyway, I want to make sure you're comfortable with all this."

"Absolutely, Mr. Decker."

"Hallie..."

Her grin returns. "Sorry. It's fun. If you want me to stop and never mention it again, then that's fine. But don't worry. I wouldn't do it in front of Sophia, and you don't need to worry about my professionalism. I have one hard and fast rule. Never sleep with someone I work for. Never get involved with them. It only ends up destroying things."

Why do those words destroy *me* a little? They're exactly what I should want to hear. She'll keep this professional, and she can be the nanny—and woman—my daughter needs.

What about what I need?

Ha. My needs. I gave those up when I had a kid.

"Well, we should talk about compensation, then. Not a sex joke, I promise."

She laughs a little. "Let's crunch some numbers."

IT'S ALMOST ten by the time we're finished talking through things and drawing up an online contract. I was ready to say screw it, but Hallie reminded me that contracts protect both parties and they're essential.

We came up with a pretty good system overall. I can't afford to pay her a ton, but since Frannie isn't charging her rent, she says she doesn't need a lot.

Hallie sets her mostly full cup of tea on the table and fidgets in her spot like she's done several times over the last twenty minutes.

She just signed the contract. Now I'm reading through it all on her tablet so I can sign it too.

"Are you okay?" I ask.

I finished my tea a half hour ago. Maybe she's just tired or nervous—though that doesn't seem like her. Either way, something's wrong.

"Just been a long day. Still getting used to a new apartment." She gestures to the tablet. "Finish reading."

I finish up and sign. It's more thorough than I ever would've thought of, but she's right. It protects us both.

I lean forward to hand her the tablet, but she pushes to her feet. "Fuck."

Then she's bolting toward the hallway. I jump to my feet and follow her.

She runs into the bathroom and drops to her knees in front of the toilet. She barely gets it open before she throws up.

I drop to my knees beside her and grab her hair, holding it back.

After a couple of minutes, she sits back, wipes her mouth with some toilet paper, then swipes her hand over her eyes, sniffling.

"Sorry. I hate throwing up."

I gently run my hand down her back. "It's okay. You don't have to apologize. Is it something you ate? A stomach bug? Can I get you anything?"

She waves a hand. "No. It's... I'll get some crackers in a minute."

"Let me get you some water."

I run back to the kitchen before she can say another word and return with a glass of water for her.

"Thanks."

"It's okay. Do you need any medicine? Pepto? Or I think I have some antiemetics from when Soph was sick last."

"No. It's fine. I don't think I can…"

She trails off, breathing heavily.

I stare at her for a moment.

She said no when I asked about the stomach bug or food.

She doesn't know if she can have meds.

"Hallie…?"

All fragility disappears, and she sits up straight, looking me in the eyes. "I'm pregnant."

It's mine.

I know it before she opens her mouth to say it.

She's pregnant with my baby.

She's. Pregnant.

Fuck.

Shell-shocked, I stand up, mumble something about seeing her in the morning, and bolt.

CHAPTER TEN

I GLANCE at the clock for the tenth time in the last two minutes.

On the list of things I don't want to do today, facing Deck is all of them.

I told him I was pregnant, and he ran his ass out of here like it was on fire.

I get that it was a shock, but what the actual fuck?

When I saw how he was with Sophia yesterday morning, I was briefly hopeful. Maybe my baby would end up with a good dad.

Now I have no idea where we stand, but that's why I wanted the contract signed. I don't need to know what's going on with us. I have a job to do, and I'm going to do it.

Grabbing my keys, I make my way across the hall and knock on the door, pleasant—if slightly robotic—smile in place.

The door swings open almost immediately, and I'm greeted by Deck's stupidly handsome face. It's annoying how hot he is. Especially right now.

"Hallie—"

"Good morning, Mr. Decker. Is Sophia here?"

He opens the door a little farther to let me in. "She is, but we need to—"

"Miss Hallie!"

I smile brightly when Sophia dashes into the room and runs over to give me a hug.

Deck can go fuck himself as far as I'm concerned, but being Sophia's nanny requires no effort. She's a sweetheart.

"Do you know how to curl hair?"

I laugh at that. "I do. But curling irons can be a little dangerous and burn you." Her little face falls, so I continue. "But I have a secret magic way of curling your hair while you sleep."

Her eyes light up. "Really?"

"Yes. I can bring my secret weapon here tonight when you get ready for bed." I look over at Deck. "If your dad's okay with that."

"That's fine. We should—"

"Daddy, you need to go to work."

I check the time, and she's right.

"You do. I've got things from here." Walking toward him, I keep my most professional face on. "Does she have any allergies I need to know about?"

Decker's jaw ticks for a second before he answers. "No. Her only issue is she has sensitive skin and occasionally breaks out in hives. Don't use any lotions or soaps that we don't have here in the house. And if you do her hair, don't add any products. If you notice any hives, usually a cool compress will do it, but we have twenty-four-hour allergy meds for mild cases and Benadryl for worse ones. If it seems really bad, obviously—"

"Call an ambulance or get her to the ER."

Dad mode seems to take over for him, and that's fine by me because it's much easier to work with.

"You're CPR certified, right?"

"Yes. I renew it yearly to make sure I'm up to date on any new recommendations. Also, let me know if you think her hives are severe enough that I should carry an epi-pen. Now, Sophia's right. You should get to work. But at this point, I should probably get your number. If that's okay with you."

The bite to my voice makes his brow furrow. He stares at me for a beat, then points to the fridge. "My number, my mom's number, AB Construction's number, and my boss's number are all there, along with her pediatrician and school numbers."

"Okay then. We're all set. You can head to work."

As I spin to walk away, he grabs my arm, pulling me back.

His hot breath tickles my ear as he leans in. "Tonight, we're going to talk."

Then he lets me go and walks over to Sophia while I try to ignore the shiver that moves through me.

Wilson Decker can go fuck himself.

SOPHIA IS A VIBRANT, whip-smart kid.

She talked the whole morning, telling me all about an art project she's working on and the dance classes she's going to take. Then the entire walk home today, she practiced her multiplication tables, regularly looking at me for affirmation that she was correct, which challenged the math side of my brain I haven't used in a while.

Since her dad hadn't had time to change her pick-up and drop-off routine yet, I walked her over to the daycare Deck's boss's wife runs—or so Sophia says—to get her on the bus, then picked her up there this afternoon.

I went to the store while she was gone and got some food for their apartment and for mine.

Last night, while we were working on the contract, Decker said he's trying to get Sophia to be open to new foods, so I'm going to try one of my favorite recipes and get her in the kitchen with me. Hopefully that will help.

"Do I get to cut something?" Soph asks, as I get all the ingredients out.

"Well, the only thing to cut is these vegetables, and I have to use a really sharp knife for that. But how about you wash the green beans for me. Then we can be like an assembly line."

"Okay."

She grabs a stool and takes it over to the sink.

"Wash your hands first." I set an onion on the cutting board, then grab a colander for her to use to wash the beans. "All set?"

She smiles up at me. "Yep."

"Okay, so you don't need to use soap while washing these, just run them under the water and scrub off any dirty bits with your fingers. If you notice there's a long stem on the end, you can break it off." I pull one out and show her. "Like this."

"Got it!"

She gets to work, and I head for the cutting board, swallowing back some nausea. I kept Sophia from seeing it so far, though I almost had to throw up in a bush while I was walking her to the daycare to catch the bus.

"So, how come you moved here?" Sophia asks.

"Most of my family and friends moved to other places, and I felt a bit lonely. Did your dad tell you that Miss Frannie is my sister?"

"Yeah."

"Well, I wanted to be closer to her. Have you gotten to know her much?"

"A little. Daddy says she's a safe person. Someone I can go to in an emergency."

"She is. And now I am too."

"Was it fun growing up with a sister?"

I tilt my head back and forth. "Most of the time. I actually kind of grew up with two."

"Really?"

"Yeah. Want to hear something silly?"

"Mhm." She gives a sharp nod.

"Before I was born, my aunt and my uncle got married. Then my aunt introduced her sister—my mom—to my uncle's brother —my dad. And *they* got married too. They had so much fun that they bought a house with two apartments in it. One on either side. And they lived there together. So I grew up with Frannie and my parents, but I also grew up with my aunt and uncle and their daughter, my cousin Kennedy. Since both sets of our parents are related, we're super cousins. But she was always more like my oldest sister instead."

Sophia's smiling brightly at my story. "That must've been so cool." Then her eyes drop back to the sink. "Sometimes I wish I had a sister. Or a cousin. Someone else."

My hand instinctively drops to my stomach, then I rip it away again.

"Sometimes I feel really lonely."

My heart breaks for her for so many reasons. I know how she feels, and here I am carrying her little sibling and I can't even tell her. This is so fucked up.

"Are you crying?"

My gaze darts to her. "It's the onions. They always hurt my eyes."

She nods like she gets it, but the onions are nothing compared to my feelings right now.

"I know how it is to be lonely. That's how I felt before I moved here."

She drops the last bean in the colander, then turns the water off and walks over to me, throwing her arms around my waist.

"Now we have each other."

I set the knife down and turn to her, squatting down so I can give her a proper hug.

"You bet we do."

She holds me tightly, and it takes everything in me not to break.

But after our little vulnerable moment, she's back to being a chatterbox while I prep the beans and onions, then get out the ingredients for the pasta.

"What else are we making?"

"It's one of my favorite things. Pasta. But not just any pasta. It has a special sauce that's pink. Now, remind me, do you like pink?"

I already know that answer. She loves everything glittery, pink, orange, and yellow. But she likes to pair them with black because it makes the colors pop. A girl after my own heart.

"I love it."

"I thought so. It also has a fun ingredient." I hold up the mustard seeds and she frowns.

"What are those?"

"Mustard seeds."

"I don't like mustard."

"Trust me. These don't taste like mustard. The flavor is mild, and they do a cool trick. When you put them in the hot pan, they dance."

"Dance?"

"I'll show you, but move your stool back toward the sink. The hot oil hurts if it splatters."

She diligently does as I asked, while I pour some oil in the pan and get it heating up.

When it's shimmering, I smile at Sophia. "Here we go. Can you see inside the pan?"

"Yes!"

I pour the mustard seeds in, and they immediately start popping and bouncing around.

"Oh my gosh. That's so cool!"

"Cooking is fun, right?"

She nods boisterously.

"Want to know a secret?"

"Hm?" she asks, eyes bright.

"The food tastes even better when you help cook it."

I wink at her, then get ready to add the next ingredient.

The rest of the meal comes together quickly, and since Deck isn't home, I put it all in the oven to stay warm.

"Can I watch TV?"

I almost say yes because I'm exhausted, but then I spot the *Investigators* book series on the nearby bookshelf.

"How about we read for a bit?"

"Okay."

With that, Sophia and I get cozy on the couch and read.

All the other craziness aside, it's moments like these that I live for—that bring me peace.

CHAPTER ELEVEN

I'M A FUCKING TWAT.

That's the conclusion I've reached about fifty times today.

And a hundred more last night.

I almost stormed back into Hallie's apartment multiple times after I left like the asshole I am.

She told me she was pregnant with my baby, and I walked out.

She mumbled those words while I stood there catatonic, then I just left.

Fucking moron.

It's no surprise she didn't want to talk to me this morning, but seeing her uber professional mode was jarring. And hot.

I grip the steering wheel tighter. Two more red lights and I'll be home to face the dumpster fire anew.

Especially because this revelation changes everything.

Hallie's no longer a woman I once hooked up with and still run hot for. She's not Sophia's nanny who I want but shouldn't get involved with. She's the mother of my child. And while I wasn't willing to cross professional lines because Sophia needs someone like her, it's all different now.

If there hadn't been any continuing chemistry with Hallie—if she hadn't made me feel alive the way she did—I wouldn't even let my mind go where it's going.

But fuck.

It's Hallie. My hellion. *Mine.*

Now that I know exactly what's at stake, I want her to be. I want a chance at being the man who takes care of her. Who supports her. Who cherishes her. And that's fucked up because I haven't wanted anything like that in a long, long time.

It was there, deep in my gut, the night we spent together. But I knew I couldn't have it. Or I thought I couldn't.

I keep going back to fate.

Did it throw us together for a reason?

I pull into the parking lot, at odds with the idealistic side of me I don't let out often.

But damn it all if I don't want Hallie to be mine, and I'm willing to grovel to prove to her how sorry I am for how I handled this.

I trudge up the stairs to the apartment, cursing the fact that we have to wait to talk until Sophia is asleep. I haven't even let my mind wander to what we're going to tell her or when, but we'll have to figure it out eventually.

The second I open the door, Hallie spins around and starts moving quickly through the apartment.

"Hey, your dad's here."

"Daddy."

"So, I'm going to head home."

I kiss Sophia's cheek and set her down.

"Hallie."

"I'll be back in a couple of hours with my special tools to help curl your hair."

"You're not going to stay for dinner?" Sophia asks, eyes big.

Hallie looks from her to me. Then her eyes shift and her gaze narrows. I follow her line of sight to my hand. Where my keys are. Where the half heart she gave me is. For some stupid reason, I kept the damn thing and put it on my keychain.

My eyes meet hers.

Maybe it wasn't stupid at all.

"We'd love for you to stay," I say gently. Then I lean in and whisper, "If you think you can stomach it."

She lets out a sigh. "I'll stay."

I'll consider that a win. Especially since she hasn't slapped me or told me to go fuck myself. Both of which I deserve.

"I'll get changed, then we can eat."

"We'll dish it up," Hallie says, and before I can say anything else, she and Sophia start plating things up.

After changing, I head back to the kitchen, but I pause at the edge of it, staring at the set table and two girls waiting for me.

My heart quakes.

I want this.

I asked Hallie to stay because that's what I was always planning on. It's stupid for her to cook for us, then go home and cook for herself. And maybe it was me letting my professionalism slip because I was hoping we'd feel a bit like a family.

It's completely stupid, but... fuck. As much as my mother harped on me about finding a partner, I always shut it down. Looking at it now, though, I realize it wasn't because I was against the idea. I was afraid to admit I wanted it.

Now fate threw it in my lap.

The possibility of it, at least.

I make my way over to the table and sit down. It all looks amazing.

As we eat, Sophia tells me all about her day and how she helped Hallie cook everything. Then she eats the whole meal without a hint of coercion or leveraging dessert.

I can't remember the last time that happened with something other than chicken nuggets and fries.

In case I wasn't sure before, it's clear now. Hallie is magic.

Once we've finished, Hallie heads home, promising to come back and bring whatever hair accessories she has planned.

I get to work on dishes, and the evening goes by quickly.

When Hallie returns, wearing a tank top and sweats, I have to force my eyes off her. She's so gorgeous it hurts.

Sophia settles on the couch with her, and I try to distract myself with a book while Hallie twirls Sophia's hair around some silky things that she'll leave in all night.

"Thanks, Miss Hallie," Sophia chirps, throwing her arms around Hallie. "Goodnight."

"Night." She smiles and gives a little wave as Sophia scampers down the hallway to get ready.

I turn back and look at Hallie, unsure of what to say, but hoping my eyes convince her how badly I want her to stay.

SOPHIA IS asleep when I walk by her room after taking a shower, and when I get to the living room, I'm shocked to find Hallie sitting on the couch, reading.

She puts her book down when she sees me.

"Hey." I do my best to keep my voice even.

"Hi."

Slowly, I walk over and drop down on the couch, leaving a little space between us. "I'm surprised you're still here. I figured I'd have to hunt you down tonight. Rightfully so."

She clears her throat. "Part of me wanted to make you do that. But I saw the keychain. It reminded me of that night. Who you were with me. Not the guy I saw last night." She's quiet for a moment. "Why'd you keep it?"

"That night was one of the best of my life because of you. I wanted to keep that connection to you alive. Did you keep yours?"

She stares at me for a beat. "It's hanging from my mirror. I kept the bunny too. Named it after you." She smiles when I arch a brow. "Veranda."

I chuckle and shake my head.

"I really did name it that."

I move closer, splaying my palm over her thigh. "Hallie, I'm sorry. I'm sorry for how I reacted last night. That's not who I am, and that's not the man I ever want to be. I panicked and handled it very poorly."

"You think?"

"You have every right to be pissed, but I promise you, that moment is not who I am."

She stares at me. "That's why it surprised me. You're grumpy, but I didn't think you were an asshole. I'm still a little pissed, but I haven't handled it perfectly either. I should've told you before we talked about the job or signed the contract."

"I understand why you didn't."

"I appreciate you apologizing. But I get it. This is messy. After I found out, I laid around and avoided life for three days."

"When did you find out?"

"Last week. My period was late, and I kept trying to ignore it, but when I started getting really nauseous, I finally went to the doctor."

She leans over and grabs her bag on the coffee table, pulling it closer, then takes something out. Slowly, she hands it to me.

An ultrasound picture.

My breath sticks in my throat as I stare at it. It barely looks like more than a grain of rice, but it's the beginning. The beginning of us.

I pinch the bridge of my nose, completely overwhelmed.

I did this once before, and while it was emotional, I was a nervous wreck. When they put Sophia in my arms, I melted, but there were still so many logistics. Just like there are now.

But this time they don't worry me. Everything is upturned and twisted, but it all feels right to me. This is where I'm supposed to be.

Hallie runs her hand down my arm, drawing my gaze back to her.

"You okay?"

I nod and wipe my eyes. "Yeah. God, I can't believe I get to do this again." Then I remember the hard parts about the first time. How unsure Sophia's mom was. "Is this what you want?"

Tears well in her eyes. "I've never wanted anything more than to be a mom."

The way her vulnerability unlocks something feral in me is slightly terrifying.

"I will be here for every step. I will take care of you. I'll be at every doctor's appointment. I'll make middle of the night food runs. Every bill will be taken care of, and I'll make sure you have everything you need. When you're with Sophia, if you need to rest, that's okay. I can cook when I get home. Just know I will be by your side, fulfilling every need the whole time."

She leans back slightly, a mix of surprised and frustrated.

"I'm not incapacitated. I can still take care of Sophia and cook. Obviously, I'll rest if I need to." She shakes her head. "I appreciate that little speech, but all I need is a supportive co-parent who pulls their weight."

I sweep some hair behind her ear. "No. That's the bare minimum of what you deserve. I want you to have everything you could possibly need. I want you taken care of in every way. And I want to be the man to do it."

"Why?"

One simple word that tells me everything.

She doesn't trust what I'm saying. And I don't think it's because of how I walked out.

She was wild and free the night we met. When there were no strings.

I'm here for fun, and that's all.

Now that it's serious, it's something else. She's guarded, and that means I have some walls to dismantle.

Luckily, I can take a wall down just as well as I can build one.

"Because I felt something for you the moment I saw you. I said one night because I thought that's all I could have. I said I wouldn't cross professional boundaries because that's what Sophia needed. But all the while, my insides have been screaming at me to find you again. Stay close to you. If I'd known then what I know now, I'd have chained you to my bed and made you mine for good."

"Deck..." Her breath is shuddery, and her eyes are half closed. Then she snaps them open and shakes her head. "I don't do love. That's not what I'm looking for. We can be co-parents and maybe friends eventually. And with Sophia, we'll keep things professional." She stands quickly. "I should go."

I watch her as she hurries across the room and out the door.

Fuck me. I'm down bad.

She can say she doesn't do love, but that's not how love works. Love finds us.

It may not be love yet, but there's no denying the connection between us, as much as she might like to try. My mind is reeling, but my heart's never been more sure.

When I looked into Hallie's eyes, I didn't see locks and chains. I saw intense vulnerability. I saw a girl who wants to be loved, but is terrified to accept it.

Guess that means I have my work cut out for me.

But if I was a quitter, I wouldn't be here. Sophia wouldn't be who she is.

Hallie Baker is mine. She just doesn't know it yet.

"SOPH! Give me a hug. I'm leaving."

Sophia bolts into the room and runs over to her dad.

So far, nannying her is going really well. She's a bright burst of sunshine, she's creative, she's got a billion ideas about everything, and she loves to dance. I'll never say no to a random dance party.

And as for Deck... I've kept things professional. I help out, talk with him about how Sophia is doing, try to keep all the focus on her. It's become mandatory in Sophia's eyes that I stay for dinner, but she's such a chatterbox she keeps all the attention on her. As soon as dinner's over, I escape back to my apartment.

Deck never knocks on my door, but I swear sometimes I can feel his intense energy through the wall. It doesn't help that our rooms are so close together. Only a thick wall between us. It's not even brick. But that's fine. There's a wall there, literally and metaphorically, and that's all that matters.

"Love you, sweetheart. Have fun today," he calls as Sophia

leaves the room. Then he clears his throat. "Have a good day. Let me know if you need anything."

"Thanks. You too... Mr. Decker."

He freezes with his hand on the door, and I hide a smile as I turn back to the sink. Once the door closes behind him, I let myself laugh.

Okay, maybe I'm blurring the professional lines a little bit, but I like having fun with him. And having fun keeps me from thinking too hard about that little speech he gave me the other night.

I was dangerously close to breaking my rule. Multiple rules. Only hookups, and don't get involved with the client—though really, it's a little late for that.

But I almost gave in to the wild chemistry between us. The sparks that fly every time he touches me.

Falling for Wilson Decker is a recipe for heartbreak.

I need to keep him in the fun zone. Fun friend zone. Fun, boss, friend, co-parent zone. Sounds totally manageable.

"I'LL SMOTHER him in his sleep. Find out where he's working and make sure he has an *accident* on the job site. I—"

"Calm down and come back from the murder place," I say to Justin, who looks like he's about to blow a gasket. "I'm not mad at him anymore."

I'm sitting in the corner of the couch at his and Jade's apartment. He's sitting a couple spots over, fuming.

"Well, that makes one of us."

"There's more to the story."

"Does it include an evil twin being the one who heard that and reacted like a fuckwad?"

"Oh, I hope not. I hate an evil twin plot," Jade says as she walks into the room.

"No evil twin. He apologized and gave me a whole speech about how I deserve to be taken care of and that he's the one who's going to do it. And maybe a few things in there about how much he wants me and wishing he wouldn't have let it be one night in the first place."

"And then what? You threw your underwear at his face?" Jade asks playfully.

Justin's brows lift. "What did you say?"

"Thanks. I don't do love. Let's co-parent and keep this professional. Bye."

Justin throws his head back, laughing. "Aw, Hal. You *like* him."

"How does anything I just said give you that idea?"

"You only run from things that scare you. And nothing scares you more than lo—"

"Don't you even say it, or I'll punch you in the nads."

Jade laughs, then hums the chorus of *Love Story* by Taylor Swift as she walks into the kitchen

"I hate you."

"You love me," she sings, pulling the refrigerator open.

Technically, I'm still getting to know Jade, but she's awesome. And she makes Justin ridiculously happy.

Jade walks over to the couch and hands me a cup.

"What's this?"

"Homemade banana vanilla shake. Justin made it earlier."

I stick my lip out. "Thanks, buddy."

"So much nicer than threatening my balls."

"Would it be the worst thing to actually have feelings for this guy?" Jade asks.

"Yes," I say dramatically. Because not only am I chaotic, I'm a massive drama queen at the moment.

They share a look, then they both whisper, "Afraid to fall."

Jade glances at me, smirking. "And he fell first and hard."

"He's going to break through her walls."

I take a loud slurp of my milkshake and glare at them.

"Glad you two are having fun with your romance tropes. I'm going to keep living in the real world."

"No, you're living in delusional Hallie land if you think you can keep the feelings you don't want to admit you have for him locked down," Justin says.

"You're annoying." I take a sip of my shake. "But I've really missed you."

Jade and Justin exchange a glance, then Jade hops up again and kisses Justin on the cheek before she leaves the room.

Justin slides closer. "You okay, Hal? Besides the obvious chaos right now. Are you okay?"

"I'm fine."

"Don't lie to me. I've known you too long, and it's never worked. All this aside, the last few times I saw you, you had more of an edge than normal."

"Well, that's what happens when everyone leaves you behind."

"Hallie."

Fuck the stupid tears in my eyes.

Justin wraps an arm around me. "Hey, I'm sorry."

"Why? You needed to do what was right for you."

"But I didn't reach out enough. Didn't call or visit enough. I'm sorry for that. We've always been close, and I consider you my little sister. I hate that you ever felt left behind."

I shrug. "It is what it is. I've been dead set on avoiding love. Everyone else left to find where their hearts were supposed to be. With mine closed off, it's no wonder I ended up there alone."

"You didn't close off from us, though. You act like love is something to be scared of, but that's the exact thing you've been missing from all of us."

"You're my family. It's different."

"I don't think it is. And one day, you're going to have to make a choice—do you want to become bitter and closed off or do you want to open your heart to something more? Either way, we'll all still love you, but you should be happy too."

"Can I tell you a secret?"

"Always."

"This isn't how I saw anything going. Sometimes it's scary. Everything's chaotic and I have no idea what I'm doing. But despite all that, I like where I am now. As crazy as it sounds, I think I'm happy."

He chuckles and ruffles my hair. "I love that for you."

"TWIRL ME!" Sophia grabs my hand, and I spin her around as we dance to Taylor Swift.

We should start making dinner soon, but I can't deny Sophia a little dance party. Plus, they liven me up too. By this time of day, I'm usually exhausted, and a dance party gets me energized again.

I jump when the apartment door swings open a solid hour before Deck should be home.

I fumble for my phone to turn off the music as Sophia runs toward the door. "Nana!"

I spin around quickly, a smile plastered on my face, and look at Deck's mother.

She's about my height, though her body is fuller with beautiful curves. Her medium-length hair is graying brown and perfectly styled, and she's wearing a bright smile that matches Sophia's.

"Hi, Mrs. Decker. I'm Hallie."

Her warm smile grows a little. "It's nice to meet you. And please, call me Linnie. I hope you don't mind me stopping by. I brought some groceries and thought I might make some dinner."

Sophia frowns. "But we already have food to make."

"We do, but we can make that any night. Let's see what your nana brought. It's probably even better. And maybe the three of us could cook it together."

Sophia's eyes light up at that, and Linnie walks over to me and rests a hand on my arm.

"I like you already."

We share a laugh, then she follows Sophia into the kitchen where she starts unpacking the bag she brought.

I pull out my phone and quickly text Deck.

> Hey, no emergency. Your mom is here. I just want to know what she knows, so I'm prepared.

It's not until she's explaining to Sophia how to make the spinach and ricotta pasta bake that he texts back.

DECK

> Sorry. Usually she mentions when she's planning to stop by. As of now, she only knows you're the nanny Sophia loves, who is also saving my ass.

> Good to know. Thanks.

I stare at my screen for a second, thinking of how sexy his ass looked naked.

Nope. I need to get my shit together, and thinking of Deck's ass is not going to help me do that.

With that, I tuck my phone away and get to work helping in the kitchen.

LINNIE IS LOVELY, and it's clear where Sophia gets a lot of her energy and charm from. I see some of it in Deck too, but from the way Linnie has been talking, he takes after his late father.

He only briefly mentioned that his dad passed away before Sophia was born, but it's clear from the way his mom talks that the three of them were very close.

The door swings open, and Deck walks in, soaking wet. Sophia is halfway to him when she thinks better of hugging him.

"Why are you late and drenched?" Linnie asks.

It's only then that I put it all together and glance at the window.

"Crap. When did it start raining? I didn't put the top back on the Wrangler—"

"I did it." Deck looks at me, a drop of water dripping off his hair and running down his cheek.

He reaches up and pushes his hair back from his face.

"That was sweet of you, honey," Linnie says.

"Yes." I clear my throat. "You—you didn't have to do that."

"It's better than you cleaning out a wet car or struggling to put it on in the rain. It started raining when I had mostly finished, so you should be okay."

I stare at him, and the expression in his eyes is so... earnest. It hits me right in the chest.

He wants to take care of me.

And there's a part of me that's soft for him and wants to let him.

That fear of having my heart crushed dances in the back of my mind. With him, it would be complete and total devastation. If I let him care for me the way he wants to... it would end up destroying me.

I can't go there with him.

"Thank you, Mr. Decker."

He goes rigid and his eyes flit to mine as he flexes and releases a fist.

He clears his throat. "No problem. I'll just wash up, and then we can eat."

I watch him walk out of the room and fight the urge to follow him. To thank him for real. But being alone with him—especially in his bedroom—would be a very bad idea.

I keep telling myself I won't give in to the pull between us. But in moments like this, holding out feels like an impossibility.

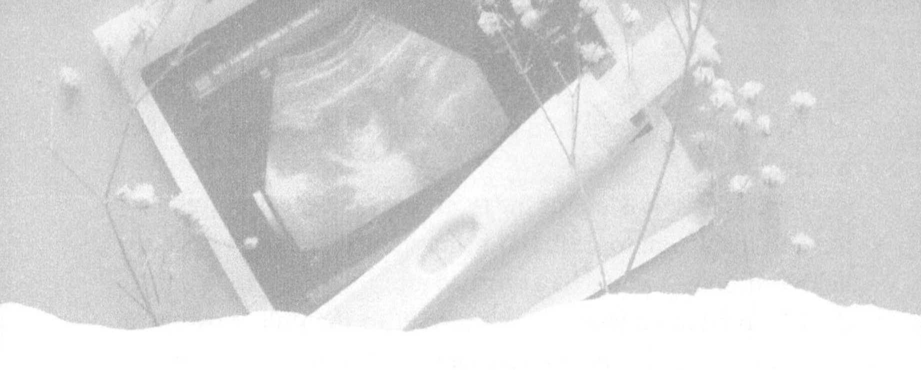

CHAPTER THIRTEEN

Wilson

I'M EXHAUSTED, but I can't sleep.

Story of my life lately.

I'm always thinking. Thinking about Hallie and the fact that she's only a wall away from me. Thinking about how to break through *her* walls and prove I'll be here to support her in every way, not just as a co-parent. Co-parenting with her would kill me when we could be together. We *should* be together.

I'm pretty sure most people would say I'm delusional. But my dad wouldn't have. He would've understood completely. He believed in fate and the power of true love.

My mind goes to that half heart on my keychain.

I kept it because I felt more than chemistry or intense attraction that night. I felt settled.

I have to believe there's a reason for that. She didn't come into my life the way she did, then show up as my neighbor ready to be

Sophia's nanny while pregnant with my child by pure coincidence.

Someone or something had their hands in it.

Maybe it was the threads of fate, or maybe my dad helped orchestrate it himself. Nothing would surprise me.

Despite the softness I see in Hallie, she puts up rock-hard walls.

I wouldn't blame her for being cautious, but how guarded she is surprises me.

If I could just crack through her walls, see what's going on underneath, maybe I could figure out how to get all the way through.

Grumbling to myself, I grab my pillow and roll over. I probably shouldn't be thinking this much about Hallie. I should be worried about Sophia. How will finding out she's going to have a sibling affect her? Will a complicated relationship between Hallie and me set an example for relationships I don't want her to have?

"Fuck," I mutter, rolling onto my back and sprawling out like a starfish.

I'm a mess.

I throw the blankets off, ready to call it, grab a snack, and eat my feelings all night. But I haven't even made it a step when I hear a groaning noise on the other side of the wall.

Hallie.

Then footsteps thunder down the hall of her apartment.

I'm moving before I realize what I'm doing. I grab her spare key off the side of my fridge and the video monitor for Soph's room and bolt out the door.

Fumbling with the key in her lock pisses me off so much I almost kick the damn thing open, but finally the handle turns, and I run inside.

I find Hallie on the bathroom floor, crying as she throws up.

She jumps when she hears my footsteps.

"It's just me."

Before she can hit me with a sassy remark, she dives forward and throws up again.

I drop to my knees beside her. "Breathe, Hellion." I run my fingers through her hair and pull it away from her face.

She sits back on her heels and flushes the toilet.

"How did you get in here?"

"We exchanged keys the other day, remember? I heard you groan and run down your hallway, and I... I just wanted to make sure you're okay."

Her eyes meet mine. "I'm okay. You don't need to stay."

"I'm not leaving you here like this."

"I'll be fine." She pushes herself up to standing, but her legs wobble.

"Convincing." Standing up, I wrap my arm around her back and guide her out of the bathroom. "What can I get you? You should eat something."

She shakes her head. "I'll be okay. I have water."

"Water isn't enough when you just threw everything up."

We get to her bedroom and she sits down on the edge of her bed and takes a drink from her water bottle.

I squat down in front of her. "Let me make you something."

She shakes her head again. "Everything turns my stomach except—"

"Except what?"

"Vanilla milkshakes and french fries. I ran out of vanilla ice cream earlier. I was going to go to the store in the morning—"

"I'll go get you what you need."

"Now?" She whips her head to look at the clock. "It's almost midnight."

"I don't care. Please. Let me do this for you." I stand up and take a risk, brushing my knuckles over her cheek. "Let me take care of you."

Her bottom lip wobbles, but she stiffens it quickly. "Okay."

I hand her the monitor. "Can you listen for Sophia?"

Her eyes widen. "Of course. But what should I tell her if she wakes up?"

"Tell her you're sick and I went to get you food to help you feel better."

She blinks at me, then nods.

"Lie down and rest."

She stares at me for a beat, then gets under the covers.

"I'll be back soon."

I kiss her forehead—another risk—but she doesn't push me away or even bristle at the touch.

She feels this too. I know she does. And somewhere deep down, she wants it.

WHEN I GET BACK to Hallie's apartment, I pop the two gallons of ice cream I got at the grocery store in her freezer before heading to her bedroom.

I jogged through the door of the supermarket four minutes before closing and got some very dirty looks, but I paid by card at the self-checkout and ran out the door with thirty seconds to spare. Then I hit up McDonald's drive-thru for fries and a milkshake.

Hallie is sitting up in bed, knees up to her chest, eyes glazed as she stares at the small TV on her dresser.

"Hey."

Her gaze darts to me. "Hi."

"How are you doing?"

She shrugs. "Okay. Didn't throw up anymore. Still queasy. My stomach hurts." She blinks a couple of times, then looks away.

I ache to reach for her, cup her cheek, comfort her. But I'm not sure she finds me comforting.

Instead, I pull a container of fries from the bag in my hand and offer them and the milkshake to her. "Eat."

She swallows hard as she takes them from me. "Thank you."

"You don't have to thank me. I'm happy to do it. Do you need anything else?"

Her eyes roll over my face. "I—I'm okay. But did you want to stay?"

My heart leaps at her words.

"I could stay." I couldn't hide the smile creeping up my lips if I wanted to.

"Okay then."

I walk around the side of the bed and sit down next to her.

"Anything you want to watch?" she asks.

I toe my shoes off, then kick my feet up and pluck my own container of fries—and nuggets—from the bag. "Whatever you want."

"Okay. Hope you don't mind fast-talking, sarcastic women." She turns on *Gilmore Girls* as I arch a brow at her.

"*You* are a fast-talking, sarcastic woman."

She laughs. "Perhaps."

Finally, she relaxes, and I feel like I can too.

"Fries and nuggets?" she asks.

"Don't tell Sophia, but I'm a sucker for McDonald's fries and chicken nuggets."

Hallie elbows me. "Maybe *you* should tell Sophia. Let that playful side out. It's good for her." She swirls a fry through her milkshake and pops it into her mouth. "And maybe I like seeing it too."

She nestles into her pillows, then to my shock and delight, leans against me.

I think I've made the first crack in her walls.

Maybe I'm not completely delusional after all.

CHAPTER FOURTEEN

"THEN DADDY TOLD me we could pick one night a week to go out to eat," Sophia says, bouncing in her booster seat in the back of my Wrangler. "Maybe you could come with us."

In the rearview mirror, I give her a little smile. "Maybe. But I think you should enjoy time that's just you and your dad too."

I love that Deck took my advice and told her he secretly loves McDonald's chicken nuggets.

Seeing him this morning was the ultimate test of my willpower.

They usually spend all day Sunday with his mom, so today was the first time I saw him after what happened Saturday night.

When he took care of me, even though I tried to push him away.

I hate pushing him away.

I hate fighting my feelings for him.

The night we met, I felt a hum of awareness. A buzz of electricity. Like something was drawing me to him.

It should've made me panic, but I told myself it was just one night, and if it was the best night of my life, I'd have it to look back on.

But it's so much more than one night now.

And while I enjoy the playful side of him, the caretaking vulnerable side is enough to undo me. I almost burst into tears when he offered—insisted—to get me the food I needed.

My parents or friends would get me whatever I needed if I asked them to.

Frannie and Kennedy would've gone out without me asking back when we were living together.

But since then, this is the first time someone was so insistent on caring for me. He wants to be my person. The one I can rely on. He wants me, but I don't know how to give him that.

Because I could never give him a part of me. He'd want it all. And giving him all of me would mean handing over my heart. That's dangerous, and it's sure to come with heartache.

But with the way he looks at me sometimes—the way he makes me feel—my resolve is wearing thin.

At this point, giving in to him might be inevitable.

I help Sophia out when we get to the parking lot across the street from the apartment building.

As she puts her backpack on, I notice her scratching at her wrist, and it looks a little red.

"Okay?" I ask.

She looks up at me, eyes a little wide. Then she smiles. "I'm good."

"All right. Let's head inside."

I take her hand to cross the street. I'll be keeping an extra close eye on her this afternoon because there's something about her answer that I don't trust.

We head across the street and into the building, though Sophia is a little quieter than normal.

"Why don't you go wash up, then we can come up with a good snack, okay?"

Sophia hangs her backpack on the hook near the door, then nods.

"Okay. Could we listen to music too?"

"Of course."

She hurries off to the bathroom, and I head for the fridge. My mind wanders to my own kitchen and the two containers of ice cream sitting in my freezer.

Deck left me a note yesterday morning, telling me to check the freezer. I texted him right away and thanked him. He didn't have to do that. He went to McDonald's to get me a shake and fries. He didn't have to go to the grocery store too.

He's making it a point of caring for me in every way he can. I wasn't expecting him to be so happy to do it. And it makes it even harder not to let my guard down and let him all the way in.

He cares incredibly deeply, but where does that get me in the long run?

Heartbroken, one way or another, probably.

I rest my hand on my stomach. *He's going to be in my life no matter what.*

"Miss Hallie?"

I close the refrigerator door and spin around at the sound of Sophia's panicked voice.

My eyes flare as I take her in. Where her wrist was red, her hand, wrist and lower arm are now red, puffy, and splotchy. Same with her other side. And around her mouth and her lips are swollen too.

I squat down in front of her, stomach churning. "Hey, sweetheart. Can you take a deep breath for me?"

She nods and does it.

"Did that feel okay?"

"Yes."

"Not hard to breathe at all?"

"No."

"Okay. Open your mouth really wide." She does it. "Now stick your tongue out, but don't touch your lips." I relax a little at seeing her tongue looks normal. Not swollen or splotchy.

Deck said she doesn't have any food allergies, but she has sensitive skin. Since it's mostly her hands, she probably got into something that irritated her skin, then touched her mouth—because kids can't keep their hands away from their mouths.

"Did you try any different soaps today? Did the ones in the bathroom at school smell different?"

Her eyes get a little wide, but then she looks to the side, avoiding eye contact.

I tug on her shirt. "Hey, you're not in trouble, but I need to know what happened. Just tell me, okay?"

She turns back to me with tear-filled eyes. "My friend Maria... while we were waiting to be picked up, she shared her lotion with me. And I know I shouldn't have taken it, but it smelled so good, and I want to be her friend and—"

I wrap my arms around her. "It's okay." She's nearly blubbering, and I need her to calm down. We don't want anymore swelling. "Keep taking deep breaths for me. Everything's going to be okay, but we're going to go to the hospital."

She steps back, eyes huge. "The hospital?"

"Your lips are swollen, and we need to be safe."

"So we have to tell Daddy?"

I cup her cheek and give her a reassuring smile. "Yes. But he's only going to care that you're okay. I'm going to grab my purse and a couple of things. Can you get your shoes on?"

"Yes."

"Okay, do that. And do your best not to lick your lips."

"Okay."

Her voice is uncharacteristically small, but I get it. She's embarrassed and scared. I think she'll be okay, but with that much swelling and especially with it being around her mouth, going to the hospital is a better idea. I don't want to give her anything here and have them say that's not the right treatment.

I grab the insurance card and the paperwork Deck had done listing me as someone who can take her to the hospital or doctor and give and receive medical information, then pull my phone out and call Deck.

He answers exactly how I'd expect him to since I never call him.

"Hallie, what's wrong?"

"Breathe. Everything's okay. Sophia's friend gave her some hand lotion today that made her hands and wrists break out and swell up. She touched her lips so they're swollen too, but her tongue is fine and she's breathing like normal. To be safe, I'm taking her to the ER."

"Fuck. Okay. I'll meet you there. Thank you. Is she—you're sure she's okay?"

"Yes. She's breathing and talking fine, but I'm taking the liquid Benadryl with me, just in case."

"Okay. Go. I'll meet you there."

"Hey. Take a deep breath. Don't rush. You're close, so you'll probably beat us there. But I need you to be careful. Sophia needs her dad. Don't drive stupid because you're worried, okay?"

He lets out a long breath. "Okay. I'll meet you there. Be safe."

"We will."

I hang up, grab the Benadryl from the bathroom, then aim for the door.

Sophia is waiting there, and is still doing okay, but she looks miserable.

I slip my feet in my shoes, grab her hand, and head out the door.

"BREATHE," I whisper to Deck as a nurse takes Sophia's vitals.

She's still doing good, but her upper cheek and eye are swollen and splotchy on one side too since she rubbed there.

Deck is bent over in his chair, elbows resting on his bouncing knees as he hangs his head.

"She's okay." I gently rub my fingers over his upper back, lightly massaging the tense muscles in his shoulders.

This is who Deck is. A good man, who loves hard. He's a great dad. Sophia is lucky. So is our baby. *So am I.*

Deck slowly sits up, eyes on me the entire time. His large palm comes to rest on my thigh, sending shockwaves up my leg.

"Thank you."

"You don't need to thank me. I'm already wrapped around her finger. I'd do anything for her."

He slowly shakes his head. "Not just for that. For staying. Being here for me."

Our eyes meet, and something stirs deep in the pit of my stomach—a word that sounds an awful lot like *mine.* But that can't be right.

Without thinking, I take his hand, threading my fingers through his. "You need support too."

He stares at me for a beat, then opens his mouth to say something, but the nurse turns to us and starts asking questions before he can.

My stomach whirls.

Wilson Decker has an unshakable hold on me. I'm in so much trouble.

SOPHIA IS DOZY and loopy as we get back to the apartment building.

I open doors for Deck, who is carrying her, while she intermittently mumbles.

They gave her corticosteroid cream and Benadryl, plus some pain meds, and her skin looks a lot better now. She's also being sent for specialized allergy testing. Which is good, but if it's skin sensitivity, it may not show anything.

I unlock Decker and Sophia's apartment door and swing it open, then step to the side to let them through. When I don't follow Deck in, he turns back to me.

"Did you need anything else? Want me to pick you up some food?"

He stares at me for a beat. "No. There are leftovers. Do you have enough?"

"I got fries at the hospital, and my freezer is full of ice cream. Plus, I have a few other things that sound okay to my stomach."

"Okay. I guess I should..." He nods toward the hallway of his apartment.

"Yeah. Call if you need anything. Or if she does. Okay?"

"Will do."

We stare at each other for a beat longer. I can tell he wants to ask me to stay. But unless he needs something, I can't do it. I have to put some space between us before I do something stupid.

Like break my cardinal rules and get tangled up with him.

"Have a good night, Hallie."

"Night. Keep me updated on how she's doing."

"I will."

One more agonizing moment passes between us, then he closes the door.

I let out a rush of air, then turn to my own apartment, my heart beating too fast.

My mind spins as I walk inside and collapse on the couch.

What am I doing?

I have no idea.

All I know is that I'm screwed because the more I get to know Deck, the more time we spend together, the harder it is to ignore the steady thrum of desire for him welling inside me. That desire is so much more than physical.

I *want* Deck in every way, and that's a dangerous place to be.

CHAPTER FIFTEEN

Wilson

EXHAUSTED IS NOT a strong enough word for what I am right now.

Getting that call from Hallie yesterday afternoon gave me a nice preview of what a heart attack is like.

Not a fan.

I'm grateful Sophia was okay. Even more grateful that Hallie was there and diligent. Not that I'm surprised. Most of the time I see Hallie's playful side or her guardedness, but she has a calm, commanding side too.

I needed that calm yesterday. Sophia did too. And after the doctor got her set up with all the medications, Hallie kept Soph laughing and entertained—until the meds kicked in and Soph started getting sleepy.

She was out cold by seven last night, but I wasn't.

Part of me wanted to beg Hallie to stay when we got home, but that's not fair to her. She'd already done enough for us.

All I did was get Sophia into pajamas and plunk her in bed. She wasn't coherent enough to eat, so I let her sleep, then warmed up food and sat by her bed all night.

I couldn't take my eyes off her. I kept checking to make sure she was breathing okay and the swelling didn't come back.

Then she woke up ready to go at five this morning and ate a huge breakfast.

I texted Hallie and told her to get some extra sleep because I called out today. Going to work at a construction site when I haven't slept the night before is a great way for me or someone else to end up injured.

I slept for a couple of hours after I dropped Sophia off at school, but now... I'm buzzing. Still exhausted but hyped on caffeine and the leftover adrenaline from last night.

Which must be why I run my hand through my shower-wet hair and pull open my door.

It's only three strides to Hallie's apartment, which is good because it doesn't give me time to think before I'm knocking on her door.

I don't know what I'm doing. I don't know what I want. I just want her.

I need her.

The door swings open, and I'm greeted with Hallie's beautiful face. Her long, dark blonde hair is pulled up in a ponytail and her cheeks are slightly flushed.

"Hey." Her smile is bright and more genuine than she's given me since that first night. She's spent so much time closing herself off and holding herself back that I haven't seen the joyful side of her as much. "Come on in."

She opens the door all the way and steps aside, making room for me.

I still don't know what I'm thinking or feeling as I walk into her living room.

She slowly shuts the door, watching me carefully. Which isn't surprising since I'm giving off caged-animal vibes.

"How's Sophia?"

Her voice cuts through my delirious haze.

"She's good. Woke up early, ate a good breakfast. She's still a little embarrassed, but agreed she'll never take lotion, soap, hand sanitizer—anything—from someone else ever again."

"That's good." She moves closer. "And how are you? Don't say fine. Tell me the truth."

Her eyes meet mine, and the intensity of her gaze suffocates me.

How do I breathe when I want her this much?

"Yesterday scared me," I choke out. "Seeing her like that was overwhelming." I let out a weak laugh. "I didn't sleep last night. I just stared at her. Counted her breaths."

Hallie reaches out and rests her hand on my arm. "I understand that." Her touch is meant to be comforting, but it makes me more unhinged.

"Thank you for being there."

"I already told you that you don't need to thank me for that."

I shake my head. "No. Thank you for being there and calming Sophia and calming me. I—I've never had that before. I've always held it together on my own. Even when my mom was there, I always felt like I was holding it together for her too. You were calm and supportive. You gave me a safe place to land." My voice nearly breaks. I'm aching to feel that safety again. I'm fighting to restrain my need for her, and I'm losing.

She moves closer again, her hand gliding up my arm and coming to rest on my chest.

Her gaze locks with mine, and she swallows before she speaks, low and breathy. "I don't mind being your safe place."

Everything snaps.

In half a breath, I have her pinned against the wall, my chest heaving with heavy breaths as I wrap my hand around the side of her neck and look into her eyes.

"Tell me not to do this."

My mind dances with the reasons why I shouldn't.

Sophia. Hallie works for me. We haven't figured anything out between us.

But when her breath hitches and she doesn't break the connection of our gaze, it's impossible to care.

I want her. I want to be with her. I want to be the man who cares for her in every way. I'm determined to figure the rest out, to break her walls, to protect her heart.

But only if she's okay with it.

"Tell me not to touch you and I won't." I dip my head, looking deep into her wildcat eyes. "Tell me to stop."

"No."

I freeze. "No?"

"Don't stop. Please, don't stop."

My mouth crashes against hers, and a whine of need escapes her.

I growl in response, lifting her off the wall and into my arms as I carry her to her bedroom.

"Tell me what you want, Hellion." I set her in the middle of the floor and kiss up her neck. Her hand lands in my hair as she gasps.

"You. I want you. Everything."

I step back and pull her shirt over her head, then the sinfully lacy little bralette she's wearing.

Her perky pink tits are fuller now, and I can't wait a second longer to have my mouth on them.

As I push down her tiny little shorts, I lick and flick at her nipple with my tongue, then switch to the other, teasing and tasting her as she moans.

"Climb on the bed," I mutter, reluctantly lifting my mouth off her.

She does, eyes on me the whole time as I pull my shirt over my head and drop my sweats to the ground.

I reach into my boxer briefs and stroke myself, groaning loudly.

"Deck," she whines.

"You need something, Hellion?"

I drop my boxers to the floor and climb onto the bed, taking in her glistening pussy.

Slowly, I drag two fingers up her center, and when I get to her clit, she nearly launches off the bed.

"Sensitive?" I lean down to kiss her stomach.

"Yes. So sensitive."

I move my kisses down until I'm hovering above her clit, then I lift her legs and suck her clit into my mouth.

"Yes," she cries.

Damn. She's so sensitive. I'm barely going to get to play. But I guess there's always round two.

I swirl my finger around her opening as I lick and suck on her clit. She claws at my hair, bucking against me.

That's right. Take what you need. I'll give you everything.

"Yes, yes... Deck!" She falls apart as wave after wave of pleasure hits her.

She's a shaking mess as she finishes and finally lets go of my hair.

I'm grinning like an idiot as I stare down at her beautiful, flushed body.

Her eyes flit to mine, and she reaches for me.

Stroking my hand down my hard length, I rub my thumb over the tip, smearing the pre-cum. Then I put it to her mouth, and she greedily licks it off.

"You're going to kill me, Hellion."

She grins up at me, and I grab her hips, lining myself up at her entrance, but she stops me with a hand to my chest.

"What do you think you're doing?"

"I... just assumed. You're pregnant. We don't need to use a condom." Seriously, why would we?

"Condoms don't just protect against pregnancy."

Oh, right. Is it bad I didn't even consider that?

She pins me with a glare. "When was the last time you were tested?"

"Honestly? I don't fucking remember. But it was after the last time I hooked up with someone before you."

"And since we were together?"

I let out a little growl at that. "If you think I'm the guy out fucking someone new every weekend, you haven't been paying any attention at all. I haven't been with another person since I was with you. I haven't thought of anyone else. Because I wasn't done with you yet. Since that night, it's been me and my hand and memories of you."

She arches a brow. "And you're not worried about me?"

"Should I be?"

With a swallow, she shakes her head, her face softening. "No. But... I've never gone bare with anyone before."

My grin is practically feral. "Are you saying I'm special?" I tease her entrance with my tip.

She lets out a shuddery breath, then locks eyes with me. "I'm saying you should appreciate how lucky you are."

"Oh, I appreciate that every single day."

Leaning down, I fist my fingers in her hair, staring into her gorgeous eyes as I press inside her.

Her eyes slip closed. I know she wants to hide from this. From us.

It's scary how good this feels. How right. And there's no way she can deny she feels it too.

"Open your eyes. Look at me."

Reluctantly, she does it.

"Good girl. Keep them open. Keep your eyes on me. I want you with me for every perfect second of this."

Her eyes stay on mine, and I slowly pull out and thrust back in.

"Can you work your clit for me?" I whisper, sucking on her neck.

"Yes."

Her breathy voice sends a chill through me, and as much as I want this to last, I'm barely keeping it together. I've been dreaming of this for weeks, and my cock is about to jump the gun.

"Oh, Deck..."

"Hellion, I'm too close."

"So am I," she whines. "I need this. Please."

"Only if you promise me round two."

"Yes, I'm all yours. Please."

I thrust harder, tilting my hips.

I give her a rough kiss, then with our eyes locked, I thrust my hips. Her pussy gives the tiniest pulse and I almost lose my shit.

"I'm so close. Please."

"You want me to fill your pussy, Hellion? Want me to mark you? Prove I'm the only man who's ever taken you like this?"

If I have it my way, I'm the only one who ever will.

"Yes... oh..." She cries out, her fingers dragging down my back as her pussy strangles my cock.

"Just like that. Fuck," I groan, my forehead dropping to hers as I fill her pussy.

I collapse next to her, then pull her lips to mine for a kiss.

I know all too well that might've been the last time I get to experience this. She agreed to another round, but I'm not going to hold her to what she said in the heat of the moment.

Ripping her lips away, she stares at me. "You want more of me?"

"I want everything."

Then she rolls on top of me and kisses me like she owns me. Which is convenient because she's owned every part of me since the second our eyes met across the bar.

CHAPTER SIXTEEN

Hallie

DECK'S LIPS roll over my neck, and even after two rounds, it's impossible to hold back my moan.

My restraint has been slipping over the past week-and-a-half, and seeing Deck so vulnerable and open made the last of that restraint slip away.

Fighting the pull toward him is exhausting.

Which must be why we're tangled naked in my bed as he lazily strokes my clit.

And my new sensitive, hormonal, *desperate* body likes it.

"You just like making me break my rules," I mumble.

He props himself up on his elbow and smirks at me. "You mean not hooking up with a client? Because the way I see it, we hooked up first, then I became your client, so technically, it's not breaking your rule."

That's annoyingly true.

I hook my leg over his and move closer. "As long as you understand it can't be more than this. Just sex."

He stares at me for a long moment. "I'll take whatever you'll give me."

I bite my lip, dragging my finger down his chest. "As long as you're giving me more orgasms."

Again, his lips go to my neck as he pushes two fingers inside me.

"As you wish."

DECK KEPT me in bed until right before he had to leave to get Sophia. Hopefully, the bulge in his pants died down before he got to the pickup line.

I had no idea what to expect when he walked into my apartment this afternoon, but everything was immediately charged between us.

He's intoxicating. When I'm around him too long, it's like I get drunk and stop thinking clearly. Except I'm completely sober and constantly fighting my instincts.

The instincts that tell me to burrow inside him and let him have me.

Sounds like a recipe for disaster.

But since my willpower went out the window, here I am.

Sophia asked me to go for a walk with her while her dad was cooking dinner and then she convinced me to eat with them.

Though Deck and I exchanged a few looks, it's not like we could discuss anything in front of Sophia.

Maybe today was him needing comfort and seeking it in me. Maybe it was the explosion that was bound to happen.

Or maybe it's the start of something.

Nope. Nope. Nopity nope.

Because I'm a glutton for punishment—and need either validation or a distraction—I grab my phone off the table and open the group chat.

> I slept with Deck again.

No point in hiding how chaotic I am from them. They have to love me no matter what.

FRANNIE

You broke your rule!!

> As he explained it, technically I'm not sleeping with a parent. I already slept with a parent and now I'm working for him.

KENNEDY

Alexa, play Usher's U Got It Bad.

KENNEDY

FRANNIE

Hallie and Deck, sitting in a tree…

> F-U-C-K-O-F-F

JADE

Just a reminder that I'm an author and anything you say may be used in a future book.

JUSTIN

But make it angstier!

> You two are nauseating.

MARK

I feel like you all need your own text group. I don't need my phone blowing up in my locker all practice.

HARDY

Speak for yourself, Markie Mark. I need the TEA.

BRIAN

When Bridgerton isn't on, he has to take his need for drama to the real world.

There's no drama. I don't know what you're talking about.

[Taylor Swift Anti-hero meme]

DEVON

Of course you're the problem. The Baker girls are troublemakers. This isn't new information.

Thanks for the love.

BRIAN

We all love you. Seriously, though, are you okay?

Hahaha. What's that?

No sooner have I sent the text than there's a knock on my door.

It could be Frannie.

But as I get off the bed and walk out to the living room, I know it's not.

When I open the door and find Deck on the other side, I know I'm in trouble.

"Hi."

"Hi."

We stare at each other for a second longer, then we collide in a kiss.

Because when Wilson Decker is involved... I am weak.

CHAPTER SEVENTEEN

Hallie

SCHOOL PICK-UP LINES are the bane of my existence, but at least it's a nice day, so I can take the top off and blare Fall Out Boy.

Nothing like the wind blowing through my hair while I belt out the words to *Sugar, We're Goin Down*.

I'm trying to enjoy every second left with my Wrangler because I know our time together is coming to an end. As soon as I figure out how best to finance a new-to-me car, I need to get one. A Jeep Wrangler isn't the most practical car for kids—especially a baby. But I found a different Jeep model I like. Maybe I'll save up and have it painted baby blue to keep the love of my first car baby alive.

I drum my thumbs on the steering wheel as I jam—more quietly now—to Fall Out Boy.

I get an approving look from a guy walking by, and where in the past that might've been something that would be an icebreaker or lead me to a hookup, as I predicted the night we met, Wilson Decker has ruined me.

Since we finally gave in to the tension between us the other day, we haven't been able to stop. We did it three times that day and again that night. And last night, Sophia convinced me to stay for dinner, then read her a book before bed. Before I could even try to leave the apartment, Deck had cornered me, begging me to stay.

Because I now apparently turn into a pile of mush when he hits me with sex eyes, I did, then ended up in his bed. I fell asleep there because my body felt like jelly, and when he wrapped his arms around me, I didn't have the energy to fight him. I had to do the walk of shame back to my apartment at five in the morning so Sophia wouldn't see me.

Talk about messy.

And yet I'm getting surprisingly comfortable in my little mess.

Would it be so crazy to keep hooking up with Deck, co-parent our child, and continue being there for Sophia?

It could totally work, right?

Some new-age version of family that would make old people roll their eyes and say "back in my day, we had respect for what a family is." All while at least one partner was cheating and women were forced to be childrearers and nothing else.

Sometimes I feel like a bad feminist because that's what I'd love to be—a stay-at-home mom, not a cheating-at-home wife. But feminism is all about women having opportunities and freedom of choice. I'm allowed to want to stay home with my kid. On my terms. Obviously, I'd want to have my own things and find things outside of being a parent that fulfill me and bring me joy, but I'd love being a stay-at-home mom. I just have to figure out how to finance that.

Sophia's bright smile catches my eye from up the walkway, and she pauses to give a hug to a friend and say goodbye. That makes my heart happy. I want her to form those kinds of bonds. Though I'm closest with Frannie, Kennedy, Justin, and now the football boys, I had my bestie Lena growing up. She was the first to leave me when she moved to Oregon after high school, but she's happy there, and we settle for monthly video calls to maintain our friendship.

I turn off the music as Sophia gets to the car. "Are you okay climbing in by yourself?"

"Yep!" She hops right in, drops her bag on the floor, and buckles herself up.

"Ready to go?"

"Yes. Let's go home."

"So, how was your day?" I carefully pull out of the spot I'm in, hand on my horn in case someone tries to cut me off. People are maniacs in the school pick-up line.

"It was good. I had grilled cheese for lunch!"

"Yum. That's one of my favorites. Who was that you were hugging when you left?"

"Oh, that was Maria. She's my best friend."

I put on a fake pout in the rearview mirror. "Replacing me already?"

She laughs. "No. You're more than my best friend."

"Oh? What am I then?"

As I come to a stoplight, I glance in the mirror and look at her contemplative face.

"I don't know exactly, but you're... like family."

Oh, my heart.

"I feel the same way, kid."

She laughs again. "That's what Daddy calls me."

She's quiet for the next couple of minutes until I get back to the parking lot across from our building.

As I help her down, she looks up at me tentatively. "Are you and Daddy friends?"

I glance down at her. "Yes. We are."

"Are you more than friends?"

Shit.

I don't want to lie to her, but telling her I'm pregnant with her half-sibling and crawling into her dad's bed at night isn't the right call.

"We're friends."

When the road is clear, we cross the street and head inside the building.

"But do you want to be more than friends with Daddy? Because sometimes he looks at you... the way he looks at me. Kind of. Not exactly."

I pause at the apartment door and meet her eyes. "What do you mean?"

She shrugs. "I don't know. He always looks like he's really happy you're here. He doesn't look at anyone else like that. Besides me."

Damn, she's perceptive. It's a good thing I've been able to hide my puking from her, otherwise she probably would've figured out I'm pregnant by now.

Unlocking the door, I push it open.

"Do you want me to be more than friends with your dad?"

She sets her bag down and takes her shoes off, then runs over and gets comfy on the couch.

"If it means you'd stay with us forever... that you'd always make him smile like that, then yes. And... I wouldn't mind if you were my stepmom. Even though I'd probably call you my mom since I don't have one of those. Exactly."

Yikes.

Deck gave me a basic rundown of the situation with her mom last week, just so I'd be prepared. Sophia seems pretty well adjusted with all of it, but still, I'm sure it's getting harder to understand that as she gets older.

"Well, I don't know if I can promise all that, but I can promise I'll always be here for you. Deal?"

She nods happily. "Deal."

"Good. Now, what do you say we have some apple slices with peanut butter and chocolate chips, then start getting the quiche ready for dinner?"

"Chocolate chips? Yes, please."

SOPHIA YAWNS as I finish reading her a book.

I wasn't planning on staying late tonight, but apparently me reading to her at bedtime is becoming a thing. I'm not sure if I should let it become a thing or not, but... I'm right here. One day, maybe she'll help me read to the baby at night.

I'm getting way ahead of myself.

"I think it's time for someone to go to sleep."

She nestles against me. "Mhm."

I look down and find her eyes closed as she snuggles close. My heart melts into a puddle.

I've never really done this. Occasionally when babysitting, but as a nanny, I was always off the clock by dinner time, usually earlier. Sophia has attached herself to me quickly, too. But the feeling is mutual. She's already stolen a piece of my heart.

I carefully climb out of her bed, pulling her blanket up and putting the bear she loves so much right next to her.

Switching her lamp off, I creep out of her room, only to find Deck waiting in the hallway for me.

"You're good for her," he says, looking reverently into Sophia's bedroom.

"What do you mean?"

He turns to me, a gentle smile on his face. "She's been lonely. She's needed connection. A different kind than I could provide."

"My brand of chaos?" I ask with a light laugh.

"Your tenderness and warmth. She was instantly comfortable with you. And it's not because you're a woman or give off maternal energy—though you do. It's because you're you. From the first moment you met her, you made it a point to see her. To see who she is and what she needs. In a short time, you've become another safe place. For both of us."

He stares at me with those smoldering dark eyes, and my body heats. That melty, tingly feeling tries to overtake me, but I steel myself.

After a quick glance into Sophia's room, I shove at Deck's chest. "Stop with the sex eyes. We need to talk."

CHAPTER EIGHTEEN

IT'S BEEN A WHILE, but usually the words "we need to talk" are not good words.

"Okay. Let's go sit."

We end up in the living room, and while she takes the corner of the couch, I plop down in the middle and lift her legs, resting them on my lap, then I gently massage them.

"What's up?" I try to keep my voice even. I'm afraid she's going to tell me she wants to stop whatever we're doing. That's the last thing I want. Mostly because while she says it's just sex, she's been letting down her guard. She doesn't just want orgasms, she wants comfort. The closer we become, the easier her walls become to break through.

I'm getting closer.

I look over at her, only to find her staring at my hands on her legs as I move them down toward her feet.

"What are you doing?"

"Helping you relax."

She stares at me for a beat, and I'm expecting her to argue. She's used to handling things herself. She's closed herself off to love for some reason—and that includes letting someone outside of her family care for her.

"Thank you."

Well, fuck me. A smile sneaks onto my lips before I can stop it.

"Don't look so smug."

"Not smug. Happy. I like taking care of you. And I think you like it too. Why else would you be here?"

She sighs dramatically. "I wanted to talk to you about something, remember?" But I don't miss the smile she tries to hide.

I give her calf a squeeze.

"What did you want to talk about?"

"Sophia. What you want to tell her and when. And when you plan to tell your mom or anyone else in your life."

I inhale deeply. All of that has been on my mind too, even if that's not all I want to talk to her about.

I'll talk to her about anything. I'll talk to her all night.

"Sophia asked me today if we're more than friends."

My eyes go wide. But I shouldn't be surprised. She's a smart kid.

"What did you say?"

"That we're friends. Then I asked if she wanted us to be more than friends and... she's hoping for that."

I am too.

"Okay, that adds another layer to this. Let's come back to Soph and talk about everyone else first. What about in your life? I assume Frannie knows?"

She nods. "I told her when I got to town."

"What about your brother? Where does he live, by the way? You haven't mentioned it."

She stares at me blankly for a second, like she has no idea what the fuck I'm talking about, then some sort of realization hits her.

"Oh. Justin." She bites back a smile. "Yeah, he's not my

brother. Not technically. That's just a thing we'd do to stay safe when hooking up. We look enough alike that we pass for siblings. He's my cousin Kennedy's bestie."

"Was she the one with the dark hair there that night?"

"No, that's Justin's wife, Jade. And the other two were—"

"Ryan Hardison and Brian Ackley."

She laughs. "Right. I forget people recognize them. No, Kennedy lives out in California with her lifelong bestie turned boyfriend, Devon. But we all lived together in New York for a while. She and Dev met Justin in college, so I met him for the first time when I was thirteen. We immediately had a sibling-like relationship. He moved to Woods Junction, where Jade is from, over the summer."

"No wonder you ended up here."

She swallows. "Yeah. Missed my people. Still miss Kennedy. She's like another older sister. Our moms are sisters and our dads are brothers, and when we were little, we lived in a duplex next to them. She and her parents moved to California when I was six. I cried every night for two weeks after she left." She laughs sadly, then shakes her head. "Sorry. I don't know why I'm telling you all that."

"You can tell me anything."

She nods absently, then continues on. "Anyway, that whole friend group knows, but that's it. Does anyone in your world know?"

"My boss. Leo. He was a single dad, and he's really great with family stuff, so I gave him a heads up I'd have to be out here and there for appointments. I was planning to stop by and tell my mom tomorrow night, and... I was going to ask if you'd come with Soph and me to dinner at her house on Sunday."

I hold my breath. It's a risk. She said it was just sex, but nothing about what we're doing is *just* anything.

Slowly, she nods. "Okay. I'll go with you. I'd like to get to know your mom better. You two seem close."

I smile at that. I wouldn't be the man I am without my mom.

"We are. Growing up, she and my dad were my biggest supporters."

"What was your dad like?"

Emotion grips my chest, both because of the topic and because she's asking about him.

"Upbeat. He was the brightness everyone needed. He was all about fate and having faith that you'd end up where you were supposed to be. Not gonna lie, I've been holding on to that lately."

She reaches over and squeezes my hand, and I clear my throat.

"He would've liked you. Anyway, what about your folks? Do they know?"

She shakes her head. "No. I'm planning to tell them soonish."

"If you need support, let me know."

"Thanks." She sighs, then looks up at the ceiling and laughs. "How did this happen?"

My stubble scrapes across my palm as I rub my cheek.

"I might... I don't know. That last round, I felt like the condom was going to burst from how hard I was and how badly I wanted to come. Normally, I'd just chalk a thought like that up to hormones and ego, but my eyes were already closed when I pulled it off. Maybe it broke or punctured... I don't know."

"Maybe, but I'm sure we... cross contaminated a bit with all the playing around we did. It doesn't really matter. Here we are. Time to figure out how to handle it. I know you know this, but we've got to be careful with Sophia. I don't want to confuse her."

"Me either." But I also want to truly be with Hallie. She isn't there yet, but Sophia is picking up on what's obviously between us. "Let's just take it a day at a time. I think we should wait until after our twelve-week ultrasound, at least, anyway."

"I agree."

That's scheduled for a little over three weeks from now. Maybe it's stupid to hope we'll have made some progress by then, but I hope we will.

"So, let's get through that, and then we'll talk about it more."

"Sounds good."

I gently rub both hands over one of her bare feet, and she groans.

"That feels so good. No one's ever massaged my feet before."

I get the feeling that's because she doesn't let anyone close enough. Not in this way.

I'm breaking down her walls and she doesn't even know it. Or maybe she does and despite her protests, that's what she actually wants.

"I'll do it every night if you want me to."

"Don't make promises you don't plan on keeping."

"I don't say things I don't mean. Whether it's here or at your apartment, I'll massage your feet, your back"—I wiggle my brows —"whatever you want."

"You're trouble."

"You bring it out in me."

"You should let that side of you out more. The guy from the carnival—and I don't mean the Ferris wheel. As soon as you let your guard down, your smile got ten times brighter."

"That's because I was with you."

Cheesy, but it's the truth.

Her jaw sets as she stares at me, but then something soft filters into her expression.

"It was a special night. But I'm serious. You should let that side out. Let Sophia see it. Let yourself have some fun—*outside* of the bedroom." Her cheeks heat. "I know you have fun in there. But on a regular day... give yourself permission to loosen up a bit."

I snort at that. "There will be time for that when Sophia is older."

"Then there will be this baby. Some unsolicited advice... if the only thing you ever do is focus on Sophia—and eventually our baby—all you'll end up with is emptiness when they live their own lives."

It's hard not to glare at her. She hasn't been through all this yet. She doesn't understand it the way I do.

"I'm not going to apologize for prioritizing Sophia."

But Hallie stays completely cool. "You're not prioritizing her. You live your entire life for her at the cost of yourself. That's different. And it only leads to bitterness. I've watched parents do it. Either live for their kids or live for their jobs so much that they miss out on everything else. Finding balance and maintaining who you are as a person and the things you enjoy are important. Sophia should be your priority, but you should be a priority too."

Damn. "That's... insightful."

She chuckles. "You sound annoyed."

"No," I say quickly. "Just... never really saw a difference until you put it like that. You're right."

She flips her hair dramatically. "Of course I am."

I roughly move my thumb along the bottom of her foot, pressing hard.

She throws her head back and groans. "Deck..."

"Call me Wilson," I blurt.

That's what I've wanted since she walked back into my life, but I've been too chicken to ask.

Her gaze snaps to me.

"Deck or Decker is what people who don't know me as well call me. Sports buddies, the guys I work with. Anyone who knows me well calls me by my real name. Please, Hallie. Call me Wilson."

She swallows hard, then leans forward, pulling her legs off me and tucking them under her.

She runs her fingers through my hair.

"Wilson. Hm. I could get used to that. But what about Mr. Decker?"

A low growl slips from me and I wrap my hand around the side of her neck.

"The only time you get to call me that is if you're riding my cock."

Her face morphs into a wicked grin, then she runs her finger down my chest. "That can be arranged."

MY GUT IS tight as I pull into my mom's driveway.

Mom is one of the most supportive people on the planet, but she also has opinions and isn't afraid to share them. Fuck, I'm still the mama's boy who doesn't want to upset her. I want her to be happy about this.

It's hard falling for Hallie when I feel like I'm trying to convince her to fall for me. Though I see glimpses of it, I don't fully understand why she's afraid to let someone in. Her parents are still together. Her sister and cousin are both in happy relationships. And she makes it sound like she's never been in love. So who or what hurt her?

That's not a question I can answer tonight.

Running a hand through my hair, I climb out of the car. I texted Mom right as I left the job site that I'd be stopping by, but didn't mention why.

She swings the door open as I walk up the front steps.

"Well, what did I do to earn a visit from my son with no Sophia?"

I wrap her in a hug. "Just wanted to say hi."

She pushes out of my arms and gives me that mom look that tells me she's on to my bullshit.

"Fine. I need to talk to you about something."

She waves me inside, and I close the door behind me.

"Good something or you killed someone and don't know what to do with the body something?"

"Mom, I work construction. There are literally so many holes to put a body in."

She rolls her eyes as she heads for the kitchen. That tends to be the gathering space in this house more than the living room.

"I take it that means something good, then?"

I blow out a breath. "I think it's good."

She leans against the kitchen island and gives me her very serious expression. "Stop being cryptic. I'm too old for that shit."

"Okay. You remember when I went down to the city for the wedding? And before I left, you implied I should have some fun —of sorts—while I was there."

She shrugs. "I don't know what you're talking about." But finally a smile comes through.

"Well, I took your advice, and I met an amazing woman and spent the evening with her. It was Hallie." I hold my hand up before she can say anything. "But we didn't know that at the time. We only exchanged nicknames. Nothing else. Frannie and Mark weren't with her that night, and I had no idea she had any ties to Ida. She didn't know where I lived. Then she showed up at my door as the new nanny. Neither of us had any idea. Frannie didn't either. It was completely random."

Mom tilts her head slightly. "You know what your father would've said. It's fate."

I swallow hard, emotion socking me in the gut.

The idealistic, romantic side of me, I mostly got from my dad. Whether it was the outcome of a football game, the timing of an important moment, or the people who come into our lives, he always believed it was fate.

I miss my dad. I hate that he never got to meet Sophia, and that I've had to raise her without him. I've wished I could ask his advice so many times over the years. He was the best.

"I hope it is. Maybe it's Dad looking out for me. And Soph. Sophia adores her."

Mom squeezes my arm. "And so do you."

I sniff, trying to keep the overwhelming emotions at bay. "I do. I have since the moment we met. And now she's here and...

Mom, she's pregnant. With my baby, from that night we spent together."

She grabs my other arm too, her eyes filling with tears, and I stop trying to sniff back my own.

"Oh, honey. That's..."

"It has to be fate. It's everything I've wanted, but was too afraid to admit to or hope for."

"And she wants this too?"

I chuckle at that. "She's excited about the pregnancy. She's always wanted to be a mom. But she's got a guarded heart. I can see the longing in her eyes. I know she wants this too. But I'm going to have to break through some walls."

Mom's smile grows. "I don't think that'll take long. You have a big heart, and it won't take long for her to see it."

"I hope so. Anyway, I'd like to bring her with us for dinner on Sunday. It will only be as Sophia's nanny and my friend. We obviously haven't told Sophia any of this yet."

"How far along is she?"

"Eight weeks now."

She covers her mouth with her hand. "Eight weeks. Amazing. Another grandbaby to love." She pulls me into her arms. "I love you, honey."

"I love you too, Mom."

"And don't you worry. Hallie will come around in time. I can see the joy being around you and Sophia brings out in her, and I only saw it for a little while. She'll get there."

"I hope so. I really, really want this."

"You'll have it. I believe that. And I think you're right. Dad's looking out for you."

I let out a shaky breath.

It's hard to admit how badly I want this. The fear of getting my heart broken if she doesn't come around is always there in the back of my mind. But she's scared too. So if I can be vulnerable with her and show her how much I care, I'm going to do that. I want her to know she's safe with me. If that means risking my heart to show her I'll always keep hers safe, I'll do it without a second thought.

CHAPTER NINETEEN

"THIS IS SO CUTE."

Deck—no. Wilson. *Wilson.* He asked me to call him that, and I'm working on shifting it in my mind. Even if calling him Mr. Decker in bed the other night was steaming hot. Which was great, since it was the only good night I've had. Last night, he couldn't even touch me I was so nauseous. We sat in his bed and ate french fries dipped in sour cream together while watching *Yellowstone*.

What's that? Sounds a lot more like a relationship than just trading orgasms?

Well, what can I say?

I'm *fucked.*

Every time I think I can keep my heart safe and keep my walls up, *Wilson* goes and grabs a chisel. Or a sledge hammer.

That man is coming for my heart, and I'm not sure there's anything I can do to stop him.

For the first time in my life, I'm not sure I want to.

It's an endless internal war for me. To give in to something I used to so desperately crave or to hold on to the walls I put up... because they're there for a good reason. Right?

I have no idea anymore.

Wilson laughs at my description of his mom's house. The house he grew up in. But it is cute. A little white Tudor-style home with a small stone front porch and perfectly manicured front gardens. There's what appears to be a small yard in the back, and a part of me wants that kind of idyllic life. I love the apartment I'm living in because it gives me city vibes without being in the city. It's calmer and quieter, but still with more life than this little street.

Maybe one day. When I'm a soccer mom and have figured out a career that gives me a solid enough income to buy a house instead of "renting" from my sister for zero dollars a month.

"Wait till you see the inside. It's even cuter," Wilson says, climbing out of the car.

It's still a little strange to call him Wilson. There's something inherently intimate about it. But I'll get used to it.

I think.

"It's so pretty inside!" Sophia says, jumping out of the car and hurrying toward the front porch.

Deck—Wilson—moves slower. Waiting for me.

He not so subtly takes my hand, and I almost freak out for a second, but I tell myself it's fine. He's helping me up the stairs. Like a gentleman.

Sophia doesn't bother knocking or waiting, and when we get to the door, Linnie is already walking toward it.

I instantly tear my hand from Deck's. *Shit.* Wilson's. My throat feels thick as I glance over at him, finding his eyes shifted to me, and his hand... he's flexing it. Like a full-on Mr. Darcy hand flex.

Son of a bitch.

Forget a sledge hammer. The man is coming for my heart with a bulldozer.

"THAT WAS the most delicious meal I've had in a long time. I love moussaka."

Linnie smiles warmly at me. She's an incredible cook, and it's the first home cooked meal I've had in a while that didn't make me nauseous.

"It settled okay with your stomach?" Linnie asks.

We came up with a story that I have a sensitive stomach issue that flares up sometimes for Sophia's sake.

"Yes. It did. Thank you."

"It always settles good in my tummy," Sophia says. "Nana's a great cook."

Wilson gently runs his hand over my upper back, subtly enough that no one would notice. But I notice.

I could be in the pitch black with no idea which way was up, and one touch from Wilson and I'd know it was him.

There's nothing like the sparks that go off in my body when his skin touches mine.

I lean into it, just the tiniest bit, and as I do, my eyes drift past him to the window on the back door and the backyard beyond.

"The backyard looks beautiful. Tell me you do idyllic things like sit on the back porch and drink iced tea or play yard games. If I had a yard like that, I'd force everyone outside to play yard games each night."

Linnie's gaze narrows slightly. "Hm. When was the last time we played a yard game?"

Wilson meets her gaze, emotion swimming in his eyes. "Must've been before Dad died. He usually instigated that. Game of croquet or bocce."

"Oh, I love bocce ball. Sometimes after family dinners, we'd go to the park nearby and play."

But then I fully process what he said.

It's been a decade since they played?

I'm not sure exactly what it is about it that makes me sad. Maybe because it was clearly something special they did once, and it was special to me growing up. Sophia should have that. It's clear she wants the big, boisterous family. Maybe, in some small way, I can give it to her.

"I still have the bocce ball set out in the shed. Should we dig it out?" Linnie asks.

"Yes!" Sophia exclaims.

Wilson laughs. "You don't even know what it is."

"Well, I want to learn."

"You play as teams of two. There's a little ball you throw, then heavier big balls that you have to try to get as close to the little ball as possible. You can even use your balls to knock the other team's balls out of the way. It's all about figuring out the perfect throw."

Sophia is transfixed as I explain.

"Can I be on your team?"

"Of course. I'll teach you how to kick their butts."

"Shots fired," Deck says. *Wilson.*

I have to retrain my brain to say the right name. Unless I'm looking at him. When I can see his warm eyes and that restrained smile that always wants to bloom into something bigger, I see him. The man beneath the nicknames. The one who isn't always in control. The one with a playful side.

"Let's go," Sophia says, jumping from the table.

Linnie laughs and follows her toward the back door.

Wilson helps me up from my seat, pausing to whisper in my ear.

"This was a great idea. Thank you."

"Just trying to remind you how to have some fun."

I wink at him, then follow Sophia and Linnie out the back door.

"YES! I KNOCKED YOU OUT, DADDY!"

Wilson playfully grumbles at Sophia, then smiles. It's the big, wild one that I'm desperate to see more of. It makes Sophia smile too.

"I'll get you back next round," he says.

She looks at her fingernails like she's too cool for school. "We'll see."

I chuckle at that. "Brutal."

His smoldering eyes land on me, and a flush creeps up my body in response. "Well, maybe we should make a little bet, then."

He steps closer to me, mischief dancing in those heated eyes.

"A bet, huh?"

"Gotta keep things interesting." The tone of his voice is practically indecent.

"What kind of bet?" Sophia asks, butting in and cooling off the moment. In the background, Linnie laughs.

"Dessert," Wilson says simply. "If we win, you two make us a dessert of our choosing."

"Oh, nice one," Linnie calls.

"Okay. If we win…" I look at Sophia.

"We go out for ice cream!"

Wilson holds out his hand to me, and I shake it.

"Deal."

His fiery gaze cuts right through me. "Deal."

"Let's get on to the next throw then. Hallie, you and Sophia start this time," Linnie says.

"Can I do it?" Sophia asks, dancing toward her grandmother.

"Of course."

I glance up at Wilson, who falls into step beside me. "Just a random little bet?"

His smile melts me to my core.

"Just trying to let the fun side of me out again, Hells Bells."

"Mhm." I elbow him, then lean in closer. "For the record, I love seeing that side of you, Mr. Decker." Then I scamper over to where Sophia is waiting, knowing I just added more fuel to the fire burning between us.

"THERE ARE SO MANY FLAVORS," Sophia breathes, looking around the frozen yogurt shop with wide eyes. Since this was one of the few indoor places open and it wasn't too far from Linnie's house, this is where we ended up, and I'm not arguing because there are a *ton* of flavors. And endless toppings. "How many can I get?"

Wilson smiles. "Three. But don't go too crazy with how much you put in your bowl."

"I won't," she calls, running off to check out the different flavors.

"What are you getting?" he asks me.

"I'm thinking cake batter and oatmeal crème cookie."

"Sounds delicious."

Don't whimper.

I take a breath. A shaky, hitched breath. But I don't whimper.

Still, he smiles at me like he knows exactly what he's doing.

Then he winks and walks after Sophia.

I get my frozen yogurt, then sit down at the table, where Linnie joins me a couple of moments later.

"Tonight was wonderful. More fun than I've had in quite a while. Thank you," Linnie says.

I smile at her, glancing out of the corner of my eye at where Wilson is helping Sophia.

"I'm happy I get to share a family tradition of mine with all of you."

"Me too. You're our family now. You should share the things that are special to you."

My throat thickens with emotion. "Thank you."

She reaches out and rests her hand over mine. "I've always wanted a daughter. And I know you and Wilson are still figuring things out. I'm not going to meddle or push, but regardless of all that, you're bringing my grandbaby into the world, and you make my granddaughter and my son smile in a way no one else ever has. That alone makes me consider you a daughter. You bring out Wilson's joy in a beautiful way, and I'm incredibly grateful for that. It's like getting a little piece of his father back. You're so good for both of them."

My eyes get a little teary, but I blink them back, giving her a soft, grateful smile. "Thank you. That means a lot to me."

"And you mean a lot to them. Hold on to that."

She gives my hand a squeeze and we both go back to eating our frozen yogurt.

My eyes drift over to Wilson and Sophia again.

I'm not sure when the two of them became such a big part of my world, but I know I'm in trouble.

It's not only Wilson trying to break down the walls around my heart, it's Sophia too. It's the family we could be. And for just a moment, I let myself imagine what that would be like, and I make it almost a full minute before my brain reminds me of the crushing pain my heart will go through.

But the more I imagine it, the more I wonder if it's a risk worth taking.

CHAPTER TWENTY

MY LITTLE HELLION likes to snuggle.

We haven't done anything sexual in a few days—her desire for that comes and goes, often in a short time span, and I happily respect it. Especially because when we aren't *doing* anything, we cuddle in my bed and watch TV together. Inevitably, she falls asleep before we finish what we're watching, and I tuck her in and lie down beside her. Like there's a magnetic pull between our bodies, she instantly rolls against me, snuggling up to me every time.

It's yet another little thing that gives me hope.

I'm chipping away at the walls around her heart, and that's a damn good thing because she's completely infiltrated my heart. I'm done. Gone for her. There will never be anyone else who makes me feel alive the way she does, and I never want there to be.

I see a future with her. Now I need her to see it too. To not fear it.

She rustles in her sleep, then groans, and I sit up, immediately on alert. That's a surefire sign she's feeling nauseous.

She sits up suddenly and stumbles out of bed.

"Oh, shit."

She hurries down the hall on shaky legs, then lets out a whimper before freezing as she pukes all over the floor.

She falls to her knees, crying, and I drop down beside her, rubbing her back.

"I'm sorry," she sobs.

"You don't have to apologize. It's okay."

She wipes her eyes, but more tears come.

"Hey…" I'm about to kiss her head, when a voice comes from behind us.

"What's going on?"

I turn to look at Sophia, who is standing in the hallway, tiredly squinting at us.

"Why is Miss Hallie here?"

Thank God we're fully clothed tonight. Well, Hallie is. She's got on a tee and shorts. I'm only in sweats, but that's typical.

I stand up and look at my daughter. "You know how Hallie said her stomach bothers her sometimes?"

"Yeah." Soph still looks so tired, I wouldn't be surprised if she didn't remember this tomorrow.

"She wasn't feeling well tonight, so I wanted her to stay so I'd be here if she needed someone to take care of her." Not a lie. "She started feeling sick really suddenly and couldn't quite make it to the bathroom."

Hallie stands and wipes her eyes, trying to put on a calm exterior for Soph, though her eyes are still red and puffy.

"I'm sorry if I scared you or worried you." She lets out a weak laugh. "I hate throwing up."

"I do too." Sophia yawns.

"Did you get any on you?" I ask Hallie.

She looks down and shakes her head.

"You two go lay down, and I'll take care of it."

Hallie's eyes go wide. "But—"

"Don't worry about it. I've got this." I wish I could kiss her to drive the point home. "Go."

"Come on," Sophia says, taking Hallie's hand. "And I don't care if you cry. Throwing up makes me cry too. It sucks."

"Yeah, it does."

Hallie gives me a thankful, emotion-filled look as Sophia leads her away.

I reach out and give her hand a tiny squeeze, the most I can do to reassure her right now.

Our hands slip apart slowly, and I savor every tiny touch before our contact is broken.

Now it's time to clean up.

My poor little hellion. Luckily, once she gets it out, she usually feels okay for a while. She looked so panicked when it happened, but it's just a little puke. I wouldn't have survived Sophia's early years if I hadn't gotten used to cleaning up vomit.

If you've never caught your kid's puke in your hands, are you even a real parent?

It's not like it's my favorite thing to deal with, but I've dealt with a lot worse.

I get it all cleaned up, then grab a couple of rags, cleaner, and some fresh water and quickly clean the spot on the floor, then rinse it.

It takes about twenty minutes all-in, and once I've washed my hands and put everything away, I aim for Sophia's room. Depending on how awake she was, she might need another story or some music on her sound machine to help settle her in.

But what I find when I get there makes me stop in my tracks.

Hallie and Sophia are asleep in Sophia's bed. Soph is curled up against Hallie, and Hallie's arm is wrapped around Sophia.

Emotion grips me as I stare at my girls. And they are both mine. My whole world is right there in one tiny bed.

I want it to last. I want to keep this. I want to give Sophia the mother she deserves. I want us both to have the family we've needed. I want to wake up beside Hallie every day and worship her.

If only she'd let herself believe in how amazing we could be together.

She'll get there, I tell myself. And I force myself to believe it. Because I'm not giving up hope that we can have it all.

I RUN my hand gently over Hallie's stomach and kiss her cheek.

"Time to wake up, Hellion."

"Hm?" Her eyes flutter open, and she looks around, eyes landing on me kneeling beside Sophia's bed. When she puts it all together, she covers her face with her hands and groans.

"Hey, none of that." I pull her hands off her beautiful face.

"I threw up all over the floor. You had to clean it up. That's *mortifying*."

"Why?"

"Because I don't want you to associate me with throwing up."

I stare at her for a second. Is she fucking serious?

"Hellion, that is never how I see you. That's a thing that happened. Just a part of life."

"It makes me feel very... not sexy."

Again, I rub my hand over her stomach, firmly resting it there. "I don't need you to be sexy all the time. I like your smile, your humor, and your vulnerability too. In case you haven't figured it out yet, I like all of you. Every version."

She rests her hand on my cheek, eyes dropping to my lips.

"Where's Sophia?"

"Putting the finishing touches on breakfast."

Leaning up, she presses a soft kiss to my lips, but the softness doesn't stop the heat. The rush of... something inside me whenever we touch. When she seeks out my comfort.

We break our kiss too quickly, but until we tell Sophia anything, it's too risky to continue.

Standing up, I hold my hand out to her. "Come on. We're having a special breakfast."

"I stayed the whole night," she murmurs.

"Yeah, you did. And you slept hard. I won't take too much offense if you tell me Sophia is a better cuddler than I am."

She blinks at me. "Is Sophia okay? Like... was she weirded out by any of this?"

"No. Our logic was sound enough for her. Plus, I don't know if you've caught on, but she *really* likes you. She's just happy you're here." She slips past, but I reach out and grab her hand, holding her in place as I whisper, "So am I."

A little shiver runs through her, but she straightens, and I let her go, smiling to myself at the effect I have on her. She can deny her feelings all she wants, but I know they're there. Whether she realizes it or not, every day, she gets a little closer to letting me in.

I follow Hallie out to the living area, and she stutter steps when she gets to the kitchen and finds Sophia at the table, smiling brightly.

"Breakfast is served. I wish this was all my stomach wanted so I could eat it all the time."

Three cups are filled with milkshakes, and each one has a plate of fries next to it.

Hallie whirls around and looks at me, emotion dancing in her eyes. "You did all this for me?"

Though I long to cup her cheek and look into those intoxicating amber eyes, I keep my hand tight at my side. Still holding her gaze, but not too intensely, I pour every bit of what I'm feeling into my words.

"Of course I did."

She swallows hard, then blinks twice and cracks her knuckles before turning back around and smiling at Sophia. "Thank you for helping. And for making sure I slept so good last night."

Sophia bounces over to Hallie and throws her arms around her. "Thanks for snuggling with me. I liked it."

Hallie strokes her hand through Soph's hair and laughs. "So did I."

The connection between those two is proof that love forms in an instant. It may take longer to grow, but those two formed an instantaneous bond that easily turned into love.

Now I'm hoping I get as lucky.

HALLIE YAWNS as Sophia heads to her bedroom to get ready. Then she sighs and groans. "I think I'm still hungry." She aims for the refrigerator. "Is there any more ice cream? Or maybe I'll go home and make some tater tots." But as she pulls the freezer drawer open, her eyes go wide. She closes it again and turns toward me. "What is all that?"

I bite my lip as I walk over to her. "I think you know."

"There are three cartons of my favorite vanilla ice cream in there. Bags of french fries and tater tots. Why—"

Checking to make sure Sophia isn't in the hallway, I wrap my arm around Hallie, tugging her close.

"Because they're the foods that settle your stomach. You should always have what you need, and you're here more than you're in your own apartment. And if you run out there, you'll have some here. I told you I was going to take care of you. This is a fraction of that."

She stares at me, just stares, emotions flitting through her eyes too fast for me to read.

"Hey, Dad?"

I step back and clear my throat as Sophia walks into the room. "What's up, kiddo?"

"Can you put more hair ties on the list? I broke another one."

"Do you need more right now? I can bring some over. I need to change quick before I take you to school."

Sophia shakes her head. "I'm all good for now. Thanks, though."

Then she scampers out of the room again, and Hallie slowly makes her way toward the door.

Her hand stills on the doorknob, and she glances over at me. "Thank you."

It's so quiet I barely hear it, and she leaves before I can say anything, but it hits me straight in the heart.

IT'S BECOMING a routine for Hallie to go to her apartment for a bit after dinner, then come back and do Sophia's hair before bed. Sometimes she also reads her a story. And when Sophia is finally asleep and I make my way out to the living room, she's always sitting on my couch, usually reading something on her e-reader.

"What's the book of choice tonight?" I ask, taking a seat next to her.

"A romance for the Baker girls book club. We finally finished going through Jade's backlist, so we're digging through her friend Zoey's books now. They're really good so far."

"Justin's wife Jade? She's an author?"

"Yep. That's how they connected. Justin narrates books. And is on the cover of a bunch too."

"Wow. Authors, narrators, football players. Any other high-profile people you know?"

"I know the Metros newest pitcher."

I gape at her. "The New York Metros... You know Jamie Henderson?"

She laughs and sets her e-reader aside. "Not well, but yeah.

I've met him a couple of times. He and his girlfriend rent the apartment above my old one in the city. My parents own the building. But that's not actually how I met him. You do realize he's from Ida, right? Mark's cousin is a friend of his, and Jade knows his girlfriend."

I blink at her in disbelief, and she laughs again.

"You're the small-town boy. Shouldn't you know this is how they work? And Zoey, the other author, is from Lacy Creek."

"Wait. Seriously? What's her full name?"

"Zoey Holloway."

"She was a grade ahead of me in school."

"You really need to get back in the small-town groove. You're out of touch."

I grab her legs and swing them onto my lap, massaging them. Another part of our routine, though I can tell she's trying not to get too used to it.

"You're probably right about that. After Sophia was born—hell, when my ex was pregnant with her—my sole focus became being a provider or caretaker. I stopped going out with friends or really doing much of anything. And once I had Sophia... I made her my entire focus. When you said that, I wanted to deny it, tell you how wrong you were. But there was truth to your words. Soph is my life. I've let go of a lot of myself without realizing it. I don't want to do that. Because you're right. She deserves to see the fun side of me."

"It came out over the weekend."

"Because of you. You... give me the safety to let that side of me out. To find it again. Thank you for that."

Her gaze lingers on me. "It's the least I can do for all the ways you take care of me." She nods toward my hands on her legs, then her eyes go to the refrigerator. "It might seem like nothing to you, but you stocking up on the foods I can easily eat means a lot to me. It's so simple, but it's also thoughtful. If we're admitting things, I didn't want to believe your words about taking care of me could be the truth. It would've hurt too much if they weren't.

But I'm glad they are." Her eyes meet mine. "No one besides my parents has ever taken care of me like this. Thank you."

"You don't ever have to thank me. It's my honor to be the man who gets to do it."

She stares at me for a moment, then in a swift movement, pulls her legs from my hands and climbs onto my lap.

Dragging her fingers through my hair, she stares down at me, emotion brimming in her eyes. Then her lips land on mine in a desperate kiss. The first one she's initiated since the night we met.

I lose myself in her lips and tongue. In the passion she pours into me.

The sinful groan I let out spurs her on, and she grinds against me, kissing me deeper, almost frantically, like if she stops, I'll disappear.

I wish she'd trust I never will.

She breaks our kiss, slowly pulling her lips from mine as if it's impossible to stop. Then she brushes her nose over mine and looks into my eyes. It's not only heat that swells in her beautiful amber eyes, it's vulnerability. Another lock cracked.

Her voice is soaked with desperation when she speaks. "Take me to bed."

My hands wrap around her ass, and I'm on my feet a second later, her body wrapped around mine as I carry her down the hall.

Our lips collide again, and the neediness of her kisses leaves my chest tight and aching with the same kind of need.

She's letting me in. Letting me care for her. And whether she realizes it or not, she's giving it all back to me.

My cock thickens as she molds herself to me. She's mine. I'm hers. And one day soon, she's going to stop fighting against herself. She'll see it too.

I'm a patient man. I can wait.

And until then, I'm going to take care of her in every single way.

CHAPTER TWENTY-ONE

WILSON DECKER IS DESTROYING me day by day.

No. He's destroying my walls.

Soon they'll be nothing but a pile of rubble, and I have no doubt he'll step in, charming smile on his face, and whisk me into his arms like I'm the princess in some sort of fairytale.

Not a helpless princess. A badass princess. And he's the knight who had to earn my trust... and my heart.

I'm scared. Every day, this feeling of falling for him gets a little more overwhelming, and I'm torn between wanting to give in or run away.

It all ends with heartbreak. I have to choose what kind I want to face.

My stomach whirls because it's not really a choice.

It hasn't been since Wilson's eyes landed on me from across the bar. Since I felt the heat of his gaze, then spent the night learning the intensity of his touch.

I always knew he was going to ruin me, but I expected it to be my body, not my heart.

A slight wave of nausea falls over me, and I almost shake my head. This baby is lucky. Wilson is a great dad, and it's clear he wants to be the same way for our baby.

When it rains, it pours.

I thought that when I was sitting on my couch, no clue what to do next.

I had no idea how right I was about that. The downpour hadn't even started yet.

Now I'm running around in the rain, still hoping my entire world doesn't flood. But there's also a bit of sun shining through.

And that's why it's time to tell my parents.

My parents are realtors and run their own business together out of their home. I still have access to their calendar, so I checked and they should be free right now.

I ate lunch not too long ago, so I shouldn't have to puke.

Flicking my phone on, I pull up my mom's number and hit call.

A prickle of nausea forms in my gut, but this time it's from nervousness. My parents are both supportive people, and since my mom got pregnant with Frannie before she met my dad and hid that fact from Frannie for years—pretending our dad was her biological father—she has no room to be judgy.

"Hello, my second prodigal daughter. How are you?"

I smile and instantly relax at the warmth in my mom's voice.

"I'm good. How are you? Is Dad there? I have something I want to tell you guys."

"We're good. Yes, your dad is right here. Putting you on speaker."

"Hey, honey," Dad says. "How's Ida treating you?"

"It's good. I'm a little surprised by how much I like it." I swallow hard, not sure where or how to start.

"What's going on?" Mom asks, cutting right to it. She always knows.

"Well... I'm pregnant."

There's silence for a moment, and I close my eyes, drawing my knees up to my chest.

"Say something," I squeak. I'm still the baby of the family who doesn't want her parents to be mad at her.

"Sorry," Mom says quickly. "We're processing. I might've expected that from Frannie. Maybe. But... what, uh—"

"Who?" Dad asks.

I chuckle lightly.

"Make sure you're sitting down, because you're not going to believe this story."

Pulling a pillow onto my lap, I snuggle up in the corner of the couch and tell them everything—well, not *everything*—but the majority of it.

"And Frannie had no idea..." Mom laughs in disbelief. "But you're happy? And this... Wilson... you're together?"

"Yes."

I don't like lying to my parents, but honestly, I'm not sure what the answer to that is. If Wilson had it his way, we would be together. And in some ways, we are. This is what the Facebook status "it's complicated" was invented for.

What am I supposed to tell them? That I'm broken and afraid to fall in love?

"And that's what you want, right? You're not just doing this because you're pregnant with his child?" Dad asks.

I shake my head vehemently, even though they can't see me, and the truth spills out. "I felt something the first night we met, but I was afraid to admit it. I... really care for him. And Sophia."

"We want to meet them. Both of them. Can you come down for a dinner? This weekend or next? We could come to you."

I saw that coming. "I would love for you to meet them both, and I'm happy to come down there, but for the moment, you'll have to settle for only meeting Wilson. We want to wait to tell Sophia until I'm further along, and... we're still easing her into the extent of our relationship." I'm a little lying liar. "But by Thanksgiving, she'll know, so maybe we could all be together then. And I could bring Wilson down next weekend?"

"We totally understand, and we'd love that," Mom says.

"We look forward to meeting him. And seeing you," Dad says.

"I miss you guys. I can't wait to see you. Oh, and can you not mention this to anyone else yet? I'd like to hit the twelve-week mark first. Obviously, you can tell Kend's parents. And I'll tell Gran. But otherwise—"

"We've got it. Our lips are sealed. We'll let you go, but take care of yourself. Let us know if you need anything. We love you, honey."

"Love you," Dad calls.

"Love you both. Bye."

I hang up, then go over to the messaging app I use for Gran, so I can reach her wherever in the world she is.

> Where in the world are you right now?

The three dots appear instantly.

GRAN

> I'm in the Netherlands right now. Just after dinner time here.

> Sounds fun.

GRAN

> You know me. I'm always having a good time. Have you been having a good time?

> You could say that.

GRAN

> Sounds like my sweet little Hallie is getting into some mischief.

> Working on it. I'm pregnant.

GRAN

My youngest grandbaby is having a baby?

Yep.

GRAN

Who's the lucky man? Or is this a turkey baster situation? You've joked about it in the past.

There's a man. His name is Wilson. He's sweet and caring, but he's got a fun side that he rarely shows. He's also got an 8 year old daughter who is beautiful and brilliant… and I'm her nanny.

GRAN

Don't tease me like that. Tell me the whole story.

Well, it all starts with a carnival…

AFTER A FUN CONVERSATION WITH GRAN—WHO made the same romance book comparisons I'd expect from Justin and Jade—I'm walking up the stairs to Frannie's apartment.

She meets me at the outer door and leads me inside, then gestures to the couch.

"I'm loving working from home more, especially now that you're here. Breaks to hang out with you are so much better than blinking at my laptop screen in an overly air-conditioned office."

I laugh at that.

"Good to know where I rank on your list of things to do." I clear my throat. "I told Mom and Dad."

"And?"

"They're excited. Instantly asked to meet Wilson and Sophia."

Her eyes narrow. "Wilson, huh?"

"That's his name," I say coolly.

"Mhm."

I swear to God she sounds just like Mom when she does that.

"He asked me to call him that. And we're becoming… closer."

"Oh, you are so gone for him. I love this for you."

"Well, bite your tongue. I'm not falling head over heels in love with him or anything."

She nods dramatically. "Whatever you say."

"Shut up. Has anyone ever told you how annoying you are?"

She smiles wickedly. "You. Every day of our lives."

"That just proves you're a bad listener."

"So, are you going to introduce them?"

"I'm going to ask Wilson to go with me to see them next weekend. Sophia doesn't know yet, so that's complicated. And… I was hoping maybe you'd be willing to stay with her or have her up here while we're gone. I figured you're sort of like her aunt-ish person now and you two should know each other better."

Frannie puts her hands to her heart. "Hal, I'd love to. She's a sweetheart, and of course I want to be a part of her life."

"Thanks," I say, but it comes out a little too high.

Frannie's smile grows again. "You're falling for him."

I stare at her for a moment, but saying anything other than yes would be a lie. So I do what any girl does when their sister is being annoying. I stick my tongue out at her.

"I hate you."

"You love me," she sings.

"Whatever."

She laughs and we fall into an easy conversation.

But my mind keeps wandering to what I told my parents today, then back to Wilson.

I want him to be mine, but I also know… I don't get to keep him. And setting myself up for that kind of heartbreak… that's not something I want to do.

But at this point, it might be too late.

I CLAP my hands as Sophia does a beautiful pirouette to finish up dance practice.

She runs over to me and throws her arms around me, and I hug her back. It's probably a bad thing that I'm thinking of her as mine.

I've always loved the kids I've nannied for, but this is different. This love is different. Maybe it's because I'm growing a baby right now or because the bond between us was instantaneous. I don't know. But there's something more maternal in there. A deep, protective love that's bigger than anything I've felt for a child I've nannied for.

They weren't mine.

Technically, Sophia isn't either. But she feels like she is.

When she breaks our hug, she looks over at Maria, who waves at her, then back up at me.

"Can Maria and me have a sleepover on Friday?"

I rest my hands on her shoulders and look at her sweet face and big puppy dog eyes.

"That's up to your dad, but if he says yes, I promise I'll come over and do your hair and nails... and whatever else you want."

"Thank you!"

"Of course. Let's go."

She and Maria boisterously say goodbye to each other, and we head out to my Wrangler.

Though it's not ideal, I'm thinking about asking Gran for a little loan to get a new-to-me car. She has more money than she'll ever need and she likes to help us all out if we need it. Since my parents and Kennedy's parents are well enough off, Kennedy is settled with Devon, and Frannie is dating a pro quarterback, they don't have much need for that money. While we do have a couple of other cousins scattered around from our other uncle, they're a little older and settled in their lives.

I'm the baby. The chaotic one. The one who got knocked up by the guy who made me come on a Ferris wheel. Whose daughter I'm now nannying for.

Chaos is exactly right.

SOPHIA FELL asleep in record time tonight. As has become common, I read to her while Wilson showered, but she fell asleep halfway through our second book. While it was tempting to snuggle in and fall asleep beside her, I shouldn't make a habit of that. I don't want to confuse her. It'll be confusing enough when we tell her about the baby. Plus, I need to talk to Wilson about next weekend.

Don't lie down.

I'm exhausted and can't stop yawning, but if I lie down, I'll fall asleep. Then Wilson will carry me to his bed, and I'll lose any remaining shreds of hope of not completely falling in love with him.

How do I protect myself from the inevitable hurt?

I can't. I'm a lost cause.

Wilson walks into the room, shirtless, in gray sweats, with his wet hair mussed—only proving my point.

"Waiting for me, Hellion?"

I narrow my eyes, even though I love when he calls me that.

"Maybe. I wanted to talk to you about something."

He drops onto the couch and pulls my legs onto his lap, massaging them like he's been doing pretty much every night lately.

"What's up? If it's a sleepover request, the answer is yes—at least if it means you sleeping in my bed."

I shake my head. Sophia was beyond thrilled when Wilson agreed she could have a sleepover here with Maria on Friday.

"Well... kind of? I told my parents today."

He freezes. "And?"

"They were great. Supportive. They're excited to meet you and Sophia." I clear my throat. This is the complicated part—mostly because he's probably going to be thrilled. "I told them we were together. For simplicity's sake."

The smile this man gives is unlike anything I've seen before. He's beaming so brightly you'd think he's incapable of frowning.

"Oh, really?"

"Don't let it go to your head."

"Impossible."

I roll my eyes, trying to play it off, because what I have to say next only heightens my vulnerability.

"Anyway, they asked me to come down and see them next weekend—and to bring you."

"Your parents want to meet me next weekend?"

"If we can make it happen."

"Of course. I'll make it work. No question. But Hal, do they know how old I am? I don't want to walk in there with them thinking I'm your age and see an older guy and think I'm a predator—"

"Wilson. Stop. They know the whole story. With certain parts redacted. It's all good."

He lets out a long breath. "Meeting your parents."

"Yep. They wanted to meet Sophia too, but I figured we should wait until after—"

"I agree. Plus, it'll be good for them to meet me first and get any questions or worries out of the way."

I practically snort at that. "All it'll take is them spending five minutes with you to know they don't need to have any."

"I'm the guy who got their youngest daughter pregnant."

"And the one who takes perfect care of her every single day."

His hand pauses on my leg. "Did you tell them that too?"

"Maybe," I whisper. "I wanted them to know I'm safe and happy."

He shifts on the couch, moving closer and brushing his thumb over my cheek. "Are you happy?"

"Yes. It's impossible not to be when I'm with you and Sophia. You say I bring out the fun side of you, well you two bring out my joyful side. Even if my parents hadn't asked to meet you, I would've wanted you to come." I look to the side, forcing my emotions down. "You make me feel safe."

"I will do everything in my power to make sure you always feel that way."

He lets out a long sigh, his hand slipping from my cheek, and damn my stupid, ignorant heart. It wants to beg for more.

"When do you want to leave next weekend?"

"Saturday morning? We can meet up with them in the afternoon, have some dinner, then stay at my old apartment. My parents haven't rented it out yet. Then maybe I could take you to a couple of my favorite spots in the city before we come home later on Sunday?"

"Sounds good to me. I'm sure my mom can watch Sophia."

"Actually, I was thinking maybe Frannie could watch her. Soph could go up there or Frannie could come down here. That way Sophia can pretty much be at home, and she and Frannie can get to know each other better. It's good for them to bond since Frannie will sort of be like Sophia's aunt."

My cheeks heat a little, and he watches me, a slow smile spreading up his face.

"Hellion, are you imagining us as a family?"

The mix of intensity and joy in his eyes is hard to ignore. Especially because I'm tired of lying or trying to convince myself it's not true.

"Something like that."

His warm eyes stay locked on me for another moment, then he sweeps a strand of hair behind my ear.

"I think that's a great idea."

"Good," I breathe. Then I yawn because I'm still exhausted.

"You need to sleep."

"I—"

"Nope." He stands up and holds out his hand, pulling me up from the couch. But he doesn't make a move toward the bedroom. Instead, he wraps his arms around me, breath tickling my ear. "Let me take *perfect* care of you."

I gulp at the devious promise in his words. Not because of any sexual implications. Because I know he means every syllable of every word. He's going to tuck me into his bed, wrap himself around me, and make sure I have everything I need all night. Then he'll do it again tomorrow. And the next day. And...

He guides me down the hall, arm wrapped around me in a way that's both comforting and possessive.

The last of my resolve is washing away, and as if it's the glue holding my walls together, I can already feel them starting to crumble.

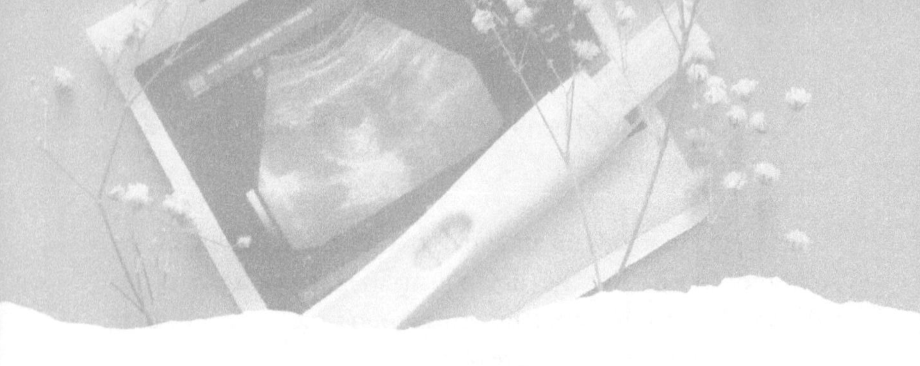

CHAPTER TWENTY-TWO

"WE'LL BE FINE, DAD," Sophia says dramatically when I give her another hug.

I rarely leave her overnight. Other than the weekend I met Hallie, I can't remember the last time I wasn't there. And back then, we lived with my mom, so she was still home.

She'll be home now. With Frannie.

"She's right. We're going to have a super fun girls' weekend," Frannie says. "It's only a few hours away and for one night. You can do it."

She smirks at me, and I roll my eyes. I'm an only child, but I get the feeling Frannie is going to show me what it's like to have a sister. In the most frustrating of ways.

"She's so annoying when she smirks like that, right?" Hallie teases.

Frannie sticks her tongue out, making Sophia giggle.

"I want a sister someday."

I swallow hard and try to keep a calm, steady face. She's going to go nuts when she finds out about the baby.

Frannie comes to the rescue, giving her a gentle smile. "Maybe you will."

"Right, well, we should get going." I resist the urge to hug Sophia a fourth time. She's already hugged Hallie twice too.

"Okay. Have fun!"

Hallie chuckles at Soph's blasé attitude.

"I know when I'm not wanted."

"Daddy... I love you." From across the room, her sweet smile melts my heart. One day I'm supposed to let her leave and go to college? I don't know how I'm going to handle that.

"I love you too, kiddo. Be safe."

"Love you, Miss Hallie."

Hallie pauses by the door and turns to look at Sophia, a warm smile on her lips.

"I love you too, sweetheart."

Damn.

I never thought I'd be jealous of my daughter, but I can't help but hope one day Hallie will say those words to me.

THE SECOND we pull onto the highway Hallie connects her phone to the car's console and starts scrolling.

"What are you doing?"

"Putting on music. That's the passenger's job."

I glance at her, and her brows raise.

"Oh no. Are you a music snob? Because I might have to rescind your invitation on this trip if you are."

"No. I—I like music and I'm not an asshole about it. But I have an eight-year-old daughter. Most of the time, the music in my life is Glee, Kids Bop, Katy Perry, or Taylor Swift. And no shade to Taylor, but I'm tired of it."

Hallie just laughs. "While I love Taylor and all her angsty goodness, it's not the first thing I reach for. Especially for a road trip. Trust me, okay?"

Reluctantly, I nod, and she laughs to herself as she scrolls for another few seconds. Then she sets her phone down and turns up the volume.

The opening notes of *Welcome Home* from Coheed and Cambria flow from the speakers, and I quickly look over at her.

"Not what you were expecting, Mr. Decker?"

I flex my hands on the steering wheel. "Hallie…"

Again, she laughs. "It's not a road trip without some Coheed. I was feeling a playlist though, so you're going to have to suffer through some Taking Back Sunday, Audioslave, Yellowcard, MCR, and Dashboard Confessional. Oh, and there's a bunch of Foo Fighters on here too."

Though I want to look at her again, I keep my eyes on the road. "Solid choices."

"I'm convinced I was born in the wrong time. I was meant to be a teen in the 2000s in the peak pop-punk-emo days."

"It's a good thing music never goes out of style. Although I could live without classic rock for a bit. I know it's sacrilege, but it's all we ever have on at job sites and I can only take hearing the same Billy Joel, Eagles, Elton John, and The Who songs so many times before my ears start to bleed."

"Well yeah. If you're doing those, you need the full albums and the deep cuts. Or a live one. I have *Last Play at Shea* on here somewhere and the version of *Piano Man* on there gives me goosebumps every time."

My gaze slips to her for a second. "Okay, you've officially won music picking privileges."

She throws her hand up. "Yes!"

She settles back in her seat, smiling as she sings along to the words, and my heart stutters. This tiny moment is everything I didn't know I wanted and never believed I could have.

I PULL up in front of a duplex on a quiet street. Or what quiet is for New York City. Still crowded with more cars parked on it than even the busiest streets in downtown Ida.

We stay in our seats for a moment because you don't just stop *Welcome to the Black Parade* in the middle of the song. Hallie sings along with the lyrics while I drum on the steering wheel, and that sense of freedom—of being alive—hits me. It's what she always brings out in me, and I want to feel it more. I want it all the time. Or as often as I can. Maybe I can't be that guy at work or in certain moments of parenting, but I want to find those pieces of me again.

As the song ends, I turn off the engine and Hallie tucks her phone away.

I climb out of the car and when I get around to her side, she's sitting there with the door open, staring up at the house.

Offering her my hand, I help her out, but her eyes stay fixed on the large two-story home in front of us.

"This is where you grew up?"

She finally looks at me. "Yep. It's a nice neighborhood. There's a park not too far from here, though there is a small back-yard, it's only big enough to sit outside—not enough to play bocce in or anything like that. I'm guessing we'll eat out there tonight."

Her hand intertwined with mine, I lead her toward the house. "Did you like growing up here?"

"I loved it. Especially once I hit age ten. That's when I was allowed to run around with my friends within a three-block radius.

We'd get milkshakes at the diner a couple of blocks over or play kickball at the park. The elementary school is four blocks away, so as long as there was a group of us, we were allowed to walk there together without our parents. I had a lot of fun here. Especially as I got older and could explore the city more on my own."

We climb the front steps, and my stomach tightens. I'm not usually the type to get nervous, but meeting her parents is daunting since I'm technically also her employer and got her pregnant out of wedlock.

"Do you ever miss it?" I ask.

She pauses and looks around. "Not really. I loved it, and it's always here if I want to come visit, but it's not my home anymore."

The door swings open as Hallie reaches for it, so I don't have time to revel in her words. This place—the house and the city—aren't her home anymore. Because it's in Ida. With me. Maybe she won't admit to the second part yet, but by the very fact that I'm here with her hand wrapped around mine, I know it's true.

"Hello," Hallie's mom says with the same brightness I often hear in Hallie's voice.

"Hey, Mom. Hi, Dad." Hallie turns to me. "These are my parents, Cheyenne and Eddie." She looks at them again. "Mom and Dad, this is Wilson Decker. My baby daddy."

I'm halfway through extending my hand to her dad when she says that. I freeze in place and groan.

Her parents both laugh, and I reach out again and quickly shake both of their hands.

"You clearly haven't gotten to know Hallie well enough if you weren't expecting that," her dad says. And I know it's a little push. A question. How well do I know his daughter? How serious is this? The thing is, that's exactly what I should've been expecting, but after sharing vulnerable moments with Hallie, sometimes the playful side of her catches me off guard.

I wrap my arm around her and tug her close. "I should've

been." Lowering my voice, I catch Hallie's eyes. "You've been a hellion since the moment we met."

She gives me her sweetest smile. "It's so much fun. How could I not? Plus, I kind of love that grumpy look you get."

We follow her parents inside, and I'm surprised when she wraps her arm around my back in return.

How much of this is real to her?

How honest was she with her parents when she said we were together?

At some point, we have to talk about all that. Probably before we tell Sophia about the baby.

"This is a beautiful home." I take in the old hardwood banister and stairwell. A lot of the home has been updated, but the hardwood floors and some of the classic features remain well taken care of focal points.

"Thank you," Cheyenne says. "Hallie mentioned you work in construction?"

"Yes. I'm a project manager. I haven't been lucky enough to work on any homes like this, though. Most of them are seventies, eighties, and nineties homes that we're gutting or adding on to. Or new builds. I'll be starting work on one of those in a few weeks."

We walk through the living room that's immaculately decorated, then through a doorway and down a short hall with the bathroom off it into the kitchen at the back of the house. It's a decent size with a four-person table in it.

"We thought we'd eat out back today," Cheyenne says. "It's not a big yard, but it's a little slice of green."

"Sounds great."

We follow them outside, and Hallie's smile brightens. She likes having that little bit of green, a space where she can relax outside. Or play yard games.

I've spent restless nights thinking about how easily we could combine our two apartments. All it would take is to remove a few walls and make some upgrades, and we could have a beautiful home. But maybe that wouldn't be the home she'd truly want.

My mind drifts to a house AB Construction flipped a couple of months ago. It was four bedrooms, only a couple of blocks from the heart of downtown Ida, but it had a big yard. I don't know if it's still available, but even if it is... I'm getting way ahead of myself. I haven't even gotten Hallie to consider me her boyfriend—or partner—yet. But now that a glimpse of that future has drifted into the back of my mind, I can't help but want it.

I pull out Hallie's chair for her at the rectangular table set on the little stone patio.

"What do you want to drink?" I ask as she sits down. "Or should I have stopped for milkshakes?"

"Just some water with extra—"

"Ice. I know."

She smiles up at me, like she's saying she told me so. How I take care of her is obvious. But I don't even think about it. It's not a choice. It's what I do because I care about her.

It's not until I turn toward the door that I feel her parents' eyes on me.

I glance back for half a second, and am met with an approving smile from each of them. For a second it surprises me, but then I think about what I'd want for Sophia. I'd want someone who would take care of her the same way I do and make sure she had everything she needed.

While I may have just won some points with her parents, I still don't think it'll be as easy as Hallie said to fully win them over.

WE FELL into a relaxed conversation as Eddie fired up the grill and started cooking.

Cheyenne told me all about their work as realtors and then asked questions about Sophia. Hallie spent the next half hour showing her mom pictures of Sophia while we both told stories about her.

Overall, it's been a pretty relaxed afternoon. Hallie's parents seem great. Caring without being overbearing or embarrassing. And it's easy to see Hallie gets her lighthearted playfulness from both sides. I'm curious where she gets her edge from, though. So far, I haven't seen a hint of it from either of her parents.

Cheyenne and Eddie made a delicious lunch of steak, asparagus, and grilled garlic bread. It's been mostly silent because we've all been savoring the food, but when I look over at Hallie's plate, I realize she's pushing around the same piece of steak she had on her fork ten minutes ago. She picked at the asparagus and garlic bread.

I rub my hand down her back. "Okay?"

Her eyes flash to me, and she tries to force a smile, but I can tell she's fighting back nausea. "I'm fine. Just not much appetite."

"Did you tell them—"

She cuts me off with a look, but Cheyenne has already tuned in to our conversation.

"Is the food not settling okay?"

"It's fine," Hallie chirps.

"She has a hard time eating most foods these days. She has a shortlist of stuff that settles well."

Cheyenne's gaze narrows. "You told me anything would be fine."

"I didn't want you to worry about what I can and can't eat."

I push my chair back. "Okay, that's it. You said there's a diner a couple of blocks away? I assume they have milkshakes and fries. What's the name?"

"Frank's. But you don't—"

"You need food you can eat."

I move to stand, but she presses her hand into my thigh. "No... I mean, you don't have to go there. You can order online and they'll deliver." Her eyes drop from mine. "That way you can stay here."

I drop back down and scooch my chair back in, then wrap my arm around Hallie's back, pulling her chair closer to me while I find the website for the diner on my phone with my other hand.

If she wants me to stay with her, there's not a chance I'm leaving her side.

I put in the order, and Hallie rests her head on my shoulder. She's still fighting the nausea, which for her usually happens if she doesn't eat enough or if she eats something that doesn't settle well with her.

She grabs her water and sips on it, and I notice Cheyenne watching her carefully.

"I wish you would've told me. I would've made sure you had what you needed in the house."

Hallie tries to shrug it off. "I usually just roll with whatever there is and then get food that settles for me later."

"Or you end up making yourself sick. Don't do that." I kiss her cheek, right by her ear, and a little shiver rolls through her.

Not one touch today has been pretend, and it's how I want to touch her all the time.

Maybe this weekend will put a little more pressure on her walls. I'm ready to see them tumble down, so I can find the depth of her and her beautiful heart beneath them.

"So, Wilson, how will things work between you and Hallie as your relationship grows? Or once the baby is born? Will you continue paying her to be your nanny?"

Hallie's eyes fly wide. "Dad!"

But the question doesn't faze or surprise me. It's what I'd ask too.

"Honestly, we haven't spoken in depth about that yet. As you might know, Hallie is quite independent, so I don't want to try to dictate anything. I know how I feel, and the most important thing to me is that she feels comfortable and knows she's taken care of in every way. How we handle things in the coming months is something we'll continue working through together."

Every word is the truth. If I had it my way, no, I wouldn't be paying her to nanny for Sophia. She'd be there in the mornings and afternoons because she'd live with us, and she could take on additional babysitting or nannying jobs or whatever she wanted to do. And I'd make sure everything she could possibly need was taken care of. But that's not up to me. Hallie has to want that too. So until we get closer to that place, I'm taking it a day at a time.

Under the table, Hallie squeezes my hand.

After a moment, Eddie gives me an understanding smile. "That may be the nicest way I've ever been told to mind my own business."

I put my hands up in surrender. "Hey, I get it. I'm a dad too."

"Speaking of that—and feel free to tell *me* to mind my own business—is Sophia's mother in the picture? I made a lot of mistakes in handling that with Frannie and her biological father, so I'm curious what Hallie will be dealing with."

Hallie gave me the rundown on Frannie not being Eddie's biological child—and not finding that out until she was in her early twenties—and how it affected Frannie and Cheyenne's relationship.

"Soph's mom is not involved in her life. That was her decision. The door is always open if she wants to come back—and she feels she could be consistent about that—but I don't see that happening."

"Not an area of drama to worry about," Hallie says to her mom. "Even though you should know by now, I can handle anything like that. All that matters to me is that Sophia knows how loved and special she is."

"That must've been difficult for you—raising Sophia alone," Eddie says.

"Raising kids is always hard. I was lucky to have my mom to help. We lived with her up until this past year. My dad passed a couple of years before Sophia was born, so she devoted a lot of her time to helping us."

"I'm sorry to hear about your father," Eddie says.

Cheyenne reaches over and rests her hand on mine. "Me too. I know how tough that is."

"Thank you." My phone pings, and I glance down at it. "Looks like your food is here." I move to stand up, but Eddie stands first.

"I'll get it. You stay here."

The look he gives me conveys what he really means. Stay with her. Take care of her.

Stroking my thumb over Hallie's shoulder, I glance at her. She's wearing a soft smile, like everything's going exactly how she wanted things to.

She really is envisioning us as a family.

She sees a future with all of us together.

But if that's what she wants, why does she keep holding herself back from having it?

CHAPTER TWENTY-THREE

WHEN WE WALK into Hallie's old apartment after a long afternoon and early evening with her parents, her body instantly relaxes.

So much so that she looks like she might fall over or fall asleep where she's standing.

"You okay?"

She spins to face me with a relaxed smile. "I'm good. A little tired. Today went pretty well though. Even if I wanted to kill my dad when he asked that question about you paying me."

"It's something we'll have to talk about."

"Yeah. *We*. When we get there."

"He cares. That's a good thing."

She sighs. "I know. And I appreciate it. But I'll be twenty-four soon. He has to let me grow up." She runs her hand over her stomach. "I'm going to be someone's mom soon." Looking around the room, she shakes her head. "Can you believe the last time we were here together, we made this?"

I stalk over to her and run my lips down her neck. "Of course I can believe it. Every second of that night is a vibrant memory. A perfect, unforgettable memory. The way my body moved with yours changed me. I'd never felt the things I felt with you with anyone else. The next morning, I forced myself to leave because I already knew I had feelings for you." I slip my hands under her shirt. "Feelings I thought I couldn't have." I switch to the other side of her neck. "I never dreamed I'd be lucky enough to keep you. To call you mine. Because you are. You can keep that sweet little heart of yours walled off, but that doesn't make you any less mine. Mine to protect, mine to care for, mine to touch and please..."

"Wilson," she breathes, hands sliding into my hair.

"What do you need, baby?"

"You. All of you."

"You've got me," I rumble in her ear. "I'm yours." And with that, I sweep her off her feet and carry her to her old bedroom.

I set her down near the bed and stand back to look at her.

"Strip for me."

"Only if you're going to give me the same show in return."

In one fluid motion, I pull my shirt over my head and drop it to the floor.

She sucks in a breath and stares at my naked chest, her teeth sinking into her bottom lip. Then she pulls her shirt off and unclasps her bra, dropping both to the floor.

I groan as I stare at her hardened nipples, aching to suck them into my mouth, tease them with my tongue.

I palm my hand over the crotch of my jeans, trying to calm down, give my aching cock a reprieve, but nothing helps. All I want is to be buried inside her.

"Your turn," she breathes.

I undo the button of my pants and let them drop to the floor, but don't go for my boxers. Instead, I stroke myself through the soft fabric.

"Wilson," she whines. Then her tiny shorts are on the floor, and I get the most perfect view. Her standing there, naked except for a soft cotton thong, with the tiniest baby bump on display.

Mine. The word is a feral growl in the back of my mind.

She's mine. I need to feel her pulsing around my cock. Need to paint her pussy with my cum over and over. *Mine.*

"Get on the bed."

I toe my socks off as she climbs onto the bed, lying in the center.

Kneeling on the end of the bed, I crawl over to her, settling between her legs. Then achingly slowly, I graze my fingers up her legs, savoring the goosebumps that rise on her skin. When I get to her hips, I hook my fingers in the waistband of her thong and pull it down.

Then I'm in heaven. Shifting onto my stomach, I push her legs up, inhaling her scent as I stare at her glistening pussy.

"God, you're perfect."

I circle my tongue around her opening, then trail it up her center until I'm teasing her clit.

Her hands fall to my head, and she rolls her hips toward me. I reach up, giving her perky little tits a squeeze, then find her nipples and roll them between my thumbs and forefingers.

But I barely have time to play because with one more flick of my tongue, her body goes taut, and she cries out, pulling on my hair.

"Yes!"

The way she moans and cries out has me grinding against the mattress to ease the ache in my cock.

I lift my head and slide up her body, shoving my boxers down as I do. But it's Hallie who grabs my face and pulls my lips to hers, kissing me deeply as she urges me inside her.

"Easy, Hellion."

"No. I need to feel you inside me. But I want you to go slow. I want this to last. I'm aching, and I just need to feel you. I want you inside me for as long as possible. Please."

"Baby, those words are going to kill me," I rasp. "Roll on your side."

She does it, and I lie down behind her.

Holding her steady, I push inside her, the pure pleasure in her moans igniting me as I bury myself to the hilt.

She lets out a shuddery breath once I'm fully seated inside her.

Slipping my hand between her legs, I rub her clit as I move in and out of her in short, slow strokes. Her hand snakes up and wraps around the side of my neck as I drop my lips to her neck, kissing and sucking the skin into my mouth.

It's gentle and controlled as I draw out another orgasm from her, then do everything I can to keep from coming as well.

She whimpers when I slow my movements, rolling her hips in desperation.

"Does your greedy little clit need more?"

"Yes," she whines.

"Stay just like that."

I carefully roll onto my knees, so she's still lying on her side, but I'm straddling her legs, pressed inside her sideways.

"Play with your nipples." I stroke my thumb over her clit, then slowly thrust deeper. "How does that feel?"

"Perfect."

Fingers digging into her hip, I move a little faster, holding on to the edge of my sanity. I come close, then pause, letting myself come back down again. I want this to last for her. I want her to be completely sated when we're done.

Sometimes she doesn't want anything more than me gently stroking her clit, but when she wants sex like this, she's ravenous.

I work her clit faster, slowing my thrusts.

"Yes, yes..." She throws her head back as she cries out, her pussy spasming around my cock in hard pulses. "Oh my god."

My abs burn from holding back, but I need to make sure she has everything she needs first.

"I need more. Not hard, but more…"

"I understand. Lie on your back."

She shifts, and I thrust deeper and pull out farther, though I keep my strokes gentle.

"Yes. Just like that." She claws at my back, dragging me down so I'm hovering over her.

"Do you have another orgasm for me?"

She nods vigorously.

"Good. Work your clit. Keep your eyes on me."

Her eyes widen slightly, then lock on mine as her hand slips between her legs.

"Just like that. Such a good girl, baby. I can't wait to feel your pussy squeeze my cock, to fill you with my cum."

I wrap my hand around the side of her neck.

"I need to come so badly," I whine. "Are you going to milk my cock?"

"Yes," she moans, working her fingers faster.

"Yes?"

"Yes."

"Say my name."

Her eyes flare.

It's one thing she hasn't done yet. Probably another little way of holding back, even if I don't understand why. She's called me Deck, Decker, and Mr. Decker in bed. But she's never called me Wilson.

I move a little faster, and she cries out again.

"Say my name, Hallie."

She stares at me for a moment more, then it finally falls from her lips.

"Wilson."

"That's my girl," I groan.

Her breathing quickens.

"Oh…Wilson. Wilson," she cries out as her eyes roll back and her beautiful body racks with spasms.

Her coming while crying out my name sends me flying over

the edge. My spine tingles and my balls tighten as she squeezes my cock. "Fuck. Hallie." Her name is a high-pitched moan as I spill inside her, marking her as mine all over again.

My eyes fall shut as I ride out my high, her pussy still occasionally pulsing around me.

I groan as I fall to the bed beside her, not wanting to pull out of her yet. She's still breathing heavily as she runs her fingers through my hair and kisses me. My eyes are only half open, but I wrap my arm around her, pulling her closer as I deepen the kiss.

"Mm," she mumbles against my lips.

I hold her tighter, but she wriggles against me. "I need to get up. Clean up." I groan in protest, but she kisses my cheek. "The doctor said it's important to prevent infection."

Reluctantly, I loosen my grip, and I'm rewarded with another kiss.

"I'll be right back."

I peel my eyes all the way open just in time to watch her naked ass strut away. Flopping onto my back, I stare at the ceiling. Hearing her say my name like that was—

"Wilson!"

I leap out of the bed and tear across the room at the sound of her panicked voice.

"What is it? What's wrong?"

She's sitting on the toilet, shaking, with tears in her eyes.

She holds up a piece of toilet paper with a pinkish-light red tint.

Oh, fuck.

Okay. Breathe. Calm. Think.

"Is there anything bright red?"

She shakes her head.

Okay, that's good. I think.

"It's been a while since I read up on all this, but it's probably just some spotting after sex. I think I remember that being a thing. Try to stay calm. We'll go to the ER and get you checked, just to be sure."

She looks up at me, utterly broken.

"What—what if—"

I lift her off the toilet and carry her back to the bedroom. I set her down and take her face in my hands. "It'll be okay." Tears stream down her cheeks, and I push all my fears away. I need to take care of her right now.

ALL I CAN DO IS pace.

Back and forth in this tiny room.

It's better than the waiting room we were in for two hours.

Hallie was intermittently crying for the first hour or two, but now she's just sitting in the little hospital bed, an oversized gown hanging off her body. Thick white blankets cover her legs, which are pulled up to her chest. She's resting her chin on her knees and staring blankly at the wall.

She won't talk to me. She's almost catatonic.

They came in and drew labs and ordered an ultrasound. We're waiting on the results of the labs and for the ultrasound technician.

I'm not convinced this is the worst-case scenario, but it's still scary as fuck.

My stomach is in knots, but I'm in dad mode. Compartmentalizing. That's what has to be done when everything else is falling apart and I have to be the reliable one.

I'm thirty-one and still wish for an adultier adult sometimes, but as a dad, unfortunately, I'm usually the adultier adult.

"This is why I don't do love."

I whip around to look at Hallie, who is wiping her eyes.

"What do you mean?"

She glances at me, but doesn't quite meet my gaze.

"Loving opens you up to heartbreak. And this?" She gestures to her body. "It's too much."

I sit down on the edge of her bed and grab her hand. "Where is this coming from?"

She finally meets my eyes, and she knows what I mean.

Not the fears she's feeling tonight. Why does she keep her heart walled off? Why is she afraid of love?

"Growing up, I was obsessed with my grandparents' love story. I'd beg my gran to tell me about it over and over. Finding a love like that was what I wanted out of life. When I was fourteen, my grandfather was in the hospital, recovering after some heart stuff. He was expected to make a full recovery, and my grandmother had been staying with us while he was there. One night I woke up to my grandmother screaming. I ran downstairs and found her on her knees on the floor, my mom in front of her crying. Frannie was beside me a moment later, and then our dad told us what happened. Pop had passed away suddenly." Her voice thickens, and she sniffs back tears. "I will never forget Gran screaming at the top of her lungs that she was supposed to die first because she couldn't live without him. That was the moment I knew I never wanted to fall in love because I didn't want to endure that type of pain. Losing parents, siblings, friends... those are all painful, but losing the person your soul is tethered to?" She shakes her head. "I don't want to do that." Her lip quivers as she rests her hands on her stomach. "But I didn't think about this. Losing a child—the thought is unbearable."

Well, fuck me.

I assumed someone hurt her, but really, she's terrified of experiencing the kind of pain that comes with deep loss.

My chest cracks open when I think about what that means. All this time she hasn't been afraid of falling for me. She's afraid of loving me that much. I don't know how to convince her it's okay. But that's for another time. Her feelings for me aren't what's important right now.

I put my hand over hers where it's resting on her stomach.

"We don't know what's going to happen, but even if we lost this baby, would you regret loving them?"

Her nostrils flare and tears fall down her cheeks.

"This is scary, but it's a part of life. If you try to hide and prevent yourself from feeling pain, all you'll be left with is emptiness, and I know that's not what you want. I understand your fear. I lost my dad suddenly, and I'm still grieving him. I always will be. Grief is love transformed. And it fucking hurts sometimes, but I'd rather feel that hurt and remember the way he loved me than to have never had it at all. Love is a risk, but it's the best risk you'll ever take. Without love, life is meaningless. Don't prevent yourself from experiencing it. And when it comes to this, how would you ever be able to love this little person as fully as they deserve to be if you're scared to open your heart all the way?"

She moves her hand and twines our fingers together over her stomach, resting her head on my shoulder.

"I'm really scared."

"I know you are. I'm scared too. But my dad would have told me to have hope. So that's what I'm doing right now. For myself. For you. For our baby. That's his love still here. Still getting me through." I brush my lips over her forehead. "It's okay to be scared. But don't give up. And don't regret loving this baby because I can guarantee it's the best thing you've ever done."

She turns her body into me, and I wrap my arms around her, holding her close while she cries.

I'm still scared. And though I wish it wouldn't have taken this to get her to open up to me, I'm glad she finally did. Now I know it's not about breaking through her walls, but showing her that loving someone deeply is worth the risk of losing that love one day.

CHAPTER TWENTY-FOUR

Hallie

I LET OUT a shaky breath as Wilson and I wait for the ultrasound tech to get everything set up. Right before they came to take me back, a nurse came in and said all my labs looked normal.

That's something.

I wasn't expecting to completely lose my shit and pour my soul out to Wilson, but... I know I'm safe with him. And even though he said some hard truths and encouraged me not to fear love, I never felt judged.

Though when he asked if I'd regret loving this baby even if we lost it, guilt almost overtook me. Not because of Wilson or his words, but because of how selfish I was being. How stupidly terrified I was. I'm afraid if the ultrasound shows the worst that I'll completely break, but I also know I'll cherish every time I held my stomach or talked to our baby or... any of it.

I don't want to stunt my love for them out of fear.

In the chair beside me, Wilson has my hand in his, and he's brushing his lips over it.

He's my rock.

My safe place.

And… I'm falling in love with him. There's no question about that.

I think some part of me has known that since the night we met. I've never felt a pull to someone like I do with him. And Sophia.

When we talked about coming down here for the weekend, he asked me if I was picturing us as a family, and the truth is, I have been since the very beginning. That's what I want.

It's time to stop pretending. To stop shutting out what we could be because I'm afraid of getting hurt.

After all these years, that won't be easy. I'll have to go slow. Whatever slow is when I spend every night in bed with the man whose baby I'm carrying, and whose daughter has already wormed her way into my heart.

Bit by bit they're becoming my family, and while the side of me that screams there's too much to lose, get out of there, is still loud and overwhelming, I'm never going to have what I want if I don't work to silence those thoughts.

"Okay, I think we're all set. Hallie, I'm going to hand you the wand, and you can insert it."

I hate this part. All those damn TV shows where they squirt stuff on your belly when you're not even through your first trimester are liars. To see the baby right now, I have to stick a wand up my lady business.

My hand shakes as I insert it.

This is it.

We're either going to see our baby and everything will be fine, or…

I close my eyes. I don't want to think about the *or*.

Wilson said his dad would've wanted him to have hope.

Hope.

I want to ask Wilson more about his dad. I feel bad I haven't. Part of keeping someone's memory alive is talking about them. It's clear Wilson had a strong relationship with his dad. He should keep that alive.

The tech hits a few buttons, and Wilson squeezes my hand.

I turn toward him, because I don't want to see the look on the tech's face.

A couple more clicks, and Wilson's eyes go wide.

I snap my eyes shut. *No.* I don't want to—

"Hallie. Look."

I open my eyes, but don't turn my head.

He looks at me and smiles softly.

"Trust me. Look."

Slowly, I turn, and when I do, I'm greeted with the most beautiful sight I've ever beheld. Our tiny baby is there on the screen, little nubbin feet kicking. And then the tech hits another button and whooshing fills the room.

"That's your baby's heartbeat. One hundred fifty beats per minute, which is typical for this stage. I can't say anything specific as that's up to the doctor, but what we're seeing is an overall good sign."

"Thank you," I murmur.

Wilson kisses my hand, then stares reverently at the screen as the tech takes a bunch of measurements.

"This is incredible," he whispers.

I squeeze his hand, pulling his gaze back to me for a second.

"Thank you for not letting me give up."

He smiles at me. "You've got too much love in your heart to ever do that."

EVERYTHING'S OKAY.

As Wilson said when he came to me in the bathroom, it was nothing serious. Just some light spotting after sex, which isn't uncommon. I already have my appointment with my OB next Wednesday, so they'll do another check and make sure my labs look good, but the ER doctor seemed confident there's no cause for concern.

I feel a little stupid for getting so upset, but I want this baby so much. The thought of losing them is horrifying. It felt a little too close to reality tonight.

Now I'm exhausted and want to crash, even though the adrenaline of it all has me so hyped I'm not sure I can.

Wilson has been quiet the entire ride back to my apartment. Old apartment. It still feels cozy, like a home away from home, but it's not where I'm meant to be.

When I unlock the door and step inside, I let out a long breath. The door shuts behind me, then Wilson walks past me, going to the other side of the room and staring out the window.

I slip my shoes off and make my way over to him. His eyes stay locked on the little sliver of the city outside.

"Hey," I whisper, running my hand up his arm.

Reluctantly, he turns to look at me, tears rimming his eyes.

"What's wrong?" I grab both his hands and step in front of him, forcing his full attention on me.

"I don't want to lose this."

Oh God, my heart.

His voice is achingly raw.

"Sophia's mom had a rough pregnancy, and I was always worried about what would happen to Sophia, but... maybe I was young or I didn't care enough or I was a selfish jackass, but it never occurred to me to worry that Sophia's mom wouldn't be okay. With you? I was terrified tonight."

"But you were so calm..."

He takes my face in his hands.

"On the outside. On the inside, I was barely keeping it together. Losing you or our child..."

A tear falls down his cheek, and my heart lurches.

Running my hands up his arms, I look into his eyes. "I'm okay. Our baby is okay."

He kisses my forehead, then drops to his knees in front of me and lifts my shirt, kissing across my stomach.

"I'm so glad you're okay, little one. Daddy loves you."

Then his eyes lift to mine, and my heart feels the words he doesn't say.

I curl my fingers through his hair as tears slide down my cheeks.

This is it. No more lying to myself. No more pretending. It's time to give this a chance—a real chance. That all-consuming kind of love still terrifies me, but I know I'll hate myself forever if I don't give this my all.

I've always said yes to taking risks, as long as those risks didn't include my heart. Well, fuck that. My heart is already on the line. Time to see what happens when I offer him a piece.

I tug on his hair, pulling him upright, then his mouth melts over mine in a warm, comforting kiss. Our first kiss that isn't out of pent-up desire. A kiss that isn't leading anywhere. It's a kiss that's about us. The us we could be. The us I want to be.

He breaks the kiss and pulls me into his arms, and I bury my face in his chest.

He strokes his fingers through my hair and I melt into him a little more.

"Can we go to bed?" I murmur. "I just want to lie in your arms."

He hugs me tighter, kissing my head. "I'll hold you all night."

WILSON'S warm hand rubs over my stomach as we lie in bed.

He held me all night. We fell asleep wrapped in each other's arms and we both slept so hard I don't think either of us moved.

We've spent the last half hour lying in each other's arms and talking. Kissing. Being a couple.

Telling my parents we were dating was never a lie. I know that's what we've been doing for weeks, even if I've been too afraid to call it that. Last night put a lot of things into perspective.

Am I still terrified of what falling in love means? Absolutely. But I'm done trying to stop it from happening. I'll just have to prepare myself to face the consequences one day.

"I love your little bump," he whispers, brushing his thumb over my slightly raised belly button. "I can't wait to watch it grow."

"Me either."

I brush my knuckles over his cheek, drawing his eyes to mine.

"Do you want more kids?"

He stares at me for a second. "I'm going to say this, but don't take it the wrong way. You need to hear everything first."

"Okay."

"The night we met, I was thinking how Sophia has been saying she wanted a sister, and how I couldn't even consider it. There was too much change and too much going on to even think about the idea. Then you told me you were pregnant, and after the initial shock wore off, all I felt was joy. I realized it was never about not being ready for another kid, it was that I'd convinced myself I couldn't have that. Or wouldn't. Now I know exactly how much I want it. And I wouldn't mind having more." He slides his hand up and plays with a strand of my hair. "What about you?"

"Being a mom was always my dream. I imagined using the turkey baster method to get there and probably only having one —maybe two. But..." I clear my throat. "With the right person, I'd love to have more."

I can see it. Us in a cute little house like the one he grew up in,

Sophia and a couple more kids playing in the backyard while Wilson rubs my round stomach as we watch from the back porch.

It's overwhelming, but there's no denying I want it.

I've never been more scared to want something in my life. To dream of it and hope for it.

Hope.

After what Wilson said about his dad last night, that word keeps dancing around in my mind.

I'm scared, but I'm letting hope guide me. I'm letting my heart lead, and I'm trying to ignore the devastation that could cause.

"With the right person?" Wilson rumbles.

I sweep my hand over his cheek. "Like a super hot baby daddy named after a back porch."

He throws his head back and laughs.

I love that laugh—the pure joy that spills out of him. That side of him is as endearing as it is fun.

"I thought we agreed you'd call me Wilson."

"And I am. But in the back of my mind, I'll always remember the ridiculous name you gave me the night we met. Oh, maybe we should name our baby Patio. No. Terrace."

"Hellion..."

"I like when you get growly."

His lips slant over mine, and my body hums with desire. Not for sex, but for him. To be close to him.

"Do you have any serious names in mind for the baby?" he asks after he breaks our kiss.

"Maybe. We'll see when we find out what we're having."

"Fine. Keep your secrets."

"I like being mysterious."

"Mhm." He pulls me closer. "I wish every morning could be like this."

"Lazy and cozy?"

"With you in my arms."

I swallow hard. "Maybe it should be like this every morning."

His brows dart up. "Really?"

"If you're okay with me not doing the walk of shame at five in the morning—at least, after we tell Sophia."

"I love the sound of that."

"Good."

He lets out a long breath. "What do you think? Should we get up and enjoy the city?"

Slowly, I nod. "For a little while. Then I want to go home. To Sophia... to our life."

My heart beats harder when I say the words. Maybe it's too heavy-handed. But I want him to know I'm jumping into this.

"Our life?"

"Mhm. It's unpredictable and a little chaotic, but I like it."

He stares at me for a beat, then kisses my forehead. "I like it too. Every second."

Then instead of getting up, he pulls me closer, and I nestle against him, dreaming of all the things this week might bring.

CHAPTER TWENTY-FIVE

Hallie

WAKING up wrapped in Wilson's arms is my new favorite thing.

We're still being sneaky since we're waiting to tell Sophia anything until after my appointment next week, so he's been waiting until she's in the bathroom each morning, then quickly sneaking me out of the apartment. I change and come back, and it's like I've barely missed any time with him.

I'm in way too deep, but there's no getting out now.

I still keep hearing that voice in the back of my head telling me to run or I'll get hurt, but at this point, it'll hurt regardless. I'd rather enjoy being happy first at least.

This morning, I talked to Gran, and she was happy to give me a loan to get a new car. Even though her version of me paying her back is taking that money and putting it into an account for the baby since that's what she'd do with the money I paid her back anyway. It's a load off my mind, but it's also forced me to think about what happens next in other ways.

If Wilson and I are together, and then I'm having his baby... will we start living together? Officially? As my dad noted, him paying me would have to stop at that point, so what would I do for income? I trust Wilson, but I'm not sure I'll ever feel comfortable not having some kind income of my own. I need to start thinking through what's next. Obviously, I'd take time to recover after having the baby.

I'd like to be a stay-at-home mom, but it scares me a little, relying on someone else so completely. I want to live my life in a way that fulfills me, but I also want to make sure I'm not giving up my autonomy. Time to do some thinking and planning, and have a conversation with Wilson about it.

Right now, I'm just happy to be feeling mostly good after last weekend's scare. I'm still nauseous, but I'm hoping it'll dissipate soon.

I've just finished folding and putting away my laundry when there's a knock on the door.

"Coming," I call.

When I swing it open, Frannie walks in, her phone in front of her face.

"Okay, I'm here." She grabs my arm and drags me to the couch with her, then tilts the phone toward me. "And here's Hallie. What's going on?"

Kennedy smiles brightly at us through the phone screen. "I'm getting married."

Frannie and I glance at each other.

"Uh, yeah... we know. You got engaged a few weeks ago. Did you forget you told us?" I tease.

"No. I'm getting married next month."

My eyes fly wide.

"What?" Frannie shouts. "When? That soon? Are you pregnant too?"

Kennedy laughs. "No. But I'm not opposed to it. Just... next month will be the eighteenth anniversary of when we met. It falls on a Saturday, so we figured why not? We already confirmed that it'll work with our parents, and the inn is free. So Devon's checking with Justin and I'm checking with you two. Can you come?"

"Of course!" Frannie yells. "Hold on." She hits some buttons on her phone and then… "And Mark and the guys have a bye week."

"Perfect timing," I say.

"You can come, right?" Kennedy asks me.

"That depends. Can I get a plus one? Or maybe a plus two?"

Kennedy's smile turns a little devious. "Ah, bringing the baby daddy?"

I take a big breath. "I want to bring my boyfriend and his beautiful daughter."

"Aw, Hal…" Kennedy says as Frannie grabs my arm.

"What? You made it official? When? I need details."

"I don't know. It just sort of happened." I don't want to tell anyone else about the scare. I'm okay, and since it helped me lower some of my walls and bring Wilson and me closer, I want it to stay between us. "I made a decision to stop fighting it over the weekend." I glance back at the phone screen. "Sorry. Am I stealing your thunder?"

"No! I don't care. You can take all my thunder, as long as you're smiling like that."

"He brings it out in me."

Kennedy claps her hands. "I love seeing you so happy."

"Me too," Frannie says.

"Okay, back to you. When do we need to be there? And do we need dresses? I'm so excited!"

Frannie and I get comfortable on the couch, and I grab my phone and take notes as Kennedy goes through everything we need to do and when. But as she talks, my mind wanders to Wilson and Sophia. To introducing them to everyone as my little family.

My heart lights up at the thought. I'm happy, and even though it's still scary, it feels too right to care.

THERE'S an autumn carnival happening tonight and over the weekend at the fairgrounds. I know because Sophia has told me eighteen times since she's been home, and she is beyond hyped to go.

I told her she had to ask her dad, but I'm hoping Wilson will lean into his fun side and say yes because Sophia should see that side of him. And I think he loves a carnival more than he'd like to admit. I love carnivals. There's always something magical about them.

The apartment door swings open and Sophia dashes to Wilson.

"Daddy! There's a carnival tonight. Can we go? Please? Pleaseeee? There's even going to be fireworks!"

Wilson chuckles, then glances over at me. "Yeah. That sounds like a great way to spend the night."

Her eyes light up and for a minute she stammers.

"Breathe," I say gently.

"Sorry. I'm just so excited! I'm going to go to my room and figure out what to wear."

She dashes out of the room, and I wait to make sure she's made it to her bedroom before strolling over to Wilson and wrapping my arms around him.

"Hi."

Then I grab his neck and drag his lips to mine. For a second, he doesn't move, but then he kisses me back, holding me tightly.

We break our kiss sooner than we want to because Sophia could reappear any second.

Wilson's eyes shine with happiness, though he looks a little surprised too.

"I could get used to this."

"What? Me welcoming my man home?"

Again, his eyes flare in surprise, but I don't know why. This is what we've been building toward for weeks. If it weren't for the endless joy in his eyes, I'd be worried.

"Daddy," Sophia calls as she thunders back to the living room.

We step apart before she gets there, and she bounces in with an endless amount of energy.

"What's up, kiddo?"

"Can I go on all the rides?"

Wilson laughs. "All the ones that are safe for kids your age, sure. But first you have to eat dinner."

She's halfway out of the room when she calls back. "But not too much. We have to save room for carnival food."

"She's got it all planned out," he says with a laugh.

"She's excited."

He wraps his arm around my waist and tugs me closer. "So am I."

SOPHIA'S HEAD looks like it might explode as she stares at all the rides around us.

"Which one do you want to go on first?" I ask.

She does two full spins before pointing at the large purple one next to us.

"The octopus!"

It spins and has arms that lift up and down.

"Do you want me to go with you?"

"No," Sophia calls to Wilson, already running for the ride.

"She's adventurous. Why do I get a sneaking suspicion you are too, but you just don't show it?"

A predatory smile grows on his face. "I think I showed you some of it at the last carnival we went to."

"Oh, really? Hm. I don't remember."

"Uh huh. I know there was nothing forgettable about that Ferris wheel ride."

I beam up at him. "I suppose it was pretty memorable."

I slide closer as we watch the ride start up. Sophia waves to us, and we wave back.

"Any chance you're willing to go on another adventure with me?"

"I think you could persuade me to do anything."

"Like fly across the country for Kennedy's wedding next month?"

"Next month? That's fast, right?"

"Eh. Not really. She and Dev have been in love since they were kids. They were just too stupid to notice."

"You really want me to come?"

"You and Sophia."

He glances up at the ride, then turns to me. "Are you sure?"

"Very sure. I want Sophia to meet my parents, and I want you both to meet the rest of the important people in my life. You wouldn't make your girl go to a wedding all alone, would you?"

His eyes soften, and he cups my cheek. "Does that mean I get to call you my girl at the wedding?"

"Why would you wait until then?" My eyes dance as I watch his expression change—watch the joy fill his face. "I'm not waiting until then to call you my man."

"Hallie..." His gravelly voice undoes something in me, and it takes everything to keep from jumping into his arms.

"I'm yours and you're mine."

He wraps both arms around me and is about to pull me into a kiss when a little girl whizzes by us.

"Harper, wait up. I'm not as young as I used to be."

Wilson lets me go and spins around, grabbing the little girl by the shoulders as a guy with graying brown hair and tattoos comes to a stop next to us.

"I believe this belongs to you," Wilson says with a laugh.

"Thank you." The man scoops the little girl into his arms.

"How many times have I told you not to run away from Poppa?" He tickles the girl and she screeches with delight.

"Leo, this is Hallie. Hallie, my boss, Leo Barone."

Leo sticks out his hand while exchanging a look with Wilson. "It's nice to meet you."

"Nice to meet you too. Your team did an amazing job on my sister's apartment."

"Thank you." He looks at Wilson again.

"Hey, boss. Okay if I stop in on Monday morning? There's something I wanted to talk to you about."

"No problem."

"Poppa... carousel!"

"A grandpa's work is never done. I'll see you Monday. And Hallie, it was good to meet you."

Leo strolls away toward the carousel, and we turn back to the ride, only to find Sophia dashing over to us.

"Can we go on the Ferris wheel now?"

Wilson and I smile at each other.

"We sure can."

Sophia runs a few feet ahead of us, and as we follow, Wilson wraps his hand around mine, and I get a glimpse of what my future could look like.

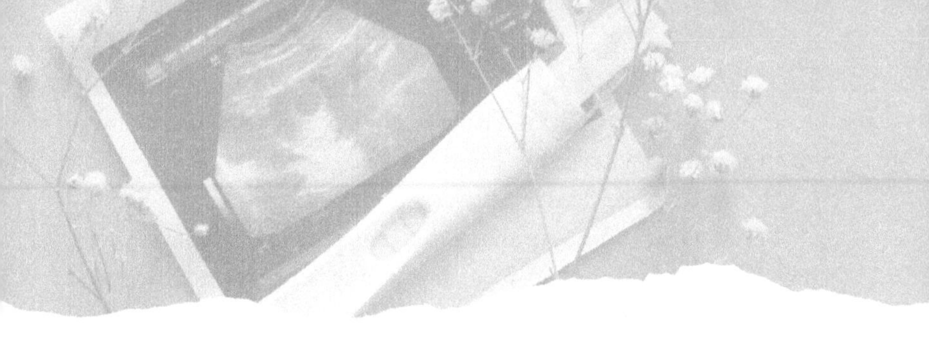

CHAPTER TWENTY-SIX

"EVERYTHING LOOKS GREAT. Your labs are excellent, and both the scan you had a couple of weeks ago and the one today show perfect growth—around the seventy-fifth percentile. And you haven't had any bleeding since the day you went to the ER, correct?" Hallie's doctor asks.

Hallie nods. "That's right."

"Then I think it's safe to say it was just some mild spotting after sex. No cause for concern. But it's good you were seen."

Hallie squeezes my hand tightly.

"So you think it's okay to share the news?" Hallie asks.

She nods. "Personally, I think it's fine to do that anytime. It's always good to have support. That said, everything looks good, so I don't think there's any reason not to."

"Specifically, we're planning to tell my daughter, who is eight."

Hallie's doctor smiles. "That's very exciting. Yes, I think now is a great time to tell her. Do you think she'll be excited?"

"Beyond belief," I say with a laugh.

"That's great. Yes, go ahead and tell people. Celebrate this time with the people you love. Everything looks wonderful, so you're good to go. They'll schedule you for your next two appointments at the desk."

"Great. Thank you," Hallie says as the doctor leaves the room.

She leans into my chest, and I wrap my arms around her.

Over the course of the last ten days, things have changed. The walls around her heart are gone, and while I can tell she's still scared, she's leaning into this. She wants this the same way I do. I can't wait to tell Sophia, so we can finally stop hiding. I want to be able to kiss her when I get home from work and not have to hide from Sophia that she's waking up in our apartment.

At some point, I want her to move in with us. Before the baby is born—whenever I can convince her. In some ways, we've moved quickly, but I know with certainty this is where we're supposed to be. We're meant to be a family.

I'm trying to believe in those thoughts—to revel in them— because they're pieces of my dad. Pieces of who I used to be. I want to be that man again. One who sees the beauty in life and revels in it. I want to live life instead of just going with the flow and trying to keep everything perfectly together and controlled. That's not who I want to be. Not for Sophia. Not for Hallie. Not for our baby. They deserve the best version of me. My dad gave me that, and I want to do the same.

"When do you want to tell Sophia?" Hallie asks, stepping out of my arms and taking my hand.

"Part of me wants to pick her up from school early and tell her right now, but the practical side of me says Friday would be better. Then we'll have the whole weekend to be a family."

My chest burns as I say the words. She could put up a wall, tell me that's too much. This stage of our relationship still feels fragile, and I'm never sure what to expect.

She looks up at me, her face blooming into a troublemaking smirk. "Are you asking me to spend the night on Friday?"

"I want you in my bed every night, Hellion. But Friday, it's official." I catch the side of her neck with my hand. "You're mine now, and I hope you understand I don't let go of what's mine. I keep it and cherish it."

"Wilson…"

Leaning in, I brush my lips over hers. "Mm, if I could, I would fuck you right here and show you exactly how possessive I can be. But it'll have to wait until we get home."

I step back, and she lets out a shuddery breath.

Pulling open the door to the room, she looks up at me. "You better speed."

Fuck, if I thought she was killing me before, now that she's mine, she's making me absolutely feral.

I CHECK the time on my phone for the tenth time in the last half hour. Usually I'm not rushing to finish work, but I'm about to yell at the guys to put their shit away and get out of here. I'm ready to go home and finally tell Sophia the truth.

I'm a little nervous because it means her heart will be involved in the equation now, but at the same time, I'm certain about my feelings for Hallie. And I don't do anything by halves. When I'm in, I'm all in.

Hallie's the wild card. But after her admission at the carnival last weekend, and how she's been for the past two weeks, I'm hopeful. Maybe too hopeful. I have a plan in the works that might be a little crazy. It's probably too much. But now that Hallie has awoken the idealistic side of me again, I can't help it.

"Hey, how's everything going here?"

I practically jump and tear my eyes from my phone.

Nick Ardito grins at me. "Dirty text?"

That's the last thing I was expecting him to say, and I burst out laughing.

"That's one thing I don't do on the job."

He holds his hands up. "Hey, man. I'd give you a pass. We can't control when our girls send us dirty things." He pauses and thinks for a second. "Actually, my wife would purposely do that at the worst possible time, so..." He shrugs. "Anyway. Everything good here?"

"Yeah. We're on track to finish by the end of next week, but I'm guessing probably Wednesday."

"Sweet. Are you okay?"

I nod. "Yeah. Just... itching to get home. Don't know if Leo told you, but Hallie's pregnant. And we're telling Sophia tonight."

His eyes go wide. "She's pregnant? You got your nanny pregnant?"

I run my hand over my face. "Technically, that happened before she was my nanny. It's a long story. But we're happy, so don't be a dick."

He laughs. "Well, from one unexpected dad to another, congrats. I hope it all goes well."

"Thanks."

"Go ahead. Get out of here."

"What?"

He nods toward the door. "I can manage these knuckleheads for another fifteen minutes. Go home."

I clap him on the shoulder. "Thanks. I appreciate it."

"No problem. Plus, it gives me a chance to heckle the guys. It's been too long."

I shake my head as he aims for the back door, then my brain catches up, and I haul ass out the front door.

Time to get home to my girls.

I DON'T KNOW why we agreed to wait until after dinner to do this. I thought I was going to explode and word-vomit it all right there at the table.

I kept my shit together, but only because Hallie threw me a few stern looks.

Now the dishes are done, and I'm bursting at the seams.

"Are we going to watch a movie?" Sophia asks.

"Maybe in a bit. There's something I want to talk to you about." I aim for the living room, guiding Sophia in that direction too.

"Am I in trouble?"

"No. You're not in trouble. This is a good thing."

Then Hallie slips her hand into mine. "Actually it's something *we* want to talk to you about."

Sophia's eyes go mega wide and she almost falls over. "Oh my gosh. Oh my gosh, oh my gosh, oh my gosh!" She jumps up and down, excitement tumbling out of her. She grabs Hallie's hand. "Are you going to be my stepmommy?"

I freeze. It didn't even occur to me that Soph would take it to that place, but of course she did.

Hallie lets out an easy laugh and sits down on the coffee table. Sophia sits opposite her on the couch, and Hallie takes her hands.

"Maybe one day."

"But you two are more than friends now? Like *dating*?"

"Yes. We are. And we have been for a little while, but we wanted to be sure it was serious before we told you."

Soph looks from me to Hallie.

"Were you dating when I asked if you were more than friends?"

Hallie tilts her head back and forth. "We were figuring it out."

"How do you feel about this?" I ask.

"Uh... awesome! I love Miss Hallie. Wait, do I still call you Miss Hallie? Are you still my nanny?"

"You can call me Miss Hallie or just Hallie. I'm still your nanny, but eventually that might change—me being here with you won't though."

"Okay. Good. I like having you here."

"I like it too."

I rest my hand on Hallie's thigh and take another big breath. "There's something else too. Hallie's pregnant. We're going to have a baby, which means—"

The scream Sophia lets out could be heard a block away. "I'm going to be a big sister!"

She jumps into Hallie's arms, wavering between laughing and crying.

"You sure are," Hallie whispers.

"I'm going to have a little sister," she cries.

"Well, it could be a boy," I say gently.

Sophia lifts her head off Hallie's shoulder, a fierce look on her face. "No. It's a girl. I already know it."

"Okay then," I whisper as Hallie laughs.

Sophia climbs off Hallie's lap, then throws her arms around me in a big hug. "I knew she makes you happy."

I give her a squeeze. "Yeah, kid. She does." My eyes drift to Hallie's. "She makes me really happy."

"Can we watch a movie now? As a family?"

Damn, that hits me right in the heart. This is what I wanted. A long time ago, before Sophia was born, if you'd asked me what I imagined for myself, it would've been this.

Love. A whole lot of love.

That's when it hits me. From the moment I met Hallie, she changed something in me, and now I know what it was. She opened my heart again. And there's no denying I'm head over heels in love with her.

"ARE you going to sleep here tonight?" Sophia asks Hallie through a yawn as we tuck her into bed.

"I sure am."

"In Daddy's bed?"

We glance at each other, and I jump in with the answer. "Yeah. Is that okay with you?"

"Well, yeah. It would be silly if you made her sleep on the couch. You told me when you date someone, they're like your best friend. Why wouldn't you share your bed with your best friend? That would be mean."

Oh, kids. Thank God she hasn't lost her innocence yet. She also didn't ask where babies come from, but I'm expecting that one at some point over the next six months.

"It sure would," Hallie says. "Good thing your dad *really* likes me."

Sophia beams at that, then yawns again as she looks up at Hallie. "You're going to be my stepmommy someday." But this time it's not a question. It's a fact in her eyes. Damn, I hope she's right about that.

"It's time for you to get some sleep," I whisper, leaning down to kiss her forehead.

Then Hallie does the same. "Goodnight."

"Night." Sophia grabs her big bear and pulls her covers up as she rolls over.

I wrap my arm around Hallie and guide her toward the door.

"I love you," Sophia calls after us.

Before I can respond, Hallie looks over her shoulder, smiling warmly. "We love you too," she says, cracking my heart open with her words.

The second we're outside of Sophia's room, I pin Hallie to the wall and kiss her like I'll never get enough of her. Because I won't. With my dying breath I'll be begging for more of my little hellion.

"I CAN'T BELIEVE you didn't tell me you were getting a new car," Wilson grumps from beside me in the passenger seat of my new-to-me Jeep Renegade.

I brought him lunch so we could spend his break together and I could show him the car. We're parked at a scenic overlook about ten minutes from his job site.

"Why? Would you have insisted on going with me? Being *the man*? Because honestly, Patio, I can live without that kind of toxic masculinity."

He grumbles, and I laugh. It's always fun to poke his buttons. Especially because eventually it helps get that cranky attitude out so we can make way for the fun.

"Still doing the name thing? I thought we were past that."

He takes another bite of his sandwich, and it's cute how he fights showing that he's enjoying it. When he gets grumpy, he really commits.

"I'm reserving the use of silly names for when you go back to being curmudgeon *Deck* instead of the man I know you actually are. Now tell me why you're grumpy."

"It's my job to take care of stuff like this," he growls.

"Do you think I can't handle it? Trust me, I got a great deal. I know when to bat my lashes and when to give a withering glare. You, of all people, should know I'm anything but a pushover."

"I know you can handle it. You're a badass and God help anyone who tries to play you. I'm grumpy because getting you a car is supposed to be my job. I'm your partner. I take care of you."

I blink at him because I wasn't expecting that. Not that level, at least.

Running my hand up his thigh, I draw his gaze to me.

"Hey, I appreciate that, but I'm still my own person. Despite how quickly we've moved, we haven't known each other that long. It's not your job to do all this for me."

"But I want to. You talk about the man underneath the curmudgeon? This is me. I don't take care of you because I have to. I do it because I want to. I like it. That's how my dad was with my mom, and I always admired that. The way he loved her was profound, and he made sure she had everything she could ever need or want. Simply because he liked to do it. For his own peace of mind and to see her smile. I want to do that for you too."

Ugh, my heart.

Where did this man come from?

How did I end up with him?

As much as I could say it's because I'm pregnant with his child, I know that's not the reason. Our connection was instantaneous from the moment we met.

I set my sandwich on the dash and turn in my seat, grabbing his hands.

"You already do all that for me, and I appreciate it more than I could ever say. There have been times in my life where I felt like an afterthought, a little left behind, but you always make me feel like I'm front and center. Even though you have Sophia to take care of and worry about, my needs are still a priority for you, and while I'm not used to that—and sometimes I'm afraid to get used to it—it means a lot to me. The way you care for me is big and beautiful. But this wasn't yours to do. No matter what's happening with us, it's always going to be important to me to maintain my autonomy. I needed my grandmother's help, but I still solved the problem on my own, picked a car on my own, and handled it all. Not because I had to. I wanted to. And I'll let you wash it, change the oil, and make all the appointments for it if you want to, but I needed it to still be mine. Does that make sense?"

"Yes." He lets out a rough sigh and runs a hand through his hair. "I'm sorry. I'm not trying to be a dick. There's just something about you that makes me a little possessive. It's like a primal urge to take care of you, and I truly love doing it."

"That's part of why you're an amazing dad. And an amazing partner. But I needed this for me."

He nods in understanding. "We need to talk about what happens when you have the baby. I barely feel comfortable paying you now, but at that point—"

"I know."

"You'll still have everything you need. I don't want you to worry about that."

"I appreciate that. I'm trying to figure out... exactly what I want. No. I know what I want. I'm trying to figure out how to make it work."

"Tell me."

"I want to be a stay-at-home mom. I love kids. I love being a caregiver to them, if that makes sense. I've even thought about homeschooling, but then I see Sophia off in the world and making strong friendships, and I want our baby to have that chance too. So I need to figure out the logistics so I can stay home but still make money."

A wave of emotion crosses his face, and he squeezes my hand. "I told you I'll take care of everything. You don't need to worry about the financial side of things."

"You're not made of money. And... even if you were, it's important to me to have something of my own. Even if it's not a lot, it needs to be something. I have some ideas—maybe bad ones—"

"I want to hear them."

Of course he does.

"Well, obviously, I could take on another child or two for nannying. But I wouldn't want to do that until this little one is a bit older. Maybe closer to a year. One thing I thought about was either being a homeschool helper or creating some kind of course-work for it. I helped two different families do it, and between my degree in early childhood education and the amount of research I've done about homeschooling, I know a lot. I'm not sure if there's really a market for that though."

"I bet there is. I'm sure there are plenty of families out there who don't know where to start. If you want to do that, you should go for it. As for paying you, let's plan on me doing that until the baby's born. Or... whenever I can convince you to move in with me. Whichever comes first."

"Just throwing that in there, huh?"

It should terrify me, but it doesn't. My fears have never been about whether things with Wilson are right. They've always been about the idea of falling in love and then losing that love and having to survive the crushing pain that comes with it.

He gives me his most charming smile. "What can I say? I'm hoping I can convince you sooner. I like waking up with you in my arms."

"I like it too." I let out a little laugh. "We didn't even know each other three months ago."

"Three-months-ago me was missing out. I wish I'd have known you then. I wish I'd known you all this time." He grimaces. "Okay, maybe not all this time. That wouldn't be a good thing."

I laugh at the tortured expression on his face. "Aw, does our age difference bother you?"

"Only when I remember that you were fifteen when Sophia was born."

"I can just tell everyone I was a teen mom, and you robbed the cradle."

He gives me a warning look. "Yeah, I don't need people thinking I robbed the cradle like that." He shudders. "No. I wish I would've known you for like a year longer."

We both laugh.

"I know it's fast, but I'm happy with where we are. Beyond the first week, I've never questioned any of it," he says, more serious now. "But what about you? How does it feel to you?"

"Right. That's how it's always felt. It scares me sometimes, but..." I laugh lightly, though I'm suddenly feeling more than a little emotional. "My grandparents were only together for three months when they got married. It truly was love at first sight for them. Falling for someone—building a relationship with them—doesn't have a timeline. It's about what feels right. I've never felt anything but at home with you. And Sophia."

"That's how I feel too. I say we keep making our own rules."

"I like that plan."

"So... moving in?"

I throw my head back, shaking it. "You finally got me to admit I'm yours. Now you want to lock me in the tower so I can't leave?"

He leans over and kisses my jaw. "No. I want to give you a warm, comfortable space to grow."

I suck in a sharp inhale, and he moves his lips slowly down my jaw, then lifts them, his breath tickling my lips as he speaks.

"You're mine, Hellion. And whenever you're ready, I can't wait to build a home with you."

Wrapping my hand around the side of his neck, I pull him to my lips.

Keep your distance. You'll only end up hurting. Don't give in.

The little voice in the back of my head is loud.

But my heart as it thumps for Wilson, Sophia, our baby, and the life we're building together is so much louder.

"HOW MANY MORE HOUSES CAN WE go to?" Sophia bounces in front of us in her adorable little witch costume.

I found orange and black striped leggings, got her a black long-sleeve leotard, a black tulle skirt, and a witch's hat. We also found an old-style broom at the antique store and last night I put her hair in tight braids while it was wet, leaving it in messy, crimpy waves for tonight.

I'm dressed as a "mummy" that accentuates my tiny baby bump with the gauze wrapped around it. And Wilson is a Frankenstein's monster type of character. Sophia said she picked it because he's so good at grunting.

He grunted in response, and the prophecy was fulfilled.

He's been the opposite of grunty tonight though. He's been smiling more than a monster should, and the happiness in his eyes is even more than what I normally see. His eyes dance every time he steals a piece of Sophia's candy. There's a lightness about him tonight.

"Let's finish this block, okay?"

Sophia gives him her poutiest face. "But that's only five more houses."

"And your candy bag is practically overflowing."

"But—"

"Besides, if we don't finish up soon, we won't be able to go to the Halloween block party."

"What?" she gasps, and I fight back a laugh. "We get to go?"

"Only if you finish up trick-or-treating."

"Let's go!" She charges for the next house, and Wilson wraps his arm around my back.

I lean into his touch, soaking in all the fall Halloween vibes around me. This is my favorite time of year, and getting to experience all the fun stuff through Sophia's eyes has made it even better.

"Stay close!" Wilson yells to Sophia as she cuts across the front yard of the next house, aiming for the porch.

I look to my right at the house we're next to. There are no lights on and no cars in the driveway, but then I think I remember seeing a for sale sign in the yard not too long ago. The whole property is surrounded by a pretty wooden fence, and there's a beautiful front porch.

"That's a cute house."

Wilson glances over at, then looks down at me, eyes even brighter than they were before. "Yeah. It is."

"Okay, I've got enough candy. Can we go to the block party now?" Sophia asks, coming to a stop in front of us.

"Sure, kid. Let's go."

A WARM HAND glides across my stomach, but I don't want to leave my sleepy cocoon.

"My girls can't hang tonight, but that's okay. I can talk to you. I know this wasn't technically your first Halloween, but I'm counting it. You were part of Mommy's costume. Next year, you'll get your own adorable costume, which I'm sure Mommy and your big sister will coordinate."

Wilson's lips brush my stomach, and I'm awake now, but I don't want to open my eyes. I don't want to affect this moment in any way.

He's talking to our baby.

Melt me into a freaking puddle.

I'm a mess on a regular basis, but hearing him talk to our baby makes me a gooey mess for him.

"Your big sister is so excited to meet you. She's also decided you're a girl, but I want you to be whoever you're going to be." He sighs. "I'm excited to meet you too. Daddy loves you so much. Having your big sister made me who I am, but meeting your mom has helped me find who I want to be. I hope when you come into our lives, together we'll find who we want to be. As a family. It's been a surprising journey so far, but I'm so happy. Meeting your mom changed everything. You have no idea how lucky you are to have her. She's brave and bold and kind. And she has a big heart."

I swallow hard, emotion swelling in my chest. Then I feel the tiniest *thunk* along the wall of my stomach.

Oh my gosh. Was that our baby?

"Keep talking," I mumble.

He chuckles. "I knew you were awake."

I slide my eyes open. "Seriously, keep talking."

His eyes meet mine, then he kisses my stomach. "Mommy says I need to keep talking to you. Do you like the sound of my voice? I can't wait to hear what you sound like."

"Oh my god," I squeak.

"What?" Wilson sits up and stares at me. "Are you okay?"

I nod. "Yes. Keep talking. The baby's kicking."

His eyes flare. "Seriously?"

He puts his hand on my stomach.

"I don't think you'll be able to feel it. I barely can. I've felt these tiny flutters for the last few weeks, but I wasn't sure what they were. These were the first few hard, specific... kicks."

I cover my mouth as I laugh.

Wilson lies down beside me, brushing his fingers over the side of my face.

"I can't wait until I get to feel it."

"I'm sure it won't be long until I'm waking up in the middle of the night to being pummeled in the ribs." Running my fingers through his hair, I look into his eyes. "Until then, I'll take being woken up to you talking to our baby."

He smiles. "I knew you were listening in on our conversation."

"What gave me away?"

"Your breathing changed."

"You notice when I breathe differently?"

"I notice every tiny detail about you."

Rolling over, I nestle against him.

"I suppose I notice the little things with you too. Like how happy you were tonight. It's not only that you were smiling more than a monster should've been, but it was in your eyes. There was this extra lightness all night."

He strokes his fingers over my collarbone. "You've brought that out in me since the night we met."

"You say that a lot, but really, I think I make you feel safe enough to let it out. You always wanted to but didn't feel you could. Either way, tonight was different. I saw that joy on a whole new level."

"Maybe I'm happy with where I am." He kisses my jaw. "Where *we* are."

"So am I," I breathe.

He cups my face with his hand, staring at me like he's memorizing every tiny detail of my face.

"I love you." *Oh my god.* "I don't need you to say it back." He shakes his head, pulling me tighter to him. "I don't want you to. I just need you to hear it and know it. Whenever you're ready, you can say it to me, but I couldn't hold it in anymore." His voice cracks with desperation. "I love you."

Then his lips are on mine, ripping the breath from my lungs and the thoughts from my brain.

Somewhere inside of me I feel a pang of guilt, like I need to say it back, but he deepens our kiss, showing me how he feels with every touch, every sweep of his tongue.

I don't have to say it back right now.

Saying it back in general terrifies me, despite what I feel in the depths of my soul, so I give in to our kiss, letting the power of it—the power of him—wash over me and overwhelm me. In moments, we're a tangled mess and he's buried deep inside me, showing me with his body how deeply he feels for me.

The connection between us blooms, the roots growing deeper with each movement, and even if I can't get myself to say the words, I can give him every last piece of me just like this.

CHAPTER TWENTY-EIGHT

Hallie

I'M LEAVING a piece of my heart in Ida. *Most* of my heart.

A depressing airport goodbye wasn't on my bucket list. Then again, neither was getting knocked up from a one-night stand then falling head over heels for that man... and his daughter. Yet, here I am.

Even if I haven't quite managed to say the words to Wilson yet.

I touch my hand to my chest. I *want* to say it to him, but every time he says them to me, the words shrivel up and die in my throat. It's stupid. It's only an acknowledgment of what I feel inside, but it's like saying them out loud will somehow trigger the universe to rip him away from me.

But if I don't say the words... will that drive him away?

No. I don't need to do this in the middle of an airport with Frannie, Justin, and Jade watching. I'm fighting my emotions enough as it is.

"Thanks for driving me to the airport."

"It's my job as your man."

I glance over my shoulder at where Frannie, Justin, and Jade are standing.

"Maybe. But I could've ridden with them. I like that you drove me."

His face is full of that same beautiful joy I see almost all the time now, though today it's tinged with some wistfulness.

I really need to get it together. This is not some tragic wartime goodbye. We'll see each other in two days.

"I want to say goodbye too," Sophia says.

Of course Sophia had to come too. There was no way she was letting her dad drive me to the airport without coming along to say goodbye.

"I can't wait to pick you up at the airport on Thursday." I wrap Sophia in a hug. "Are you excited for your first plane ride?"

Sophia squeezes me tight, then lets me go, nodding firmly. "Yes. I'm a little nervous, but mostly excited. It means I get to see you and California. And flying is good practice for when we go to Disney World one day."

This kid.

"Already planning for that, huh?"

"Of course. I have to teach my sister all about Disney."

From behind me, Justin and Frannie laugh.

"Okay, kid. Let's leave the vacation planning for another time. I still need to say goodbye to Hallie."

"Fine," Sophia says, dramatic as usual.

Wilson steps up to me and my heart gets all achy again.

He tucks a strand of hair behind my ear. "I'll miss you, Hellion."

"I'll miss you too. What are you going to do to entertain yourself while I'm gone?"

He shrugs casually, but there's a twinkle in his eyes. "I've got work and Soph."

"You're planning something."

He grins at me. "No idea what you're talking about." He presses a soft kiss to my lips. "Why would I want to do something special for my girls?"

"Something special?"

"You'll see when we get home from the trip."

"Always teasing me, *Deck*."

He pulls me close and leans down to whisper in my ear. "Don't start that shit or I'll have to spank you right here in the middle of the airport."

"Still teasing me."

He sighs and shakes his head, some of the playfulness fading away.

"Fly safe. Text me when you land. And don't have too much fun without me."

"No promises."

He stares at me for a beat, then dips me back and kisses me like we *are* having a wartime goodbye and don't know when we'll see each other again.

Justin, Jade, and Frannie all hoot and whistle.

"Daddy!" Sophia gasps.

We break our kiss, laughing, but Wilson doesn't let me go yet. Brushing his lips over mine, he whispers, "I love you." But even if I could form the words to say it back, he doesn't give me a chance before his lips are on mine for one last soft kiss.

This time when we break apart, I take a step back and stare at him. Then I throw my arms around him one more time. "I'll see you Thursday."

"Thursday, Hellion. I can't wait."

Turning, I blow a kiss to Sophia. "Have a fun first flight. Love you, honey."

"We love you too." Soph jumps into Wilson's arms, waving as I join Frannie, Justin, and Jade and slowly turn toward the gate.

I force myself not to look back.

It's only two days.

But it's two days where most of my heart will be elsewhere.

"EXPLAIN to me why sitting in the window seat is better when you're terrified of flying," I ask my sister.

She makes a squeaky noise in response. She only went on her first flight back in February—where she met Mark—because she's always been scared of heights.

From the row in front of us, Justin laughs. He turns in his seat so he can see into our row. "Seriously, how did you survive your first flight?"

"I had a hot as fuck god-like man sit down next to me and offer his hand. I knew I wouldn't survive flying without him, so I decided to keep him." Her face falls a little. "I just didn't count on him not being here for some of them."

Frannie is able to ride with the team to any out-of-town games she wants to attend, so this is her first flight without Mark. Though she's only gone to one of his games that they flew to. Despite them having a bye week, they still had some team requirements yesterday and today, so they're flying out tomorrow afternoon and leaving Sunday morning with the rest of us.

We agreed to fly out today—Tuesday—so we'd have some extra time with Kennedy and Devon, and to help prep for the wedding.

"Anyway, the window helps because it makes me feel less claustrophobic. Once we're in the air I'm sort of okay. Takeoff and landing do me in."

I hold out my hand to her. "I know I'm not Mark, but squeeze away. Try to take deep breaths and not overthink it. We're going to be fine."

Frannie's eyes meet mine.

"That's much nicer than what you said when I was panicking during my first flight."

"Sarcastic texts are my love language."

She slowly shakes her head. "I asked you to be calming and how you would respond to kids and you told me you'd put on *Bluey*."

I laugh at that. "I would. But only if there was an epic meltdown. I'd try to make it sound exciting. If that didn't work, I'd try to relate to them in some way or talk about how I overcome fears. Mostly I'd want them to know they were safe." I elbow her lightly. "You're safe."

"You're going to be a great mom," she whispers, squeezing my hand.

I squeeze hers back.

I hope she's right. But lately, I'm not only thinking about being a mom to my baby. I'm thinking about being a mom to Sophia. Being a partner to Wilson. Becoming a pillar of our little family.

At times it's overwhelming, but I've never wanted anything more.

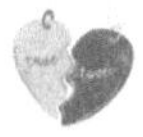

"OVER HERE!" Kennedy calls loudly, waving to us. Devon is at her side, a smile on his face as he waves.

Frannie and I take off running, and I let the two of them collide in a hug before carefully joining in.

"I missed you both so much," Kennedy says, an arm around each of us.

"We missed you too," Frannie says.

"I missed you so much, I went and got pregnant so I wouldn't be so lonely." I dramatically stick my lip out, but she ignores it, stepping back and taking a good look at me.

"Oh my god. Look at your cute little bump." She puts her hand on my stomach. "Hey, baby. I'm your auntie Kennedy and we're going to get into lots of trouble together."

"And I'll be there to send bail money," Frannie teases.

We collapse into another group hug, and my heart feels home in a different way. It's a nostalgic, peaceful home that reminds me of my childhood and how I became the person I am.

I've missed it. But it's not the feeling of home I crave anymore.

For me, home has always been where the people I love are, but who those people are and the intensity of that love has shifted.

I need to tell him.

But I shake the thought off because I can't do anything about it right now.

We separate and look over at Devon, Justin, and Jade. Justin wraps an arm around his wife.

"We finally get to indoctrinate you into the club now that the OG gang's finally back together again."

"Yes, the OG gang is back together." I wrap one arm around Frannie and my other around Kennedy, not talking about our little friend group at all, but the three of us, where it all started in a little duplex in New York City. The Baker girls.

I'VE OFFICIALLY SURVIVED ALMOST two days without Wilson and Sophia. Yesterday was spent settling in and getting a little tour of Brighton. Though I'd been here one other time because we drove across the country one summer to spend almost a month out here with Kennedy and her parents, I didn't remember much of it.

It's a cute little suburb of San Francisco, and it was fun to see Kennedy so giddy as she showed us her favorite places, introduced us to new friends, and took us to the inn Devon's family owns. It's where they're getting married, and in some ways, where Kennedy grew up. She moved out here when she was eleven, and Devon was her next-door neighbor. She spent tons of time with him at the inn. Now they live in his old house and Kennedy works part time at the inn.

She's happier than I've seen her in a long time. I always knew moving out here was important for her, but I understand it more deeply now. Not only because of how content she is, but because of how my life has changed over the past few months.

Today was spent doing lots of wedding prep. We got to see Kennedy in her dress and try on our pretty rose gold and bronze bridesmaid dresses. The inn will be getting decorated tomorrow, and our whole family will be arriving then too.

I'll be spending the day with Wilson and Sophia, but the evening will be reserved for time with my family. I'm both excited and nervous for everyone to meet Wilson and Sophia—to see my little family.

Sophia and Wilson called right before Sophia went to bed. She mentioned her dad has some kind of surprise, but she doesn't know what because they're staying at Wilson's mom's house tonight since she lives right near the airport and they have an early flight. Wilson and I didn't get any alone time to talk, and though I wish I could call him before bed, he needs his sleep.

And if the way tonight is going is any indication, it's going to be a late one. We're all in Kennedy and Devon's backyard, sitting around a campfire.

Mark, Hardy, and Brian got here a couple of hours ago, and it's been an evening of endless laughter and good food.

"It's too bad your new man couldn't be here tonight so we could grill him about his intentions," Hardy says to me.

"Yeah. You won't be doing that. I'm a big girl who can handle her own life. Accidental pregnancy notwithstanding."

"How is Baby Baker?" Brian asks.

Huh. I hadn't thought about last names. Will the baby have my name or Wilson's?

I kind of like Baby Baker.

"Baby is doing well. Growing all the time. The kicks are

getting stronger. Sophia has already decided we're having a girl, so just go with it if you hear her say that."

"She sounds feisty," Hardy says with a smile. "Like someone else I know."

I hold my hands under my chin like an innocent angel. "I don't know what you're talking about. Besides, Wilson likes it."

"Who wouldn't love a Baker girl?" Kennedy interjects.

Devon and Mark both laugh.

"Uh oh. Don't say the L-word in front of Hallie. She might spontaneously combust."

I shoot Frannie a death glare. "Shut up."

"Wait, are you saying you're *not* in love with him?" Hardy asks. "Because no offense, baby girl, but *bullshit.*"

"I... am." I throw my hands up. "I'm in love with him. The love bug bit me hard. Okay? Are you all happy now?"

"Does he know that?" Brian asks gently.

"Probably."

Mark throws his hand up. "Hold on. You haven't told him yet? Has he said it to you?"

"Yes," I huff. "He has. And I've... tried. Sort of."

"Hal, you need to tell him," Justin says.

"Go easy on her," Brian says, always the most understanding. "None of you have all your shit together. And love is complicated." He looks at me. "Sorry, I didn't mean to throw you under the bus like that."

"It's okay. It's just... hard for me. I kept love at arm's length for so long. I don't know..."

I run my fingers over the chain at my neck. The one that holds half a heart with the word I can't say on it.

Frannie watches me carefully, her expression serious. "Is this because of Gran and Pop?"

My eyes meet hers, and I give a tiny nod. "That's where it started."

"Wait. Why?" Kennedy asks, genuinely confused. "They had a beautiful love story."

"They did," I admit, heart clenching, remembering Gran telling it and Pop laughing and interjecting things.

"You weren't there the night he died," Frannie says to Kennedy. "I'll never forget the way she screamed and cried. How she said..." Her eyes drift back to me. "How she said she was supposed to die first because she didn't want to live without him. Is that what you've been afraid of this whole time? Not love itself, but loving someone so much—"

"Yes," I choke out. "And I know it's stupid. I've learned you can't stop love. And the way I love him and our baby and Sophia is so much bigger and more profound than I knew love could be, but it still terrifies me. To lose any of the three of them would destroy me. Losing him... I would be screaming on the floor. Saying it out loud to him has a finality to it. Like I'm testing the universe. *Look, I finally found love and I'm stupidly happy.* What if it all gets ripped away? I know Gran found her peace and she's living an amazing life now, but it still scares me."

"I had no idea," Kennedy says. "But I can't fault you for being scared." She takes Devon's hand. "I was terrified to mess up our friendship."

"So was I," he says, looking at her like she hung the stars.

"And I was terrified to get on a plane—and to open my heart and fully trust someone," Frannie says.

Mark squeezes her arm. "I was afraid to be honest about who I was or believe that fate could really blindside me the way it did."

"Love's good at that," Justin says with a laugh.

"He's right. It blindsided me and I was afraid to believe it could be real," Jade says.

"I was afraid to scare you away." Justin smiles at her, then moves his chair closer to hers.

"You know I get it," Brian says. "I'm scared of loving someone and not being loved in return."

There's a beat of silence, then Hardy shakes his head. "Don't look at me. I'm not scared of anything."

But the way he quickly looks away, particularly avoiding

Brian's gaze, tells me that's not true. And whatever he's scared of has to do with Brian and the connection between them.

"Minus Hardy's bullshit, I think what most of us are saying is it's okay to be afraid. But love is worth taking the risk and pushing past your fears for." Justin gives me a gentle smile, then squeezes my arm.

"Noted," I say quietly.

Thankfully, the topic of conversation moves on after that, but my mind keeps drifting to Wilson. I've admitted I love him to everyone else. I've told Sophia I love her. He needs to hear it from me. I need to get over my stupid fears because he deserves to be loved the same way he loves me.

My hand goes to my chest and through my shirt I trace the letters etched into the necklace. *L-o-v-e.*

Hopefully by the time I see Wilson tomorrow, I can grow some ovaries and finally say the words that have been twisting inside me for weeks now.

CHAPTER TWENTY-NINE

"WE ONLY GOT to see the Golden Gate Bridge for like two seconds, so we have to do that first."

I love my daughter with all my heart and soul, but she never stops talking. Especially when she's excited. And as I'm trying to navigate us through the San Francisco airport, a little less chatter would be nice.

"We'll see, okay?"

"Fine," she sighs.

"I know you're excited, kid, but let's find our way out of this chaos first."

It's apparent to me how long it's been since I've traveled anywhere farther than a couple of hours away.

I'm not used to it, and it's showing right now.

"Daddy, look!"

I swear, if it's another stand with some sort of tourist T-shirts, I'm going to scream.

But when I look up, I see something so much better.

Hallie is standing there in a white and olive-green sundress, smiling as she waves to us.

"Hallie!" Sophia goes dashing toward her, pulling up short so she doesn't collide into her.

She kisses Hallie's belly, then greets her with a hug.

I stand back, watching their sweet reunion and the happiness on both their faces.

I did something that might be completely crazy yesterday, but this moment gives me hope that it wasn't.

As Sophia lets Hallie go, Hallie's gaze turns to me, and the smile that sweeps over her face undoes me.

I make my way over to her, setting our bags down before I get to her, then sweep her into my arms.

"Hey, Hellion." Then my lips are on hers for a quick but powerful kiss.

Her smile grows as I let her go. "Missed you too."

"Hallie, can we go see the Golden Gate Bridge now? Please?"

Hallie's gaze darts to me.

"We saw a glimpse of it while we were landing, and now it's all she'll talk about."

"Got it. Well, I was thinking we should find somewhere to grab a little snack first, then we can check out the Golden Gate Bridge and whatever else you want. We just have to be back in Brighton by four so you can meet my family."

Sophia bounces on her toes. "I'm so excited for all of it." She throws her arms around Hallie's waist again.

Hallie runs her fingers through Sophia's hair while looking up at me. "I am too."

I RUN a towel over my hair as I walk out of the bathroom in our suite at the inn. There's a private bedroom and a fold out couch for Sophia to sleep on in the living room—giving Hallie and me some privacy.

"Hey, are you almost ready to go…" Hallie's words fall away as her eyes land on me.

"See something you like?"

She walks over and runs her hand down my naked chest. "Definitely." She kisses my jaw. "Too bad we don't have time for that."

I drag my lips up the side of her neck. "But it's been two whole days. I somehow survived without you. Don't I deserve a reward for that? I've been such a good boy."

"Wilson," she groans. Then she gives me a shove. "Put a shirt on."

"You're no fun."

Where I'm expecting her to stick her tongue out at me, she wrings her hands together and glances at the clock.

Oh, I get it.

Crossing the distance between us, I stop in front of her. "Is my hellion nervous?"

She meets my gaze, vulnerability shimmering in her eyes. "I want them all to like you and welcome you."

"I can handle whatever they throw at me."

"I know, but I've never brought anyone around before. I need them to understand how much you mean to me." She grabs my hand. "Because I—"

"Are we going?" Sophia asks, dancing into the room.

I hang my head. How is it that kids can ruin a moment so effectively? Because I swear Hallie was just about to say a certain L-word. Maybe not. Maybe I'm reading into it. But there's no way I'm going to find out with Sophia still standing here.

Sophia frowns. "Daddy, put a shirt on."

I hold my hands up. "Sorry. Sorry. I'm going."

Satisfied with that, Sophia leaves the room, and I lean in and kiss Hallie's cheek. "Don't worry. They're going to love us."

She smiles faintly, but she's obviously still nervous. While I don't want her to be, I also love how much this means to her. How much our little family means to her.

HALLIE'S HAND is wrapped tightly around mine as she swings open the front door to Kennedy and Devon's home.

Kennedy—who I recognize from the pictures in Hallie's apartment—appears in the entryway before we've shut the door.

"Hi! You must be the newest members of this crazy clan. I'm Kennedy—"

"Hallie's super cousin."

"That's right," Kennedy laughs. "And you must be Sophia."

Sophia's face brightens even more. "That's me."

"It's so good to meet you. We need more Baker girls around here."

Soph scrunches up her nose. "But that's not my last name."

"You're an honorary Baker girl."

"Okay, I love that." She gives Kennedy a big hug, then Frannie, Mark, and a guy I'm assuming is Devon appear.

"Hi, Frannie. Hi, Mark," Sophia says.

"Hey, want to come with us?" Frannie asks. "There's some yummy food and drinks in the kitchen."

Sophia looks up at me. "Can I?"

"Go ahead."

She walks off with Frannie and Mark, and Kennedy and Devon focus on me.

"So, you're the one who knocked up my sweet, innocent baby cousin."

"Here we go," Hallie mutters under her breath.

"If you think she's innocent, then this is all a sham and you're not really related."

Devon barks out a laugh. "I like him. And he clearly knows Hallie." He extends his hand to me. "Devon McGregor."

"Wilson Decker."

We shake hands, then his eyes narrow. "I'm assuming Justin already gave you a good withering glare and the general warning not to hurt her. But just so we're clear, Hallie's like a little sister to all of us, so just know they'll never find your body if you break her heart."

"Okay, stop threatening the father of my child."

Devon's gaze flits to her. "That's so weird. But I'm happy for you."

"Thanks," she says flatly.

"You know he's serious," Kennedy says.

"Kend," Hallie hisses.

Kennedy steps up to me, leveling me with the kind of look that would make a lesser man's balls shrivel up.

After a long moment, her eyes shift to Hallie. "I want to make sure he's taking care of you. That he'll stand by you." Kennedy turns back to me. "Because I left. A lot of us have left Hallie in pursuit of finding what we need. I want to make sure you never will."

I feel the change in Hallie's demeanor when Kennedy says that. I know it's something that's been a pain point for her. She doesn't like to talk about it, but the main reason she moved to Ida is because of how lonely she felt. I've heard all the words she didn't say. All the quiet, vulnerable remarks she played off as nothing serious.

"This might sound shitty, but I'm lucky you left her because it means she ended up in my arms, and there's nowhere else I ever want her to be. There's no amount of money you could pay me, nothing you could say, no shiny object you could offer that would make me walk away from her. She's the love of my life, and it's my honor to be the one at her side, taking care of her. That's what I intend to do until my dying day."

My eyes stay locked on Kennedy for a moment longer, then I turn to Hallie, who is smiling with tears in her eyes.

I pull her to me and kiss her forehead. "You're mine, Hellion."

"And you're mine."

To prove it, she gives me a slow, sweet kiss.

"Okay, you've passed my test," Kennedy says. "Anyone who can make Hallie melt like that—smile like that—gets my full approval."

"Thank you," I say, squeezing my fingers into Hallie's side.

"Come on. The rest of the family should be here soon, and we should make sure Frannie and Mark aren't turning Sophia into a sugar zombie," Devon says.

He leads us out of the room, and as we walk, Hallie burrows into my side, then leans up and kisses my neck.

I don't care what words she's said or hasn't said, this is all I need to know she's mine, and we've got a beautiful future ahead of us.

HALLIE'S FAMILY is full of fun with a hint of chaos.

Knowing Hallie and all of her family I'd already met, that shouldn't be a surprise, but I guess I'm used to people trying to hide that. They're all *come-as-you-are* and very warm and accepting.

Sophia has been the star guest tonight. She already decided she's calling Hallie's parents grandma and grandpa, and she announced to everyone that she's having a baby sister. At this point, she's probably willed it into being.

Hallie's grandmother is the biggest spitfire of the group. She's funny and sarcastic but also has a calming presence, and it's clear she means a lot to Hallie.

We've just finished eating dinner around a huge makeshift table in Kennedy and Devon's backyard, and everyone is chatting and catching up.

My arm is around Hallie, who is leaning against my shoulder while brushing her fingers up and down my arm.

"Hey, Gran," she says during a brief lull in conversation. Her voice is a little thick, but I'm not sure why. "Will you tell us your love story with Pop?"

That explains the emotion in her voice. I'm a little surprised she wants to hear it after how his death affected her.

"Oh, I want to hear it," Sophia says.

"It's been too long since I've told this story." Hallie's grandmother smiles. "Okay. I was just nineteen and went out for the night with some girlfriends. We were always looking for some kind of trouble to get into, though where we headed that night shouldn't have been much trouble at all. But it was for me. Trouble for my heart. The best kind of trouble there could ever be. Little did I know when I left the house that night, that I'd meet the man who would change my whole world.

"But there we were, my friends and I, playing games and laughing about nothing, when I looked up and saw the most handsome man staring at me. He had a kind smile, and he was focused wholly on me. All the music and colorful, flashing lights dimmed as we walked toward each other. We stumbled over saying hello and introducing ourselves, then he asked if he could join me. He took my hand, and that was it. There, on a summer night in the middle of a carnival, I met the love of my life."

I whip my head to look at Hallie, only to find her smiling at me. A bright, beautiful smile that tells me this is why she asked for the story. She wanted to share it with me, especially that little part.

"That's just like you two," Sophia whispers from beside us.

Hallie twines her fingers with mine, staring at me reverently. "Yes, it is."

As she stares at me with so much love in her eyes, my heart cracks open for her all over again.

I'M exhausted when I finally step into the bedroom and close the door behind me.

"She asleep?" Hallie asks, getting up from the floor where she was stretching.

"Finally." I lean against the closed door and rub my hands over my face.

Hallie runs her hands up my arms, pulling them down. My eyes land on her as she grabs the side of my neck and drags my mouth to hers.

Though her kisses are gentle, they're full of desperation. Almost frantic.

"Wilson," she breathes, barely breaking our kiss. She searches my face, looking deep into my eyes, then a look of pure peace washes over her. "I love you."

My heart stops. The world stops.

It's only her, looking at me like this, like I'm everything to her and always will be. The tenderness of her expression is seared into my mind. This is a moment I'll remember for the rest of my life.

"Hallie..."

She drops back down so she's on flat feet again, but her gaze never breaks from mine.

"Do you know what I was thinking about tonight while listening to Gran tell that story?"

"What?"

"That they were lucky. They had such a profound love, and they never took it for granted. They showed each other and told each other over and over again how much that love meant. And when Pop died, they both knew how deeply, unconditionally loved they were." She sweeps her hand over my cheek. "I realized if you left this planet tomorrow, I could never regret loving you, but I'd forever regret not telling you how much I love you. And Sophia. And our beautiful little family." Tears well in her eyes and her voice breaks. "I love you."

A tear slips down my cheek, surprising me. I don't cry easily. I never have. And I didn't think her words would hit me so hard because I already knew the truth behind them. But hearing her say them?

I lift her into my arms and kiss her deeply. "I love you too, Hellion. With all my heart. All my soul."

"Wilson," she whimpers, holding me tightly.

"I love when you say my name like that, baby. Like you're so fucking desperate for me it hurts."

"I am." She kisses up my neck, her movements frantic. "I love you."

As tired as I was when I walked into the room, I couldn't be more awake now. More alive.

I set her down next to the bed and pull the oversized shirt off her, revealing her perky breasts and little baby bump. I splay my hand over it. "You're perfect."

She threads her fingers through my hair as I suck on one of her nipples. Then I drop to my knees, kissing down her stomach as I go. Hooking my fingers in the waistband of her shorts, I slide them down with her underwear, then stand up and take in every beautiful inch of her.

"You're mine," I growl, slanting my mouth over hers in a rough kiss.

She slips her hands under my shirt and drags her fingernails lightly down my back.

Another growl slips out, and she breaks our kiss, her hooded eyes filled with desire.

"Take your clothes off. I need to feel your skin against mine."

She runs her hand up my arm, and sparks dance on my skin. She's set me on fire since the first night we met.

Once I'm naked, she skims her hands down my chest. "Sit down on the bed, against the headboard."

I kiss her cheek before doing as she asked, then she climbs onto the bed and sinks onto my lap.

I fight to keep from moaning too loud as she surrounds me.

"I wanted to be on top, but I needed to be close to you."

She wraps her arms around my neck as she lifts her hips and drops down again, throwing her head back.

Dipping my head, I suck one of her nipples into my mouth, then tease the other with my fingers.

"Wilson," she cries.

We're both trying to be quiet, but the emotion between us is explosive.

I'm leaking inside her, barely holding on. I've never needed someone so badly. Never been this close to the edge so quickly.

"Hellion, I don't know how long I can last," I groan.

"Don't hold back. I need to feel you. Us. Please," she whines.

"I'm right here, baby. I'm yours. Forever. I love you."

"I love you."

She moves faster, dropping her head against mine. Our eyes lock as we move like one, lost in each other.

Hallie walked into my life and turned my world upside down. Or maybe taught me it didn't always have to be perfectly straight. It can tilt, tip, and spin, and that's where the fun is. Where the magic is. She's helped me be freer and find myself again. She's given me more than words could ever express. And now, like this, she turns me inside out. She pulls me from the depths. She makes me better.

I'm not a grumpy single dad. I'm not Deck or Decker. I'm Wilson. I'm hers. And we're two souls tumbling through this world together.

"Hallie," I grunt, burying my head in her neck as my orgasm takes me.

"Yes. Wilson..." She spasms around me, milking my cock as

she rides her high, taking everything she needs and surrendering herself in return.

When we're both finished, we sit there, holding each other tightly, lost in the connection between us. The love.

"I'm yours," she whispers. "Forever."

Trailing my fingers down her back, I hold her a little tighter. "And I'm yours, Hellion. I have been since the night we met, and I always will be."

Her lips find mine, and we collapse in bed, tangled together as we lazily kiss and hold each other.

Maybe every night won't be like this, but as long as she's falling asleep in my arms, every night will be perfect.

CHAPTER THIRTY

I'M HAPPY.

Wholly and completely happy. Joyful.

Wilson loves to say I bring out his playfulness and joy. Well, he helped me find a piece of myself I didn't know I'd been missing.

I always had fun. I always enjoyed life. But I wasn't living fully because I was always hiding my heart. He's shown me what it is to love in a way I was terrified to. Which seems ridiculous now because that love is healing.

A few months ago, I never would've predicted that I'd be in love and building my own little family, but I'm grateful I didn't see it coming.

When it rains, it pours.

That downpour was necessary to help my life grow and blossom.

Ugh. I officially sound like a sappy card or a self-help book. I guess happiness will do that.

I'm still the same mouthy, sarcastic girl. Now I get to be her with the man I love.

Nothing is better than being the fullest version of myself.

Although this moment is pretty special.

Even though it's November, the gardens at the inn Devon's family owns are beautiful. There are late autumn wildflowers everywhere, and there are still colorful leaves clinging to the trees.

I'm standing beside Frannie at the altar, watching as Kennedy stands at the other end of the aisle with her dad.

I glance over at Devon, who is pinching the bridge of his nose, trying not to cry.

Kennedy looks stunning in an ethereal white and cream dress with her hair swept back in a low bun. Even from here, I can see her eyes sparkle with tears.

I'll never forget the first time she mentioned Devon to us. I was still little and didn't fully understand the idea of crushes, but I was getting there. Frannie, however, asked Kennedy if she loved Devon and was going to marry him one day.

Kennedy turned red and refused to say anything else, but even then, it was clear. There was something special between them.

My eyes drift to Wilson, who is wearing a brown suit—no tie. I remember how much he hated the tie the night we met. He winks at me, and my heart fills with the same giddiness of that night back in August.

I took him to that carnival to loosen him up and help him relax, but I took him there for me too. Because carnivals are always magic, and whether I wanted to admit it or not, I felt a spark of that same sort of magic with him.

As Kennedy walks down the aisle, I imagine myself doing the same thing one day, and for the first time in a long time, that thought doesn't scare me. It sends a tingle of excitement up my spine.

"WHAT'S GOING ON?" Frannie asks, voice urgent as she walks through the bathroom door in the inn.

I'm standing next to Kennedy, waiting to find out why we're in here.

"Nothing bad. I just needed a minute with my sisters. That's what you two will always be for me."

"Aw, Kend," Frannie says.

We end up in a group hug before Kennedy steps back and waves her hands. "I don't want to get too emotional right now. I know I'm going to be a mess saying goodbye to you tomorrow, but I couldn't let you leave without telling you this in person…"

"What?" I ask, thoroughly confused at this point.

She rests her hand on my stomach and smiles. "This little one is going to have a cousin."

My eyes fly wide. "You're pregnant?"

"Oh my god!" Frannie squeaks. "When did you find out?"

"Just a few days ago, so it's super early, but I had to tell you."

We both throw our arms around her.

"I'm so excited we get to be moms together. Even if it'll be from across the country."

Kennedy laughs. "Think of all the late-night text conversations we can have."

"Jeez, I guess I need to catch up with you two," Frannie says.

"No. I'm sure Wilson and I will have a few more." Then I slap my hand over my mouth. I can't believe I said that. We haven't talked about that. Not really.

"Look at you planning for the future," Kennedy teases.

I shrug. "He's worth it."

"It's pretty awesome when you find that," Frannie says.

"Yeah. It is. Even better when you actually admit to it," I say.

We all laugh at that, then share one more group hug before

heading back to the reception. We stand on the edge of the dance floor for a few minutes and watch.

"Only two more people in our friend group for the love bug to bite," Frannie says, eyes tracking Hardy and Brian at the bar.

"Think it'll get them?" Kennedy asks.

"I think it already has. They just have to see it."

I've always believed in love. I was always happy to see the people I love find it. After experiencing it like this, I want it for everyone in my life. But I especially want it for Brian and Hardy. They deserve to find that love... in each other. I hope they open their eyes and see it.

"I LOVE THIS," I whisper, swaying in Wilson's arms to a version of *Make You Feel My Love*.

"This song?"

"Dancing with you."

"I like dancing with you too, Hellion. And this song makes me think of you."

"It does?"

"Mhm. These last couple of months, all I wanted was for you to know how I felt about you. To trust those feelings."

"It would've been impossible not to."

He pulls me tight to him, singing the words in my ear and making me fall even more in love with him.

The song ends with a jarring transition to a pop song.

"God," Wilson laughs.

"Aw, look." I point toward where Sophia is with a couple of other girls. She's teaching them some of the dance routine she's learned in class. "I love seeing her make friends so easily now."

"It's because of you." He stands behind me, wrapping his arms around my waist and resting them on my stomach. "She sees you being brave and bold, and she wants to be that way too. You've brought so much to our lives."

I spin around and look up at him. "Funny, I was going to say the same thing about the two of you."

"Wow, we're really kind of gross and cheesy now, aren't we?"

"Honestly, I'll take that over drama any day of the week. You just have to promise me you'll never stop having adventures with me."

"Not for a second, Hellion. Think of all the Ferris wheels I haven't made you come on yet."

We both laugh, then I look around and sigh happily.

"I'm so glad I could be here for this, but I'm excited to go home."

His eyes dance. "Me too."

BY SOME MIRACLE, Sophia is asleep in the backseat of the car as we drive home from the airport.

She was up bright and early for our flight this morning and was wide awake for the whole plane ride. I passed out on Wilson's shoulder because I might've stayed up a bit too late with Frannie and Kennedy, but I regret nothing. Right now, though, I'm excited to get home, unpack and settle into life.

I spent so much time resisting and holding back from Wilson. I want to jump in now and really build a life with him. Become the family we're meant to be.

Beside me, Wilson drums his thumb on the steering wheel, which wouldn't be weird, except there's no music playing. I'm convinced Sophia could sleep through anything, but I wasn't going to risk playing music once she fell asleep.

"Are you okay?"

Wilson quickly glances at me before looking back at the road. "I'm fine."

"Yeah, that's not convincing. What's wrong?"

He swallows hard. "Nothing. Everything's fine." But he lets out a weird high-pitched laugh.

My stomach knots with worry. He's acting weird.

Out of nowhere, he brakes, flicks on his turn signal and pulls into the driveway of a house a block and a half from home.

He shuts off the car, panting a little.

"What's wrong? Are you okay? Are you having a heart attack? Should I call 911?"

He huffs out a laugh, then turns to me and cups my cheek. "I'm okay, Hellion. I'm not going anywhere anytime soon. You're stuck with me." He looks at the house behind me. "Depending on how you feel about what I have to show you, you might be *really* stuck with me."

The concern in my gut fades, curiosity taking over. Then I remember he was planning some surprise.

Slowly, I turn to look at the house, and I realize it's the same one I thought was cute on Halloween. I remember the mischief that danced through his eyes when I said that.

Throwing my door open, I climb out of the car, eyes still glued to the house. "What did you do?"

He laughs as he walks around the car to me. "Let's wake up our girl so I can show you both at the same time."

My heart stutters at his words. *Our girl.* That's what I want her to be one day. If she's okay with it.

Wilson opens her door and leans in. "Soph, baby, wake up."

"Hm?" She blinks a couple of times and looks around. "Where are we?"

"Hop out, and I'll tell you."

She blinks a few more times, then yawns before climbing out of the car. She looks around as we walk down the driveway toward the front porch. Finally realizing where we are, she squints as she looks up at Wilson.

"Wait, why are we here?"

"Trust me."

He leads us to the front porch, then pulls out his key ring, where his half of the heart still sits, and unlocks the front door. Swinging it open, he steps aside to let us in. "Welcome home."

I stop short as I take in the adorable living room in front of me, filled with a mix of mine and Wilson's furniture. His rug, my couch, his oversized chair.

On the walls are some of his photos, some of mine, and photos of the three of us, including a framed one of our most recent ultrasound.

Then my eyes drift to the open kitchen and backyard beyond.

"This is our house?" Sophia asks, eyes comically big. "Oh my gosh!" She goes tearing through the living room and into the kitchen and dining area that opens up to it in the back of the house, then disappears around a corner.

I look back at Wilson, utterly shocked.

"Did you buy this?"

"No. Well, not yet. I got lucky and my bosses, Leo and Noah, flipped this house. I'm renting it on a trial basis. If we like it, we can buy it."

"We?"

"If you'll move in. I want us all under the same roof. We're a family. We should be together."

Sophia skitters around the staircase that sits in the center of the house and runs over to us. "Can I see my room?"

Wilson smiles. "Sure. There's something Hallie needs to see up there too."

Sophia dashes for the stairs.

"First door on the left," he calls, leading me up the stairs behind her.

She lets out a squeak of delight, and I peek into her room, decorated similarly to her old one.

"Come here." Wilson pulls me to the next room and swings the door open.

I walk in and see a beautiful wooden dresser and a matching crib. Sitting in the crib is Veranda, the big gray bunny he won me at the carnival.

He didn't just rent this house. He made us a home, complete with a nursery for our baby. My hand drops to my stomach as I take it all in.

"I figured it was only right that the baby gets the bunny."

I let out a laugh of disbelief. "It's the perfect first decoration."

"I was going to hang the heart necklace in here too, but I couldn't find your half."

Smiling, I tug on the chain tucked under my shirt and pull out the half heart. "I put it on a new chain so my skin wouldn't turn green."

"When did you start wearing it?"

"After you said you loved me. I couldn't say it, but every time I thought it, I touched the word on the necklace."

He steps up to me, wrapping his arm around me. "I love you."

I brush my fingers over the word and smile up at him. "I love you too." Taking a step back, I look around. "And I love this. Where did you get the furniture?"

"I made it. It was Sophia's when she was little. I've kept it at my mom's ever since, hoping..." He takes my hand and twines our fingers. "I was hoping for this. Not always actively. Sometimes it seemed too farfetched to ever be a reality. But this is what I wanted. A home. A partner. A house filled with kids."

I turn toward him and wrap my arms around him. "Filled with kids, huh? You already planning for our next one?"

"Mm, sometimes I imagine doing this on purpose. Saying filthy things to you while I fuck you full of my cum and get you pregnant again."

My cheeks flush. "You can't say that in the nursery."

He chuckles. "The walls don't have ears."

"I want more kids too," I whisper.

"Good thing there's one more free bedroom up here. And

there's a beautiful attic, that with dormers and some work could be turned into a master suite."

"You've got it all planned out."

"That depends."

"On what?"

"If you're moving in too."

Oh, right. I didn't answer him.

"Hm. I might need to see the backyard before I'm convinced."

He laughs. "Of course. That's the real selling point. Not your sexy man, a cute backyard."

"Oh, can we go outside?" Sophia calls from the hallway.

"Go on," Wilson says.

He holds my hand tightly as we walk back downstairs and out to the backyard.

It's a decently long lot for downtown and wider than most of the ones around us.

"It's one of the biggest yards on the block," Wilson says.

Sophia runs along the edge of the fence, and I take it all in, imagining nights spent grilling and eating on the patio. Summer days of Sophia playing out here while I tend to the garden. Our baby sitting on a blanket in the shade of the large oak tree.

"When did you do this?"

Wilson wraps his arm around me, also taking in the view.

"I moved everything in on Wednesday." Emotion fills his voice. "But if you're asking when I decided... it was after the weekend visiting your parents. You lit up when we walked into the backyard. You deserve to have a yard of your own. A place that brings you joy."

"You did all this for me?"

"I did it for us. I want this to be where we start our family."

"I want that too."

"You're going to live here with us?" Sophia yells, dashing across the yard and throwing an arm around each of us.

"Yeah. I am. Is that okay with you?"

"It's perfect!"

"I agree," Wilson whispers. Then he gives me a soft kiss, filled with longing.

"Oh my gosh," I laugh, leaning back a little.

"What?" Wilson asks.

"The baby must know all the important people are right here. Just kicking away in there."

"I think she knows she's home," Sophia whispers.

Home.

When I left the city, I was lonely and running away, trying to find my happiness. I ended up with everything I needed and didn't know I wanted. Maybe it was the twists and turns of life. Maybe it was fate. All I know is I'm right where I'm supposed to be, and for the first time in my life, I'm settled, and my heart feels right at home.

CHAPTER THIRTY-ONE

"OKAY, we're just about ready. I want to confirm that you'd like to know the gender of the baby?"

The ultrasound tech barely gets the sentence out before Sophia shouts, "Yes!"

The tech looks from me to Hallie. "Does everyone want to know?"

"Yes," Hallie says. "We'd like to know."

"Okay, then. Let's get started."

She squirts some gel on Hallie's stomach as I turn to Sophia.

"Remember, the baby might not be what you're hoping for, but that doesn't mean you're going to love them any less, right?"

"Right. But it's going to be a girl."

The tech laughs under her breath, and I turn to Hallie.

These last few weeks of living with her have been incredible. Now that we're getting close to Christmas, I'm even more excited. I'm already imagining the perfect Christmas morning with us wrapped in a blanket on the couch while Sophia tears through all her presents. Our first Christmas in our home. We've already decided we're going to start the process of buying the house in the new year. Hallie has plans for a garden in the spring, and Sophia is excited to make a snowman in the backyard. She also made me promise to get her a sprinkler this summer.

Soph broke in her new bedroom by having a sleepover with Maria and another new friend from their dance class.

I love watching her blossom. I'm sure she could've found her way to it without Hallie, but Hallie makes both of us better, and she makes our family whole.

"All right, here's a look at your baby."

I take Hallie's hand as we both watch the screen. Our little peanut is in there kicking and flailing away.

"She's so cute," Sophia whispers.

Again, the tech laughs. "I'm going to take some measurements and then we're going to see if you're right. But first..." She hits a button and that wonderful whooshing sound fills the room. "One hundred forty-two beats per minute. Perfect."

The tech gets to measuring as Sophia watches in wonder. I roll the stool I'm sitting on farther up the bed, then give Hallie a quick kiss on the cheek.

"I love hearing the heartbeat," she murmurs.

"Me too. That's the heart the two of us created."

"Ugh, don't make me cry here."

I laugh and kiss her forehead, then turn my attention back to the screen. All the measurements show our little one is still hovering around the seventieth percentile.

"Now for the fun part." The tech basically jabs Hallie in the side with the wand, but Hallie doesn't show any signs of discomfort. Her eyes are glued to the screen. "Okay, and right here... there's no penis. Which means—"

"It's a girl!" Sophia jumps up and dances around. "I knew it."

The tech smiles and continues on.

Hallie looks at me. "What do you think? You ready to be a girl dad all over again?"

"Can I tell you a secret? I love being a girl dad. I love taking care of all my girls."

"We're going to have you wrapped around our fingers."

"Like I'm not already?"

"You love it."

"I do." I look back at the screen. "I'm excited to do this with you. The first time around... I didn't really have a partner. Especially once Sophia was born. I'm so excited to have this baby, but I'm even more excited to walk this road with you."

Hallie blinks rapidly. "Stop saying things like that in the middle of the ultrasound."

Leaning forward, I kiss her head. "Sorry. I'll never stop telling you how much I love doing life with you."

"Back at you." She lowers her voice. "Mr. Decker."

"Hal..."

"Payback," she says with a smirk.

I can't complain. I love every side of her, but especially the feisty side that drew me in the night we met.

WHEN WE WALK OUT to the waiting room, Sophia goes dashing for my mom, who also came along.

"Nana! I was right. It's a girl!"

Mom stands up and hugs Sophia. "Oh, that's wonderful." She looks at the two of us. "Congratulations."

Hallie tucks her phone away and goes to hug my mom.

As I lean in and give my mom a quick hug too, my phone goes off in rapid succession.

"Where should we go to lunch to celebrate?" Mom asks.

"Oh, what about that one with the dog on the sign? Oh, or the one that has the really yummy fries."

Sophia goes on ahead with my mom, talking her ear off about different restaurants. Hallie and I walk together behind them, and I pull my endlessly vibrating phone out of my pocket.

Ah, yes. The group chat that Hallie added me to. I've officially been accepted into the Baker girls tribe now, and while I'm grateful, their group chat is pure chaos on a good day.

HALLIE

It's a girl! And yes, Sophia is THRILLED.

FRANNIE

Yay! The first Baker girl of the next generation.

KENNEDY

Now I'm extra excited to find out what we're having.

BRIAN

Congrats. Love you all.

HARDY

It's time to start buying all the baby outfits.
Get ready for lots of dresses and bows.

BRIAN

Every time we go to the store, he's going to be looking at baby clothes now.

HARDY

I call dibs on godfather.

DEVON

You can't dibs that.

HARDY

Why not?

MARK

It's against the laws of dibbing.

JUSTIN

Seconded! And seriously, if you think you're getting to be godfather over me, who is like her brother, you are sorely mistaken.

HARDY

Don't make me fight you for it. You can't be the godfather to Kennedy's baby and Hallie's. That's against the law of godfathering.

JADE

Again, I'm here to remind you all that anything you say may be used in a story.

JADE

Oh and congratulations. I can't wait to spoil her rotten.

Thanks for the congratulations. I'm muting this chat now.

I tuck my phone away. Laughing, Hallie does the same, leaning against me as I wrap my arm around her.

Sophia and Mom are still plotting lunch, so I savor this short, quiet moment with Hallie.

"How long do you think it'll be before Soph starts coming up with names?"

Hallie laughs. "I'm sure she has ideas. But I've already got one picked out."

I turn to her. "Oh, really?"

"I think we should name her Veranda."

I stop moving, staring at her, trying to keep my face neutral because... I don't think she's kidding.

"I..."

The sound of her laughter sends relief washing over me.

"Oh my gosh. You actually thought I was serious?"

I pull her tighter to my side and keep walking. "I never know what kind of crazy ideas you're going to come up with."

She shakes her head.

"No, *Deck*. I do not want to name our baby Veranda. I'm not going to name her after a stuffed rabbit."

"Because *that* would be crazy."

"Exactly."

She stops and looks up at me, eyes serious.

"Hope."

"Hope what?"

"I think we should name her Hope. When I was in the emergency room, you said your dad would've told you to have hope. That word kept coming back to me. I think we should name her that in honor of your dad."

Her words sock me right in the chest. Yeah, my dad would've wanted that. He would've *loved* that. I sweep my hand through her hair, wondering yet again how the fuck I possibly got this lucky.

Dad, if you had anything to do with this… thank you.

"My dad would love that. I love that." Gently, I press my lips to hers. "I love you."

"I love you too."

We start walking again, the cold December air rushing around us as we walk outside.

"Plus, I think Hope Patio is a beautiful name."

I laugh and tug on her hair, shaking my head.

"Whatever you say, Hellion. Whatever you say."

EPILOGUE
FIVE MONTHS LATER

"BREATHE DEEP, NOW LET IT OUT." Frannie's calming voice reverberates around the room.

"That doesn't fucking help," Hallie growls.

Frannie bursts out laughing. "Sorry. It's all I've got."

"You suck at this."

Frannie points at me. "That's why you have him. Besides, I think I'm just as helpful as you were during my first flight. Actually, you made me more scared I was going to crash and die."

"That was Kennedy," Hallie grunts. "You're my big sister. Say something comforting."

"I may be the big sister, but you're doing the hard thing first. I'm proud of you. You're a badass. I know you can handle this. Take deep breaths. Remember why you're doing this. It'll all be worth it in the end." Frannie kisses Hallie's forehead. "And don't die."

"No one's dying," I growl.

"Oops, woke the bear. I'm going to give you two a minute. I love you."

"You're the worst, but I love you too," Hallie calls after her.

I stalk over to the bed as the door closes behind Frannie.

"Okay, *Deck*. What's wrong?"

Every time I get a little grumpy, she calls me Deck to remind me that grumpy isn't who I am.

"I don't like you two joking about you dying. It's not funny. It'll never be funny to me."

"Aw, you kinda like me, huh?" Hallie teases, but I'm not in a teasing mood.

Hearing those words from Frannie's mouth sent me over the edge, which wasn't hard since I've been worried from the very first contraction.

Looking back, I'm not proud of how emotionally unattached I was when it came to Sophia's mom. We weren't the right match, but when she ended up having an emergency C-section, in my heart, I was more worried about Sophia. With Hallie? I'd burn the entire world down to keep her safe. The thought of her being in the same position as my ex? Or something worse happening? I don't know how I'd survive it.

"It's not a game, Hallie."

She blinks a couple of times, all playfulness falling away, then she grabs my hand and pulls me onto the edge of the bed. "Talk to me."

"I don't like jokes about you dying. Everyone talks about childbirth like it's simple, but it's not. So much can go wrong. Women die. And the thought of losing you…" I shake my head. "You were scared to fall in love because you were afraid of that type of loss. I'm not immune to those fears. Losing you would destroy me, and even though I'm supposed to have all my shit together and be calm, I'm not. Everything seems good now, but I'm scared. Okay? I'm scared."

She brushes her thumb over my cheek. "That weirdly makes me feel better."

"It does?"

"I'm scared something bad will happen. I'm scared of losing her or having complications... all that stuff. I know childbirth isn't always easy. I've heard stories from families I nannied for over the years. There are a lot of scary things. And even when everything is okay, it still hurts like a motherfucker," she grunts, wincing and clutching the edge of the bed.

"Another contraction?" I ask.

She nods, and I wrap my arm around her back, bracing her.

"Fuck," she groans. "This baby is going to be worth it," she whispers to herself. "The pain is worth it for the love."

That's my girl. The one who learned to open her heart and believe love is worth the risks and potential pain. Or literal pain in this case.

She gasps out a breath as the contraction subsides. "I need to get up and walk around."

I help her out of bed and trail behind her as she paces the room.

Frannie, my mom, and Sophia are out in the waiting room, and Hallie's parents are driving up from the city. Besides Kennedy and Devon, everyone else is in the area. They're just waiting to come to the hospital until the baby is born—and until we're ready for that chaos. For fights over who gets to be the godfather and all the other nonsense. I remember being low-key intimidated by and not wanting to bother Brian and Hardy the night I met Hallie. Now they're like two annoying brothers.

Hallie braces her hands on her knees, and I gently rub her back as she groans through her contraction.

When it's subsided, she stands up and walks over to the window, which only has a view of the parking lot.

"I need a distraction. Something to take my mind off being cooped in this hospital room."

"Come sit on the couch with me."

She waddles over, looking extra adorable as she cradles her bump.

I help her onto the couch, and she rests her head on my shoulder.

"There's going to be another contraction soon. I want to be done with this part. I just want to push her out. I want to meet our little girl."

I kiss the side of her head. "So do I, but speaking of *push*. I have a little present for you."

She sits up and looks at me. "You got me a push present?"

"It's not exactly a push present. More something special that I wanted to do for you anyway and the timing seems right."

Her fingers twist into my shirt. "Hold that thought."

She groans loudly, then forces herself to take deep breaths as the contraction drags on. They're definitely getting longer now with less space between them.

Everything's okay, I remind myself.

I hope it stays that way.

Hope.

Our little girl has a heck of a guardian angel watching over her.

It'll be okay.

"All right. Give me the present. Who knows how much time I have before the next one."

I chuckle at that, then kiss her nose. "This is why I was planning to wait, but here you go." I hand her the flat, black velvet jewelry box and watch her open it.

"Wilson," she breathes. "This is beautiful."

In the box is a gold chain with a simple, flat gold heart, engraved with the words *true love*.

"I thought you deserved a better quality necklace."

"I love it. But where's your half?"

"Well, I'm not much of a jewelry guy, and a keychain wasn't good enough. So..." I pull my arm out of my sleeve and show her my upper forearm.

Keeping it a surprise from her has been a challenge, but thankfully she was focused enough on the baby coming that she didn't notice me insisting on wearing long sleeves for the last few days.

She traces the words that match her necklace.

"You told me that night that the half heart meant I'd always remember the night I met my true love—not that I could ever forget—but I want those words right there where I can see them anytime. So I can take myself back to that night and remember when I started falling for you. So I never take a second of this life we have for granted. I love you."

She meets my lips in a soft kiss. "I love you too—oh, fuck."

She grabs my arm and holds tight as another contraction hits. One contraction closer to meeting our little girl.

HALLIE IS A WARRIOR. She's had a long labor, but she never lost her resolve. And now, every push fuels her.

"Just a few more pushes. Are you ready?" the doctor asks.

"Yes," Hallie says, fiercely determined.

She wrenches my hand, and I kiss her head. "You've got this. She's almost here."

Hallie nods and pushes again. Watching her is exhausting and humbling. Women are magical beings that we're lucky to share our lives with.

"Okay, she's crowning. Big push."

Hallie grunts through the push, and then, in a whirlwind, everything changes. Hallie gasps and leans back as a sharp cry pierces the room.

I stand there, looking between Hallie and our baby, completely overcome with emotion.

A nurse plops our little girl on Hallie's chest, and I stand at the side of the bed and rest my hand on our sweet girl's back.

"You did it, baby."

Hallie looks up at me with teary eyes. "She's here."

I pull out my phone and take a few pictures. They're so intimate, I don't think I could ever share them.

"Does Dad want to cut the cord?"

I swallow down my emotions and step forward. "Yes."

With instruction from the doctor, I cut the cord. A second later, I'm back at the side of the bed with my girls.

"Does she have a name?" a nurse asks.

"Hope," Hallie says with a smile. "Hope Baker-Decker."

My brows go up. We hadn't talked about last names.

"Going with the hyphenate?"

"Yeah. She should have both of our last names. No offense, but whenever we get married, I'm keeping my last name. I love being a Baker girl. I want her to be one too."

"I would never take offense to that. I don't care what your last name is, only that you're mine. That we're a family."

"We always will be," she whispers, stroking her finger over Hope's tiny hand.

I kiss Hope's head. "Hey, sweetheart. It's Daddy. I love you."

I can't find any other words than those. I'm too overwhelmed with emotion. But really, those are the only important ones anyway.

"SHE'S SO CUTE," Sophia whispers, a mix of exuberant and teary-eyed as she looks at Hope.

"Ready to hold her?" Hallie asks.

"Yes, please."

"Let's come over to the couch." I guide Sophia there and sit down next to her, placing a pillow on her lap.

Hallie sways over, looking perfectly content and comfortable, like she didn't just give birth an hour ago.

"I'm going to rest her head on your arm so it's supported, okay?"

Sophia nods.

Hope wriggles and lets out a soft cry as Hallie sets her in Sophia's waiting arms.

"She's so tiny. Oh my gosh. Hi, little Hope. I'm your big sister, Sophia. I'm going to be your best friend and take care of you and teach you to dance." Soph leans down and kisses Hope on the forehead, and I melt. Wrapping my arm around Hallie, I pull her onto my lap. Finally, I've got all my girls right here with me.

Hope lets out an angry wail and Sophia's eyes go wide.

Hallie stands up, but I pull Hope into my arms before she can. What can I say? I'm already a goner for her.

Hallie laughs and carefully sits down next to Sophia.

"Hey, Hallie." Sophia's voice is quieter than usual, and I already know what she's about to ask.

I nestle Hope against my chest and shift so I can watch this moment play out.

"What's up, sweetheart?" Hallie gently runs her fingers through Sophia's hair.

"I wanted to ask you..." She bites her lip and looks at me, so I give her an affirming nod.

"Go ahead."

She takes a big breath, then looks at Hallie, eyes shimmering. "Now that Hope is here, and she'll call you Mommy, I was wondering if I could call you Mommy too." She rushes out the words, her big heart on full display.

Hallie's eyes fill with tears. "Oh, honey. I would love that. As long as—"

Sophia's smile is giant as she jumps in. "Daddy already said I could. He just said I had to ask you."

Hallie wraps Sophia in her arms. "I'd love that. And I love you." She looks at me and whispers, "I love us."

With one hand splayed over Hope's back, I reach for Hallie's hand with the other.

It hasn't even been a year since she walked into my life and changed everything, but I never want to go back. Not to the man I was before, and not to the life I had. There were beautiful things, but it was dull without her. For me and for Sophia. Now our lives are filled with the beautiful mixture of peace and wildness that Hallie brings, and the vibrant joy we've created together.

Hallie

I USED to think of home as an apartment in the city. A place where I laughed with my friends and family and crashed after long days of nannying.

Now this is home.

The trees and flowers in the backyard blooming. The windows cracked open, letting in the cool spring air, the birdsong outside, and the sound of cars going by. It's the place I spend my days with my family, whether there's laughter, tears, or sleepless nights.

There's been a lot of those lately.

It's only been a week since Hope was born and our beautiful little house officially became a home.

I set a cup of coffee on the table next to the couch for Wilson, who smiles up at me and catches my hand. I give it a squeeze before setting my tea on the coffee table and curling up next to him on the couch. He wraps his arm around me as he yawns, one hand constantly cradling Hope, who is asleep on his chest.

He's an incredible dad.

It's crazy to me that not so long ago, I felt completely alone and didn't know if my baby would even know their father. Fate intervened—or maybe put me on this path in the first place.

As much as I like to tease Wilson about being a grumbly curmudgeon sometimes, he has the biggest, softest heart.

He's up in the middle of the night as often as I am, usually helping me and making sure I have water or a snack while I'm nursing Hope. He's rubbed coconut oil on my cracked nipples and soothed me every time I've felt like I was failing.

I love getting to do this with him by my side. I love the way we laugh together and tease each other. Though it's easy to see now how quickly you can get lost in being a parent and nothing else, I'm determined to keep having fun with Wilson, which means scheduling date nights, and when Hope gets older, at least a couple of times each year when we have a night all to ourselves.

Sophia plops down beside me and snuggles up to me. "Mom, can we read a book?"

I still want to ugly cry every time she calls me mom.

I always knew I wanted to be a mom, but I had no idea how much becoming Sophia's mom would mean to me.

I've become sappy and ridiculous, and I'd hate it if I wasn't so happy.

"Yeah, of course. Go pick a good one."

She skips upstairs to do that, and I rest my head on Wilson's shoulder.

"How's our little Hopie?"

"Enjoying sleep now. Finally."

"Well, she's in her favorite place."

He flashes me a smile. "Her second favorite place. You have the milk, so your boobs will always be her favorite place. Can't say I don't understand."

"Oh, I know you love those."

"How are you feeling?"

"Good. Mostly." Then I sigh. "My vagina hurts."

Deck tries and fails to hold back a laugh, but he instantly claps a hand over his mouth, then watches Hope cautiously. We're both terrified she might wake up. We barely sleep at this point, so getting some rest wherever we can is important, even if it's not sleep.

Hope wiggles, sneezes, then goes back to sleep, and we both breathe sighs of relief.

"At least she's cute," I whisper, kissing her head.

"Of course she is. We made her."

"Did you think this is where that night would lead us?"

"Not for a second, Hellion. But I knew I didn't want to leave the next morning. Now I know why."

"You could already sense the baby?" I tease.

"No. Some part of me knew you were mine, and I didn't want to let you go."

"Well, you're stuck with me now. Good luck."

Sophia bounds back down the stairs, several books in her hands.

"Yeah, I'll probably go gray prematurely and question my life choices and my sanity, but you're worth it."

"Aw, thanks. You say the sweetest things."

"I love you."

"Love you too."

He tilts his head and gives me a quick kiss, making Sophia smile.

"Ready to read?"

She nods and curls up next to me.

I open the book and start reading. We take turns voicing different characters, and occasionally she makes Wilson do a silly voice.

My fingers drift up to the necklace draped around my neck. I brush my thumb over the words. *True Love.*

"Now you'll always remember the night you met your true love."

I had no idea when I said that how right I was. Or maybe some part of me did know, and that's why I picked the necklace.

My heart is home with my little family. I hate that I ever let the fear of losing love hold me back from loving in the first place, but I also know I never would've fallen as hard for anyone else.

I used to think the last thing I'd ever want to do was fall in love. Life, or maybe fate, proved me wrong.

Thank God I broke my rules—got tangled up with the man I was nannying for, and more importantly, let myself get lost in love.

Best decisions ever.

The End

Grab a Hallie & Wilson bonus chapter, check out more of the Baker Girls series, sign up for Bethany's newsletter, and more here:

Thank you so much for reading Hallie & Wilson's story. It's one of my absolute favorites that I've written, and I had so much fun writing all their banter, silly nicknames, and steamy tension. I hope you enjoyed their story too!

If you want a bonus chapter featuring a proposal (or two), you can grab it on my website.

Up next in the FINAL Baker Girls book is Hardy & Ackley's friends to lovers rom-com, *The Last Person*. I can't wait to finally tell their story (I've literally been planning it since 2023).

And if you haven't yet, go back and check out Mark and Frannie's story in *The Last Lie*, Kennedy and Devon's story in *The Last Key*, and Justin and Jade's story in *The Last Love Story*. And if you want to know more about the Ardito & Barone families including how Leo became a grandpa and Nick's story, check out the *Freaking Love* trilogy.

For more news, updates on what I'm working on, teasers, and freebies, sign up for my newsletter or hop over to my reader group, Bethany Monaco Smith's Book Besties.

Thanks again for reading!

XO,

Bethany

THE LAST THING PLAYLIST

You can find *The Last Thing* playlist on Spotify

- A Whole New World- Yellowcard, Chrissy Costanza
- I Don't Dance- Lee Brice
- Leave Before You Love Me- Marshmello, Jonas Brothers
- Sugar, We're Goin Down- Fall Out Boy
- MakeDamnSure- Taking Back Sunday
- Hands Down- Dashboard Confessional
- Only One- Yellowcard
- Carry You Home- Alex Warren
- Take It From Me- Jordan Davis
- Have It All- Jason Mraz
- Falling Like The Stars- James Arthur
- Lay Down With You- Dylan Scott
- King Of My Heart- Taylor Swift
- Control- Mutemath
- Part Of It- Jordan Davis
- Anti-Hero- Taylor Swift
- Promise You That- Trevor Martin
- A Thousand Years- James Arthur

- Can You Feel the Love Tonight- Simple Plan
- Daylight- Taylor Swift
- To Make You Feel My Love- Dave Fenley
- Faithfully- Journey
- Love You 'Til Death- Forest Blakk

ABOUT THE AUTHOR

Bethany Monaco Smith is a writer-mom. When she's not busy hanging with her boys, she's writing beautifully messy love stories.

She loves happily-ever-afters and cries at every emotional moment, whether reading, writing, or watching. When she's not mom-ing or writing, you can find her binge-reading on Kindle Unlimited, supporting fellow indie authors, and having sushi dates with her SIL. Bethany survives on coffee, rewatching the same TV shows over and over, and her KU subscription. She lives in the Southern Tier of NY with her husband and two sons.

For more about Bethany and what she's working on, follow along on Instagram or on her website, bethanymonacosmith.com. Stay in touch by joining Bethany's exclusive Facebook group, Bethany's Book Besties & signing up for her newsletter.

ACKNOWLEDGMENTS

To my right-hand girls Cassie and Lacey, who I couldn't do this without!

To my fabulous betas for keeping me on track, making sure the spice is spicing, the banter is hitting, and book boyfriends are extra swoony: Amarilys, Carissa, and Mel

To all the amazing authors who support me along the way. I see you and I'm right here cheering you on in return.

To all of you who LOVE a surprise pregnancy. You're my people.

And to all of you wonderful readers, I couldn't do this without you. Thanks for being here.

9 781963 450248